# Praise for
# *When We Return*

"Eliana Tobias has managed in this moving and intelligent novel to show us two characters who, coming from very different worlds, at the end are telling the same story. The story of disarray, discrimination, and injustice. Showing us as well that hate is everywhere and the only antidote we have is memory and love."

**—CARLA GUELFENBEIN,** Alfaguara-award winner and internationally recognized author of eight novels including the award-winning novel *In the Distance With You*

"A spellbinding narrative that spans two continents, Europe and Latin America, at pivotal times of history. We are drawn to the lives of its characters, those that escaped the fractured world of the Holocaust and those in Latin America who struggled for truth and justice. Eliana Tobias has written a mesmerizing novel where history is braided with humanity. A passionate tale of resilience and fortitude."

**—MARJORIE AGOSIN,** Wellesley College, award-winning poet and novelist, author of *The Butterfly Hill Series*

"A story about reparations and redemption, *When We Return* weaves decades and continents, victims of the Holocaust and those reeling from terrorism in Peru, with the struggles of loss and injustice. Tobias explores with insight and compassion the familial bonds that sustain us to ultimately reveal the healing that comes from family, love, and our shared humanity."

**—CLAIRE IBARRA,** author of *Fragile Saints* and *Vortex of Our Affections*

"In a novel with as many victims as there are survivors, Eliana depicts the phenomenal resilience of love that can bridge displaced families across borders and beyond lost time. A thoughtful writer, giving readers history and fiction in equal servings, her words are prime and elegant, adding richness to a beautiful retelling of an ugly past."

—**MARI JOJIE,** author of *A Hundred Silent Ways*

"In this thought-provoking novel, the author traces generational history for those who are recipients of life-shattering events. Tobias seeks and provides answers to questions of the rights of recipients of outrageous historical behavior and to what forms such reparations may take. Personalizing such problems, the novel gives a historical background from the Peruvian Shining Path guerilla movement to the European Holocaust and shows through keen characterization how the sharp light of history reflecting national crimes impacts both the recipients and future generations. Can new relationships provide solace to those long ago destroyed? A must-read for philosophical and historical students and deep thinkers everywhere. A highly original and different type of novel."

—**SUZANNE HILLIER,** author of *My Best Friend Was Angela Bennett* and *Sonia and Carl*

"As a Jewish Latina familiar with South and North America, Tobias provides penetrating and perceptive observations on the all-too-human-issues caused by displacement and generational trauma. Weaving a tapestry of trauma as experienced by a Peruvian victimized by the Shining Path guerillas and an American affected by his father's preoccupations as a Jewish Czech refugee, the author provides a unique window into life and political events. Equally compelling is the struggle of the affected individuals to confront memory and seek justice, each of which proves to be an enormous challenge. After all, the perpetrators rely on the erosion of memory and the avoidance of justice. This story may help inspire those who know that silence is not the answer."

—**ROBERT KRELL,** CM, MD, Professor Emeritus of Psychiatry, University of British Columbia, author of *Sounds from Silence*

"Eliana Tobias renders this powerful tale of a Peruvian family trying to come together after the murderous corruption of the Fujimori years unfolds with the inevitable grace of a tropical flower blooming."

**—EDUARDO SANTIAGO,** award-winning author of
*Tomorrow They Will Kiss* and *Midnight Rumba*

A NOVEL

# When We Return

## ELIANA TOBIAS

RIVER GROVE
BOOKS

Published by River Grove Books
Austin, TX
www.rivergrovebooks.com

Distributed by River Grove Books

Design and composition by Greenleaf Book Group
Cover design by Greenleaf Book Group
Cover images used under license from ©Shutterstock.com/ hachiware; ©Shutterstock.com/saiko3p; ©Shutterstock.com/ Adwo; ©Shutterstock.com/Anne Richard; ©Shutterstock.com/Dan Breckwoldt; ©Shutterstock.com/Who is Danny; ©Shutterstock. com/Al Serov; ©Shutterstock.com/Josep Curto; ©Shutterstock.com/ NICOLA MESSANA PHOTOS

Publisher's Cataloging-in-Publication data is available.

Print ISBN: 978-1-63299-534-6

eBook ISBN: 978-1-63299-535-3

First Edition

To the members of my family
whose stories inspired this novel.

*"One thing I think about is how humans work—the only thing that can replace one story is another story."*

—Yuval Noah Harari

(Quoted by Ian Parker, "The Really Big Picture,"
The New Yorker, February 17, 2020.)

# CHAPTER 1

## The East San Francisco Bay Area, California, 2008

The email came late one night as Jerry Gold lay at home in his bed. He rubbed liniment on his right knee before applying an ice pack and, a little apprehensively, asked himself if he should consider giving up jogging at his age. Jerry didn't make it a habit to look at his messages this late, but the pain kept him awake. When he reached for his cell, he noticed an unfamiliar name. Jerry almost deleted the message but, for some reason, opened it.

> Mr. Gold, my name is Dario Alvarez and I'm reaching out to you, wondering if you could be my relative. I was born in La Paz, Bolivia, in 1949 to my mother Soledad Figueroa. When she was close to her death, my mother confessed that I was not the son of the man I lived with and called my father, but of a foreigner she had known by the name of Milan Goldberg. If you have any information about Milan

Goldberg, I would appreciate hearing from you. Thank you for your help.

Jerry shot upright, his green eyes open wide. *Are you kidding?* Jerry thought. *I don't have time for this.* He couldn't figure out who this Dario was. Carefully, Jerry dragged his tall, slim frame out of bed, reached for his robe, and limped straight to the liquor cabinet.

He sat on the couch in his condo living room, gulping Scotch, and speculated how this total stranger could have tracked him down. *Who is he anyways? Dad never mentioned having another child. This is absolutely ludicrous. I'm certainly not going to deal with an unknown jerk.*

After finishing off his drink, he hobbled back to bed. The Advil he'd taken earlier combined with the liquor were making him drowsy and he didn't want to risk falling with his injured knee.

As Jerry lay in bed, he remembered how, at the end of his life, his father began to talk more about his time in Bolivia. Jerry tried to remember what his father had said about his time as a refugee, when he had been known as "Milan," but Jerry hadn't paid much attention. At the time, he thought it was best the old man dream about his romantic entanglements rather than what he would have faced had he remained in his homeland in Eastern Europe. Jerry's father had rambled on about his relationships with Latin women in Bolivia, extolling the virtues of one in particular named Soledad. He said he'd had a serious relationship with this Soledad, who lived in a sheltered environment and had to lie every time she sneaked out of the house.

But had his dad fathered a child? This went 'round and 'round in Jerry's mind. Would communication with Dario expose a family secret? He wondered if he should ask Dario for more information before committing to becoming involved. Young adult relationships came and went, and sometimes tough choices had to be made, but Jerry hadn't really believed his father was in an intimate relationship with Soledad. Not in Jerry's wildest dreams had he thought the

relationship his father had described—sometimes in the most sugges-
tive ways—had, in fact, taken place. Jerry had always thought they'd
just been a figment of the old man's vivid imagination.

"Were you in touch after you left?" Jerry had asked at his father's
side in the hospital, a few weeks before the old man's death.

"Some Christmas cards," his father responded, sheepishly.

"Did you hear back?"

As Jerry stared at him in the dim light of the room, his father shook
his head and didn't elaborate, instead falling asleep.

▲ ▲ ▲

After a week of resting his leg and pondering the email, Jerry gave
his jogging partner, Ron, a call. He was missing his regular runs and
his stress level told him it was time for a workout. Jerry reluctantly
said he would have to reduce his mileage, and Ron reassured him he
wouldn't mind shorter runs. They met the following day at the Lake
Chabot trailhead.

"Something odd happened last week, and I was hoping you'd hear
me out," Jerry confessed as they started their run down a paved, open
road. It was a warm day, and the forest cover would keep them cool,
so they quickly found a softer path leading into the woods. There
was nobody in sight when Jerry began to tell Ron about the stranger's email.

"It came as a shock," Jerry said.

"Jesus Christ, you better watch out; the world's full of crooks."

"I've dismissed it, but it still bothers me," Jerry said. "What if he's
telling the truth?"

"Or maybe he's a con artist looking for a sucker."

"The email made me think about my dad and the way we lost so
many family members during the Holocaust. What if I've found a new
relative? It's so unexpected."

"Think about his motive for contacting you. You might regret opening that can of worms."

"I wonder how this man knew to contact me. You know, my dad liked to give advice and often said you should always watch out for people trying to pull a fast one."

"There you go."

Jerry needed to stop for a rest when they reached a eucalyptus patch at the top of a gradual hill.

"Is it hurting?" Ron asked.

"A bit. The thing is, my dad was a product of terrible times, and he learned to distrust people's motives early in life. I didn't like this part of him and struggled to be more open-minded. I don't want to think that strangers should always be suspect."

"Is there anyone in your family who might know how this played out?" Ron asked.

"Everyone in my dad's generation is dead and, as far as I know, he didn't maintain friendships with anyone in Bolivia."

They walked back towards the parking lot in silence. By the time Jerry got in his car, he felt as confused as he had before.

▲ ▲ ▲

As Jerry went about his work building a set for an art installation in the following days, he thought about the strenuous efforts his father had made to save himself from the dangers of the Second World War brewing before his eyes in his native Czechoslovakia. He'd ended up in a Latin American country by sheer luck. Now Jerry wondered if he had abandoned a pregnant girl or if she had gone through the pregnancy without his knowing. By the end of the week, Jerry started to feel a growing urgency to find out who Dario was and if they were, in fact, half-brothers. No person's history was certain, and Jerry couldn't jump to any conclusions about Dario or his dad.

One evening after dinner, he put his dishes in the sink and went to his desktop computer. Enough worrying. He clicked on his inbox and found Dario's email. Taking a few deep breaths, Jerry felt his mind settle into the beginnings of empathy for the man.

Perhaps Dario's story was true. Maybe he just wanted to create a family tree and was looking for lost relatives. It might be somewhat risky to respond, but Jerry's father had died many years before and wouldn't be harmed, and he would be cautious. He'd say just enough to put the stranger at ease and encourage him to reveal the reason for his search.

> Hello, Dario.
> My father was a Czech immigrant named Goldberg, who did spend a few years in Bolivia before moving north. He changed his name to "Miles Gold" before I was born, and he may be the man you are looking for. Unfortunately, I know very little about my father's earlier private life. Before communicating further, I would like to know more about you and why you have contacted me.

A few days later the stranger wrote back, saying his mother had saved twenty-five Christmas cards Milan had sent over the years, which was how he'd been able to find Jerry through the internet. His mother and Milan had remained friends, and she cherished his cards until she'd passed.

After reading that first part of Dario's email, Jerry stared off into space, then leaped to his feet to pace around his mid-century modern living room.

*I can't believe it!* Jerry thought. *My father wrote to Soledad after I was born! Did she know what was going on with him? He was living a double life that included another son. What else was he hiding from me and my mom? Did he leave Bolivia to run from his pregnant girlfriend?*

Struggling to get his emotions under control, Jerry returned to his desktop to read the rest of the email. Dario had spent his early years in La Paz until his family moved to the United States, settling in Maryland. Dario was married, had two adult children, and his oldest was pregnant with her first child. His daughter and her husband were worried about their unborn child's health, and their obstetrician was considering ordering genetic tests to see if the baby carried certain genes that could manifest as a congenital disorder. As Dario's wife suffered from retinitis pigmentosa, and his daughter was married to a Jewish man, there was a high probability that the newborn might inherit the disease. If Dario could find out whether he and Jerry were related, this would help the couple decide whether to undergo an amniocentesis procedure in a few weeks. Amniocenteses were risky, and in light of Soledad's confession about Dario's biological father, the doctor wanted to gather health details from up to third-degree relatives before going ahead with the test.

Jerry Googled "retinitis pigmentosa" and found that it was a rare condition that, over time, would lead to progressive loss of vision. It was most prevalent among Ashkenazi Jewish people. Now it made sense why Dario had reached out to him to ask about his family history. They had to prove there was a genetic match to ensure that they were actually related.

As the days passed, Jerry tried to recall the stories he was told in his childhood. His dad had talked about an aunt who'd lived with them in Prague and suffered from loss of peripheral vision, eventually becoming blind. His father had said that he saw little of her, as she mostly stayed in her room and didn't interact with the children when he was growing up. This was an unmarried aunt who, as his father learned, had been transported to the Terezin deportation camp, before ultimately being murdered at a different death camp.

Jerry emailed Dario to share the few recollections about his father's family and the little he knew about his aunt. Dario responded with much appreciation and said he was grateful that Jerry was willing to cooperate during this challenging time for his family. He would share Jerry's information with the obstetrician and would be in touch if they needed to delve deeper.

In the next email, Dario told Jerry that he would be getting a call from Dario's primary care provider about giving a blood sample for genetic testing. Jerry wrote back that the test needed to be done immediately, because he would be traveling to Latin America for work in a few weeks' time. That same afternoon, Jerry received a call to arrange a lab appointment, and soon they would know the truth.

In his email at the end of the following week, Dario attached a picture of himself standing next to his daughter. The subject line read, "Congratulations." The blood sample had established identical DNA segments between Dario and Jerry, proving beyond a doubt they were half-brothers.

Dario extended an invitation for them to meet next time Jerry was in Washington, DC, adding that his daughter was scheduled to have an amniocentesis to detect chromosome abnormalities in the next few days.

Jerry wrote back immediately, asking for Dario's phone number. That evening, they had a surprisingly warm and animated call, both eager to meet up soon. Early summer, Jerry said, as he was planning to be in DC for the twentieth anniversary of his wife's death. Then the old familiar ache in his chest returned, just as it always did whenever he thought of Claire.

▲ ▲ ▲

Claire, had been twenty-three when they'd met, working towards a master's degree in public health. After she returned from serving in the Peace Corps in Ecuador, the couple got married. They talked about having children, but as their careers took off, they delayed their decision until they were more established and secure. Claire, always attracted to South American culture, went to work for a nongovernmental agency helping women and children in need. The day before she got on a plane to fly back home from one of her visits abroad, they'd talked about how excited they were to see each other again after a month apart.

"I love you so much," she had said. "I don't know why we have to be separated."

The next day that plane crashed, and Claire had died instantly.

Jerry's world fell apart. At times he felt he couldn't go on living without the love of his wife. He lamented not having a family with Claire and, most of all, not spending their golden years together.

He'd grieved for five years until he decided to take a break from work as a carpenter and go traveling in the Andean countries of South America. His first stop was Ecuador, where he visited some of the villages where Claire had worked. Then came Peru where, in a remote highland location, he consulted with a shaman for advice on how to overcome loss.

He stayed in Peru for a while to continue his healing, which included consuming a powerful plant concoction to give him the strength to confront his innermost demons. His character was deeply tested, and the intense visionary experiences made him think hard about his outlook on life. The healing and clarity he experienced during his hallucinations were the beginning of a slow process of self-discovery. He was determined to change his fate and found purpose by grounding himself in a desire to create. Over the years, he became a brilliant designer, much in demand by both architects and artists.

# CHAPTER 2

# The East Bay, California, 2008

"Get ready to come—there's talk reparations will come into effect." These were the only words Otilia Perez heard when her son tried to explain why he was calling her at work.

Seven years before, after a democratic government took power in Peru, a Truth and Reconciliation Committee was formed to look into complaints of human rights violations during years of civil conflict under past administrations. Otilia and Salvador patiently waited to be called to a hearing requesting compensation for families who'd been separated and forced to flee, as they had been.

She cut the long-distance call short because she was bracing herself to meet with her supervisor to negotiate a new position with the firm. She took a deep, anxious breath. The lunchroom was noisy with no breathing space, so she promised to call Salvador in Lima at the end of the day.

Otilia worked for a business providing electrical equipment and services to construction companies. She'd been with them for ten years, starting at an entry-level position in the accounting department and moving up. Otilia questioned whether she would be able to travel back to South America for an appointment at the Reparation Council in Lima if she got the promotion she had worked so hard for. There were many capable applicants, but she had a hunch that the accounting manager, Sharon Thompson, favored her.

Before one o'clock Otilia walked down the hall to the staff bathroom to comb her shoulder-length hair and apply her favorite coral lipstick, then on to one of the multiple private offices in the building. She knocked on the door.

"Just give me a minute, Otilia. I'll be right with you," Sharon said, smiling over her shoulder as she stood filing away some documents.

Otilia came in, sat down, and looked at the framed photograph of Sharon's family on a river hike. She bit her lip, holding back tears as she thought of her own life in Peru, when she'd lived with her husband and son twenty years back, before trouble began. She escaped all alone when escalating tensions between government armed forces and The Shining Path guerilla factions threatened her family's way of life. For Otilia, the menace had seemed remote, but her husband Manuel felt differently. He'd made the decision to take their seven-year-old son, Salvador, into hiding in a mountain village before returning for her.

"They're after the children. They kidnap to indoctrinate," he'd said, before leaving in a rush. She'd stayed behind to mind the family property and despair over them. She waited for him, but he did not return.

"Thanks for coming, it's so nice to see you," Sharon said. "How are you doing?"

Sharon always put Otilia at ease with her soothing voice. They'd worked together for a long time, and Sharon had helped her grow, pushing her to improve her English and pursue her education in accounting.

"As you know, Stu is retiring in a few months, and you are the perfect candidate for the job. You're reliable and have strong analytical skills. We would like to offer you the position of Payables Manager, and you can start working with Stu until he leaves, beginning next week."

"I am certainly thrilled to accept your offer, but I must deal with a difficult personal situation right away." Otilia could tell her Spanish accent was becoming more pronounced, which always happened when she was nervous.

"Oh, what's going on?"

"I've mentioned before that I have a pending human rights abuse case back in Peru."

"Yes, concerning the displacement your family suffered during the war."

"Exactly," Otilia replied. "Now the Reparation Council is requesting an in-person meeting to review the facts and see if I qualify for compensation."

"That's terrific!" Sharon said. "Finally, after so many years, they want to hear from you to make amends. How do you feel about it?"

"I'm anxious and a little skeptical. I don't know what lies ahead. Will it be more of the same: Bringing up the details of what happened one more time? I'm tired of filling out lengthy forms to prove I deserve justice. I'm actually dreading the process."

"My dear, you've got to go and try to get what you deserve. We can wait and you can assume your new responsibilities when you return. Stu still has a couple more months left with us."

"I keep telling myself I have to think positively," Otilia said. "There are changes happening in Peru under the new president and being called for an interview is a step in the right direction. I'm hoping that there is still a possibility of getting my family's property back."

▲ ▲ ▲

After work, when Otilia got in her car to leave the business park, she felt a cool wind whipping up from the San Francisco Bay. Settling into the driver's seat, she turned on the heat.

Driving through the quiet streets of Hayward, she glanced at the sun setting against the background of hills, still green in early March. With traffic flowing smoothly for a change, she entered the freeway, making her way to the stucco bungalow she was renting in San Leandro, a town about twenty minutes away.

Otilia cringed when her mind, once again, went to her own hasty retreat from her village of El Milagro when Manuel didn't appear and Sendero Luminoso, the Shining Path guerillas, arrived. She'd left her home, thinking Salvador was safe with his father, and she would reunite with them soon. She'd taken along some warm clothes for herself and her boy in one small bag, carrying no keepsakes and no documents other than her ID card. But life took a different turn, and each one of them was compelled to their own perilous fate.

She'd tried tracking them down but found only obstacles in her way. Within days she was trapped high in the Andes in a mining camp, working in the kitchen, housed in a cramped space with several other female workers, and agonizing over her husband and son. There Otilia met Michael Sweeny, an American geologist from California, who helped in her search. But after six months of police requests going unanswered and people being arrested and vanishing, she feared being next and took a bold step. When Michael gave her the option to leave the country, she did. Otilia agreed to find refuge in Michael's sister's home in San Francisco's East Bay, although she had only a vague idea of where it was.

It was 1989 when she arrived as a refugee. Desperate for word from Manuel and Salvador and backed by a supportive Latino community in her quiet struggle for information, Otilia joined forces with those who had fled Latin American countries and were looking for loved ones from abroad. Together, they raised their voices to demand details about those who'd gone missing. They made headway, but it wasn't through them that she finally learned where Salvador was. Five years ago, Otilia received a letter from Salvador letting her know he'd met a nurse who remembered her from the time she worked at the mining camp. Otilia clearly recalled the day before her departure telling Rosa, the nurse at the Andean health clinic, that if anyone showed up looking for her, to please give them Michael's address in California.

Her dreams had come true. Her son Salvador, a grown man, had written about being separated from his parents after his father, Manuel, took him into hiding. Determined to track them down, he was inquiring whether Otilia could be his mom. After that letter came a phone call and the next thing she knew, they had planned to meet in San Francisco when Salvador flew up for a work conference.

Looking at her side mirror, Otilia signaled and swiftly turned off the highway. Forced to come to an abrupt stop when cars began backing up at the exit, she left her thoughts to concentrate on the road and the urban jungle surrounding her. Otilia's eyes watered from traffic fumes as she drove slowly down the ramp towards the leafy boulevard. People were shopping at the corner butcher store and coming and going from the neighborhood coffeehouse. At the next stop sign, Otilia turned right and parked in her driveway. She hurried inside to call her son.

▲ ▲ ▲

A lot had gone wrong in Peru: a brutal conflict, guerilla warfare, extreme ideology, military dictatorship, oppressive governments, and enormous infringements of human rights. For decades there was no coming together from either the Left or the Right. When the Peruvian Truth and Reconciliation Commission was formed in 2001, they brought out thousands of witnesses to provide information about the horrifying events between 1980 and the early 2000s.

"Who was at fault?" people asked. "Was it the guerillas or the armed forces? Would it be possible to have justice after carnage?" It seemed unlikely—justice wouldn't bring back the dead or heal the wounded. It wouldn't comfort those tormented by loss, the women who'd been raped, or the children who'd lost their parents. But those whose lives had been devastated couldn't exist with indifference, and justice was called for to ease their pain and help them build new lives.

Trying to set the historical record straight, the Truth and Reconciliation Commission heard testimonies from thousands of survivors and prepared recommendations to restore hope and begin to repair the harm. Some were shocked and scandalized by the commission's report on what had occurred in the country at the time. Others claimed they were deeply shaken by the report's bias in favor of the guerillas destroying the nation's way of life. The polarization grew. Nevertheless, forced to face the reasons as to why such violence had come about, with a community traumatized, the commission looked at the causes more carefully and determined that a disproportionate inequality in society was to blame. Recommendations were made to ensure that all public institutions evaluated how best to ensure social justice and equality for citizens.

Then another part of the story came into play. Reports unraveled slowly, and the people learned how in 1990, they had voted in the most corrupt and criminal government in Peruvian history. Alberto Fujimori, whose administration lasted ten years, had systematically plundered the country's coffers to satisfy his own interests. After Fujimori's election, everything appeared fine, but one needed only to scratch below the surface to uncover tremendous discontent among the public.

The government blamed its inadequacies on terrorist activity causing disruptions and barring them from governing properly. When the Shining Path terrorist leader, Abimael Guzman, was captured in 1992, the people were jubilant. Cities became safer and citizens felt relief at no longer needing to fear bombing on the streets. The level of outward threat was greatly diminished, but the president continued to operate above the law, concealing his complex illicit activities. Practical and political considerations overwhelmed moral concerns.

▲ ▲ ▲

Otilia looked at her watch and thought it might still be too early to call Lima. Salvador had a late shift and would not be home from work yet. She wanted to eat and think carefully about what to say. Otilia found a few glass containers with leftover food in the refrigerator and heated them up in the microwave. Acorn squash, lentils, and rice—a vegetarian meal was best for anxious digestion. She sat on a bar stool at the kitchen counter. She didn't like eating alone at the dining room table; it reminded her of her loss.

Meals were when she and her husband Manuel sat and talked about their business and the day's events. Even as a baby, Salvador had always been at their side, sitting in his high chair in his spot at the table, babbling away while they ate and chatted. A few years later it all came to a halt. She'd been deprived of memories of her baby growing up. No more stories at bedtime, no sweet smiles, no hugs and kisses to reassure Salvador that he need not worry about the monsters behind the door.

Otilia thought about the letter she'd received a few months ago from a Peruvian government lawyer advising her that Peru was open to healing the effects of the past. They were willing to provide help to those who'd suffered displacement, encouraging survivors to fill out the enclosed application and apply for compensation. Reparations would help regain civic trust and achieve a degree of justice for victims of violence and loss. However, the letter pointed out, it was still unclear how the government would choose to compensate people. These issues were currently under discussion, and she would be hearing about them soon.

The lawyer, speaking on behalf of the government, acknowledged there was a need to "make right" people's losses, to determine a settlement for damages. But since it would be costly for the state to take on all of the responsibility for people's hardships, citizens needed to realize that there were times in a nation's history when bygones should be considered bygones.

"Forget the past and move on? No," Otilia had shouted. "What happened to providing stability and predictability for ordinary citizens?" Even today as she grappled with these thoughts, they provoked outrage in her. The past had left deep-seated marks on her psyche and had caused Salvador great distress. It had been a shock for her when she discovered that her son had suffered the loss of his family and then had to struggle against all odds to find a relative. Salvador had lived on the streets before he was able to locate his uncle, Tomás, who offered no help to track down his parents.

Reparations were important. People had put faith in their government to protect their best interest and it had failed them. Making amends was essential and she vowed to seek compensation for every one of the damages and each injury her family had endured.

▲ ▲ ▲

Otilia took a moment to glance at the belongings she now possessed: the floor-to-ceiling shelf she got at the thrift store for her books, the vintage pedestal table she fell in love with one day while antiquing at the Alameda Point antique fair, the woven woolen tapestry hanging on the wall in her living room depicting an Andean village in muted tones. Then she smelled the bright red carnations she had bought for herself on the weekend to cheer herself up. Slowly she eased herself into an armchair to make the call.

▲ ▲ ▲

"*Hola, mijo*," Otilia said.

"Mamá, good to hear your voice," Salvador replied.

"What is happening?" Otilia asked, continuing in Spanish.

"I wanted to let you know that we're ready to make an appointment with the Reparation Council. When can you come down to testify?" Salvador asked.

"I had a conversation with my boss and was offered the promotion, but I still have some work to complete before I can come down. I'll let you know by the end of the week how long it will take me."

"*Felicitaciones*, congratulations!" With hesitation in his voice, he continued, "You need to know I've discovered another stumbling block."

"What's happened?"

"While waiting for the Reparation Council to review matters, I went up north to our village to look into our property's history and got some disturbing information."

There was a pause. "Yes?" Otilia finally asked.

"Right after you left, it seems that Tomás Campos stole your land."

"¿*Cómo*? What? How is that possible?"

"There was a sham government—people were paid off."

"How could he have made a transaction without proper documents?"

"When I lived with my uncle, and perhaps because he felt burdened by having to care for me, he persuaded government clerks to transfer our family property into his name."

"*Dios mio*, that greedy thief!" Otilia cringed at his memory, and made a hasty sign of the cross.

"When I found out, I was so furious I decided to do my own investigation," Salvador continued. "I went looking for him to better understand what he did. Had he been an honest guy, we wouldn't have suffered such damages."

"He really hurt us. Is he living it up like a king? Enjoying our money?"

"Mamá, you wouldn't believe it but he's sitting in prison right here in the city."

"How come?" Otilia asked.

"I checked the database and police reports, found records for his arrest."

"The advantage of working for the police force," Otilia said ruefully. "What are the charges?"

"He got caught trying to cross the southern border with cocaine."

"That crook."

"I'll go see him on Friday. I want to hear the details from his own mouth."

"Be careful. He's the type who thinks nothing of making a deal with a thug and you could get beaten up."

"He's behind bars and will be for a while before he even gets his day in court. Trials are delayed, the prisons are full beyond capacity. Then he'll get anywhere from eight to fifteen years for smuggling drugs." Salvador paused. "Fortunately, he's locked up, but he should also be serving time for theft."

Otilia was furious and couldn't get the dark thoughts out of her mind. She was now forced to think about her brother again, the brother she'd cut out of her life for having impacted the family business interests. How could Tomás have gotten away with appropriating their property? Maybe she'd find out more details once Salvador questioned him. She was so proud of her son, who had started his career as a policeman before rising to the ranks of forensic officer, performing analysis on evidence taken from victims caught in the ongoing armed conflict.

She was stunned to discover that after all the decades of violence, both from Shining Path terrorist organizations and the Peruvian military, it was a member of her own family who was to blame for the loss of their assets. *But why should she be surprised?* she thought. *Tomás was an underhanded bastard who'd think nothing of deceiving others to live beyond his means.*

She was happy to know Tomás was rotting away in a packed, corrupt jail, where he would be sleeping on a cockroach-infested mat and was expected to pay for his daily upkeep. And with this thought another came, which she swore she would keep to herself. Had Tomás been involved in Manuel's disappearance?

# CHAPTER 3

## En Route to Lima, Peru, 2008

O tilia's heart pounded loudly as the flight attendant in her high heels and tight skirt made sure seat belts were on, seat backs were in an upright position, and carry-on luggage was safely stored away. Otilia was on her way to Peru. Sharon had been supportive, giving her time off with pay, assuring her everything would go well. Otilia was relieved that the middle seat between herself and the man on the aisle was empty. She looked out the window as the plane flew through low-lying clouds and San Francisco rapidly disappeared from sight. When she could no longer see what they were flying over, she sat back.

She was soon preoccupied with thoughts of how to find witnesses from twenty years ago if she wanted to regain her property. How could she possibly find them when, during her last visit to her village of El Milagro, she'd hardly recognized anyone? Many villagers had been displaced—some had left for other cities, others to reunite with family abroad. Who could she trust since she'd become estranged over the years? She was now considered an outsider to those who remained.

The land where they lived and carried out their business had belonged to her parents, and when they passed, it had been willed to herself and her brother, Tomás. They worked trading horses and cattle, which sometimes took Manuel and Tomás to off-the-beaten-track places. When Tomás opted out, he was well compensated. All three of them—she, Manuel, and Tomás—had gone to see the notary public to have the title of ownership transferred to Otilia and Manuel. The notary, an elderly man, had a reputation as an honest person, according to the villagers. He was probably not alive today. He'd drawn up the documents and had notified them before taking the deed to be registered in Manuel's name.

Otilia complained bitterly, letting him know that both her and Manuel's names should be recorded, since it was her money as well. But custom had it that only the husband's name would appear on official documents. She left it at that, for she knew that she wouldn't be able to fight the *machista* attitude that prevailed.

She recalled that once transfer taxes were paid and the deed recorded, the notary had said the transaction was finally complete. That night, she and Manuel went out to celebrate. But had they made a mistake? They'd been put through an ordeal, with months of delay before the filing had taken place, as no matter how hard they tried to move the process along, the excuse always was that the offices were understaffed because personnel had to deal with vague regulations that were difficult to interpret.

Had all this business of blaming the so-called cumbersome procedures been a pack of lies? Were she and Manuel inadvertently to blame for not checking the papers more carefully? Had a poorly executed title transfer turned into a costly mistake? If there had been room for fraud afterwards, the key was to figure out if there was still anyone in the village who could vouch for the bogus conveyance. Pushing back festering memories, Otilia decided she'd leave all her worries behind until she was forced to face them head-on in the next few days.

She reached for the issue of *People* magazine she'd tucked into the seat pocket in front and, resting her head against the window, began flipping through the pages. When a child a few rows behind started to cry, Otilia heard the mother telling the flight attendant she wanted a Coke with ice for the child.

"A Coke for a toddler?" the man sitting next to her said, shaking his head.

Otilia looked at him, raised her eyebrows and smiled.

Dinner was being served as the man closed his laptop and placed it under the seat. "Where are you flying?" he asked. This was a polite icebreaker for an anxious flyer, and she appreciated it.

His name was Gerald Gold, close to her age, possibly in his early fifties, tall and slim with salt and pepper hair curling below his earlobes. A potentially awkward social situation turned pleasant while they ate. He was a designer who had started as a carpenter, building sets for the theater before slowly making his way into the art scene. He was stopping in Lima for a few days before going to Santiago, Chile, for work.

"Is this your first trip to Peru?" Otilia asked.

"I've been there before," Gerald replied. "The last time was after my father passed away in 1999. Went traveling in the highlands and the Amazon. Swam with the piranhas, then went on to Bolivia to take some of his ashes."

"Oh, I'm sorry," she said with a polite smile and went back to her meal.

After the meal, the lights were dimmed for the night. Rising, Otilia excused herself to edge past Gerald. He swiveled his knees towards the aisle to let her through. She walked to the back of the plane noticing a couple in their twenties, lovers kissing, snuggling in their seats. It made her think of Manuel and wish she was going home to Peru to see him again.

She stood in front of the bathroom mirror and examined her face.

Her usually lush hair hung limp and there were deep bags underneath her dark brown eyes. What would Manuel think of her now? Her image of him was still that of a strong young man. She cupped her hands to splash water on her pale face and took another look after she dried it. Otilia pulled her hair back, twisting it up into a knot, then grabbed her toothbrush from her purse. When she was done, she returned to her seat to get some sleep, wrapping herself in the airline blanket.

A few hours later, Gerald noticed she was awake and started to chat. "Are you going home?"

"Not exactly home. I live in the States. I went into exile."

"You're going for a visit."

"Yes, to see my son and daughter-in-law." Although Otilia usually spoke of her story openly, as this was her way of grieving, she remained silent this time. What difference did her story make to this stranger?

He didn't ask her for details and began telling her about his work.

"What does a designer do?" Otilia asked.

"I help artists execute their work. Sometimes I gather objects, other times I help with the fabrication—whatever is needed to get them ready for an exhibition."

"Where are these shows?"

"Galleries, museums, all over the world."

"All very abstract—modern?" She asked, feeling somewhat awkward about not having a good understanding of that world.

"Not necessarily. Artists portray things in many ways; some are very realistic."

"I often look at modern art and think that a child could have done that," Otilia said.

"That's a common reaction." He laughed. "I like to work with people who have a lot of enthusiasm and passion. Those are the artists who can express their ideas best."

"It's very . . . ah . . . how do you say? I work with numbers, very concrete." She smiled.

"Yes, it's subjective. Here, let me show you," he said, reaching for his laptop.

Gerald put on his wire-rimmed reading glasses and said, "I just came from a project where the artist created spatial waves of different kinds of metals in all sizes and colorings to interpret emotions."

"I see, unusual," she said, looking at the photographs. "And what is taking you to Chile?"

"I'm going to a ceremony where the first stone will be laid for the Museum of Memory and Human Rights. Have you heard about it?"

"I'm afraid not," she said. "But it sounds interesting, I should find out more about it."

"I was a consultant to the architectural firm who bid on the contract to build it. They needed to hear from curators and designers to understand what kind of exhibition halls would be appropriate. But I'm talking too much, tell me about yourself."

*He's traveling the world, doing exciting things*, she thought, feeling they were on different wavelengths. Again, she turned away as she struggled to continue the train of the conversation.

She wasn't expecting to meet anyone on her flight, but Jerry, as he'd asked Otilia to call him, was engaging and down-to-earth with a love for adventure and art. Just a bit too intense, though.

A few minutes later the captain announced they were about to land. "Perhaps you can show me around Lima," Jerry said.

"I'll be very busy during my stay," Otilia replied politely over her shoulder.

"It would be nice if we could go out for a drink when I return in a couple of weeks."

She pursed her lips. "Maybe."

Jerry awakened an excitement she hadn't felt for a long time, but she couldn't give in to such thoughts at this time.

"Let me help you with your bag," he said, looking at her kindly as she reached into the overhead bin.

"Thank you," she replied, welcoming his attention.

Before they went their separate ways, he insisted on getting a phone number where she could be reached, and she gave him her son's home number before saying goodbye.

# CHAPTER 4

## Lima, Peru, 2008

Salvador found a seat on a bus heading out to the prison at the edge of a shantytown. He was hoping that a meeting with his uncle, Tomás, would give him some clues about what happened after his parents were separated from him. The stony mountains in the distance surrounded by sandy desert terrain made for a hot, dusty ride. No trees were in sight—only trash, stray dogs, and shacks made of cardboard and wood, covered with pieces of flat corrugated tin roofing secured by heavy stones.

As the bus went along, Salvador saw a group of women carrying buckets of water back to their huts after refilling them from the *aguateros*, water trucks. He'd read an article about how, during the winter months, one community was trying to catch fog with plastic netting, turning it to droplets of water when the *garua*, heavy mist, blanketed Lima. Salvador felt strongly that price gouging shouldn't be tolerated. It wasn't right for these poor people to have to pay such a high price for water. A fog-catcher would help them reduce the amount of water they'd need to buy.

▲ ▲ ▲

Salvador entered the prison gates, following an orderly line of elderly men carrying multiple plastic bags. When a person in the back started to yell, the advancing lineup came to a stop. Almost immediately a guard raised his baton and struck the unruly man to one side.

At the first security checkpoint, bags were opened for inspection. Since Salvador carried no package, he was told to move on. Next, he spread his legs wide for a pat-down. Up ahead, after showing his identity card, he was given a metal token with a printed number he'd have to return to the guards on his way out to account for his visit. Lastly, while shuffling along, he was asked to contribute a few *soles* for soft drinks for the guards. He reached into his pockets and found a few coins, which he dropped in a box at the end of the corridor.

In the prison yard, Salvador was keenly aware of the throng of people milling about. *These places are jam-packed*, he thought as he looked for his uncle in the crowd. Inmates talking to suited lawyers, visitors meeting up with family members, joggers getting exercise, and a group of men shooting hoops. Cooked meals, fruit, drinks, batteries, radios, and clothes for sale were set up in stalls against decrepit walls. Long lineups of raucous men waited to use a few public phones that only accepted calling cards. Among the cacophony, supervising guards moved through, keeping an eye on the inmates while yelling into their megaphones.

Salvador noticed Tomás, drawn and frail, walking slowly towards him, dragging his feet, his face grim. He seemed shorter than Salvador remembered him. It'd been years since they'd seen each other last, and the man had aged badly.

Tomás let out a deep breath, nodded, and pointed to a bench. Salvador checked out the courtyard, wrinkling his nose at the stench. Before Tomás rolled down his sleeves, Salvador noticed the naked female tattooed on his uncle's forearm. Tomás pulled two cigarettes out of his stained pants pocket and held out one for Salvador.

"No thanks, I don't smoke."

"So, you found me, kid. How about that?" His voice was loud. He lit his cigarette with trembling hands. "How's life?"

Salvador had no stomach for small talk. It was colder than usual for the end of March, and he wanted to be out of there as soon as he could.

Tomás coughed. "I'm stuck in this fucking place."

"I'm here for only one reason," Salvador said, staring him in the eyes.

"Thought you'd be wearing your cop uniform."

"Cut the crap," Salvador snapped.

Tomás looked puzzled, his face carved with age.

Salvador removed a pad of paper and pen from the inside pocket of his light jacket.

"What the fuck is that for?" Tomás sneered.

"I need facts."

"Say that again; I'm hard of hearing," Tomás said, leaning in.

"Since when?" Salvador looked at Tomás doubtfully. He knew he shouldn't make Tomás feel uncomfortable. He needed him to cooperate. He repeated the phrase, trying not to sound accusing.

Tomás griped, "Be nice. Remember that I took you in when you were an orphan—when your mother and father left you alone. You were just a grimy little beggar. Now it's your turn to take care of me—get me out of this nightmare."

"You crook."

"If you want information, you'll have to pay. You know this place is hell. Money here is everything. With cash, I can pay off guards, bend the rules, make phone calls, get a decent mattress, and buy drugs. As you can see, there is a lot of stuff to be had. I'll not be stuck in this shithole any longer without any dough. So, what do you want?"

"I want to go back to 1988, when you took me in. I want to know how you were able to transfer my mother's property to your name."

Tomás's face lost its little remaining color.

"I want to know who you talked to, who was your contact at the municipality, who prepared the documentation, the name of the notary, and who you sold our property to," Salvador said, jabbing his finger at his uncle.

Tomás took a puff of his cigarette, blowing the smoke into Salvador's face. "I don't know if I can remember that much."

"You're senile now? You better get your shit together if you want a better life. And I also want your bank statements, all of them."

Tomás laughed. "I wish I had a bank account."

"I mean it. I want to see your records," Salvador said, ignoring Tomás's smirk. It was clear his uncle had no intention of cooperating, so Salvador stood and strode away.

Realizing he would be left empty-handed, Tomás began to scurry after Salvador. "As you can see, I won't be able to get to my files," the older man simpered.

"Nevermind, I can find them on my own," Salvador said, walking straight to the exit.

▲ ▲ ▲

Salvador got a message from his uncle that afternoon saying that he had information to give him.

The next day, Salvador took an extended lunch break and returned to the endless lineup at the prison gate. This time, however, when he showed his police badge, a stern guard motioned him to pass through the turnstile.

Tomás moved slowly across the courtyard, where Salvador met up with him. Tomás reached out and they shook hands, then walked towards the same wooden bench they'd occupied the day before. Tomás pulled out a long list of items he'd scribbled on a piece of rough brown paper.

"This is what I need," he began. "I still have a long time in this dump and can't survive the way I've been living."

"Before we go there, tell me how in God's name did you end up here?"

"They got us for a defective brake light at the border. It was a sham. Me and my *pata*—a good buddy from way back—were a team. We paid his friend, a border patrol cop, to let us through, but he wasn't on duty that night, so we got locked up for carrying cocaine. But, say, how is Carmen? That's your wife's name, right?"

"What do you care? You said you have information. I want details," Salvador said.

"I want seven hundred *soles*, plus all the items on this list first."

"You son of a bitch. You think you're so smart. Don't you understand that this is not a business deal?"

Salvador saw tension in Tomás's face.

"This is a straight deal. If you don't pay, I won't cooperate."

"It's your call. Now that I found you, I can find the information."

"You're kidding," Tomás said.

They sat in silence. Salvador's cell phone vibrated in his pocket and he stepped away to take the work call. When he was finished, he did not sit back on the bench; instead, he walked away.

"Hang on," Tomás called.

"Okay then," Salvador said, looking back.

"When my landlord found out that I was in prison, he came to visit and told me I could keep a few of my belongings in his storage shed. I think that's where you'll find what you need." Tomás seemed out of breath as he walked alongside.

Salvador felt a glimmer of hope he didn't show. "I'll give you two hundred *soles* right now, and the rest of the money after I see if your information is of any use to me."

"Please give him a *propina*, the landlord could use a bit of cash— he's a good guy."

"Write down his address and telephone number. I'll get back to you," Salvador said, walking away quickly.

He hoped he would have some news before his mother arrived in Lima the next day.

# CHAPTER 5

## Lima, Peru, 2008

Once Otilia cleared immigration and customs, she went straight through the doors to exit the modern arrival building. A large crowd waited outside as airport authorities didn't allow visitors to enter the terminal. She could see Salvador and Carmen in the distance, and when they made eye contact, they rushed to her side. They hugged and kissed her and told her how much they had missed her.

"I hope you'll be able to take a rest while you're here," Carmen said. Otilia smiled. "The weather is getting warmer and you can enjoy the beach."

Salvador took her luggage as Carmen linked arms with her mother-in-law to navigate passing cars as they walked towards the parking lot.

Otilia felt tired after the long flight but was eager to make conversation with her loved ones in the car. She hesitated to ask Salvador if he'd gotten new information from Tomás, and the moment there was a lull in their chatter, she leaned her head back and closed her eyes. She wondered if the office registering her claim would even bother to view her case, since Tomás had succeeded in getting hold of their land. She did not doubt that in the shadows of war, when confusion reigned and it was a free-for-all in real estate, her brother could have bribed the officials in charge. She shouldn't concern herself right now, she was sure that Salvador and their lawyer would follow the paper trail. After all, there was the trauma of separation, the absence of a husband and father, the years of searching for one another. Their possessions and connections were gone, a family erased.

"Mamá, as soon as we get home you better take a nap," she heard Salvador say, when he noticed her eyes open, in the rearview mirror,

"I'm fine, it's just that I have lots on my mind," Otilia replied.

▲ ▲ ▲

On her first full day in Lima, midmorning, when the somber clouds hovered in the sky, adding to Otilia's sadness, she left her son and daughter-in law's apartment to visit the memorial park. Amid the bustling capital, she held a special place in her heart for this place. She waved down a *combi*, paid the driver's assistant the bus fare, and asked to be let off at Campo de Marte park. Stepping out in the middle of a residential neighborhood, she walked a few blocks, passing by older colonial houses interspaced with newly built apartments until she reached the ample green expanse at the park's entrance. Then, she followed the signs towards the path that would take her to the monument. Ahead, children playing a game of Follow the Leader, skipping from one rock to the next, crisscrossed in front of her. Their mother ran over to admonish them and pulled them away. Otilia thought of the beautiful family she'd lost, and her knees nearly buckled when she remembered how wrong she'd been to assume that her search efforts to find them would be carried out. Shivering, she pressed her cotton shawl snugly around her shoulders and hurried on.

Then she saw the newly erected fence around the area where the sculpture known as *El Ojo que Llora, The Weeping Eye,* had gone up a year ago. She walked over to look at the portrait of a man bearing his name, affixed with tape and pins to the fence, and several wooden crosses with different names written on them. She opened the gate, entered, and walked to the black granite stone statue representing Mother Earth, crying for the suffering endured by her children. She followed the spiral labyrinth pathway surrounded by thousands of stones with inscriptions of names and stopped in front of the remembrance stone she'd laid in 2005 in Manuel's memory. She was heartbroken by the site's somberness. Tears filled her eyes as emotions flared and overwhelmed her.

It was a shame that access to the area was restricted, and it was kept behind locked gates, only opened to the public a few days a month. All because it had been severely vandalized by supporters of the former president Alberto Fujimori the day he was extradited from Chile back to Peru to face grave charges of human rights violations during his time in office.

Otilia laid down the flowers she carried and removed a votive candle from her purse. It was not a proper grave, but the closest she could give Manuel, bless his soul. Salvador had not been in favor of memorializing his father this way, since he hadn't been declared officially dead. But as they would only be able to obtain a death certificate and have a proper burial site after Manuel's body was found, Otilia insisted she wanted a space where he could be remembered properly.

Making a sign of the cross, her eyes on the flickering light, Otilia bowed her head to pray. Here, she could weep and honor his name, openly displaying public grief. There was no one around. Forgotten, dismissed—those whose names appeared in this park, those who had not had a chance to say goodbye, who were killed or just disappeared prematurely from this earth. She felt sad that this new generation of young adults, born after the peak of guerilla troubles, didn't know much about what had gone on and didn't have the need to grieve for relatives they never knew.

Lulled by the rhythmic repetitive phrases she continued to utter in prayer, Otilia felt calmer. Slowly coming from prayer to reality, she looked up and noticed traces of orange paint still left on some of the hundreds of memorial stones that lay beyond. "How could these vandals have done such a thing?" she whispered angrily.

Then, she saw the smashed stones on the other side of the fence. "Don't they have any respect?" Otilia prayed that no one would ever deface Manuel's stone. Here was the only proof of his existence. She lingered for another painful hour.

▲ ▲ ▲

The afternoon had turned sunny and the streets of Salvador's neighborhood were free of cars. Up ahead the road was under repair and resting workmen in overalls gathered to smoke. On the next block she went by a couple carrying a beach chair and an umbrella to soak up the sun at the beach. She looked for a bakery and found two of them on the ground floor of different apartment buildings on opposite sides of the street. She went into the first one and saw that they mostly sold bread and a few large cakes. At the second one she found the pastries she was looking for: *alfajores*, her favorite treats, delicious cookies that tasted so different in the US. There, the dough was dense, but here, the heavenly light meringue dough sandwiched with caramel filling would melt in your mouth. She bought a dozen cookies and walked back to her son's place, looking forward to feeling a sense of belonging when the three of them sat down together for tea.

▲ ▲ ▲

Otilia was alone in the apartment when the phone rang.

"I just wanted to say it was nice meeting you." It was Gerald Gold. "Would you be free to visit *Yuyanapaq*? I don't know if I am pronouncing it correctly," Jerry said.

"It's a Quechua word," Otilia said.

"Are you free tomorrow afternoon?"

On the sixth floor of the Museum of the Nation, on neglected cracked cement walls, the *Yuyanapaq: Para Recordar* exhibit comprised some 179 photographs of graphic violence and human suffering. The images chosen for the installation represented major events that had devastated the country from 1980 to 2000, curated by the Truth and Reconciliation Commission to reflect memories of past experiences suffered.

"I'm sorry, I can't," Otilia said quickly. Her purpose in Lima was to get her personal affairs in order, not to navigate the dark visual imagery of intimate suffering with a total stranger. She wanted to see the exhibit, but needed to go by herself or, even better, to be able to reflect on the photographs with Salvador by her side.

Jerry paused. "I'm sorry, but since I'm leaving on Sunday, I thought I'd give you a call. Of course, you are here to see your family—no worries."

"Let's meet when you return. I'll still be here and will feel more settled," she said. "Have a good trip."

# CHAPTER 6

## Prague, Czechoslovakia, 1938; En Route to Lima, Peru, 1939

The winter sharpness was gradually fading in the city of Prague, Czechoslovakia, as Milan Goldberg prepared to attend a fur auction in Leningrad. For his trip to the Soviet Union, he would pack two suits, several white starched shirts, his heavy overcoat, and polished black leather rubber-soled boots, as there would still be snow on the ground in Russia in March. He became alarmed when, a few days before his departure, the German army marched into Austria, but Milan convinced himself that Hitler would not bother the Czechs. He had completed his military service before joining his father's business when his father took ill, and he was ready to defend his country from the Nazi intruders—if the military called him back.

Milan had lost his mother several years before his father's death, when he was in Leipzig, Germany, as an apprentice learning the family trade. He came from a long line of furriers and, as the firstborn son, it had been expected he would go into the business. Now, heading the company, trying to move it forward so he could provide for his blind aunt and his brother, Pavel, studying chemistry in London, he would be traveling to the most important fur auction of the time. The auction would be the first to be conducted in English rather than German, as the Soviets had recently developed a very competitive industry, under-cutting Leipzig pricing, and were keen to expand their export trade.

All of Europe would be there, plus other representatives from over 150 international firms, from Athens to Copenhagen, Berlin to the United States. He had brushed up on his English-language skills to communicate with the agents when they gathered to examine the mink, fox, sable, and lynx pelts up for sale. Milan was prepared for transactions to be slow-paced and full of protocol, which was the Soviet way. He had booked a hotel room for six nights and was ready to spend time drinking vodka and discussing politics. With the pos-sibility of war, these were troubling times for businessmen.

▲ ▲ ▲

Milan got to the Prague Central Station with plenty of time as a stream of passengers entered the main hall. He went to stand in line to pur-chase his ticket and then to buy a newspaper for the trip. He walked out of the ornate concourse to find the right track for his train. He had a long trip ahead, one that would take him from Prague to Tallinn, Estonia, then a transfer to Leningrad. He waited under the soaring steel and glass rooftop for some time, impatiently looking up at the departure board and checking his watch. When at last the train pulled into the platform, Milan hopped on his assigned car and made his way to his sleeping berth. When he heard the conductor blowing the whistle alerting passengers to departure, they were a half an hour late.

By morning the train sped through the countryside with maple and linden trees standing bare in the snowy fields. There was no sign of spring. In the late afternoon, the express rolled into Leningrad where Milan was met at the platform by the Soviet state's representative of

Sojuzpushnina, the People's Hide and Fur Cooperative. It was the day after International Women Workers' Day, and countless red banners were displayed on the lamp posts inside the station. "Emancipated Women Unite" read the signs written in both Cyrillic and Roman alphabets.

"I'm Victor Popov," the agent said, extending his arm and introducing himself in halting English when Milan approached him.

Milan removed his hat before shaking Victor's hand. "Good morning, Tovarisch Popov," he said. "I see you've had a celebration."

"Flags of liberation," Popov replied.

Milan was surprised that Victor was slovenly dressed, with a scruffy beard and bad teeth. His shabby brown trousers hung below his thin woolen coat, and he kept his fur hat on.

As they walked out of the station, Milan tried to engage Victor in small talk using his limited Russian. Victor told him that his car was waiting outside, nearby. A biting wind sent Milan's hat flying, and he ran after it. As he bent over to pick it up, icicles dripping from the roof's edge wet Milan's head.

On his way to the hotel, dim lights appeared on the lampposts. Victor pointed out important landmarks and spoke of the city's European influence.

"Peter the Great built the city after returning from the Dutch Republic. Over there you can see the Peter and Paul Fortress on the river Neva. Frozen now. Many serfs died building the city," he said.

Milan listened quietly. In Stalin's Soviet Union, Milan was stunned at the level of poverty he saw on the streets. Imposing neoclassical style buildings with geometrical columns, some in pastel colors, were in disrepair and covered with grime. There were few cars on the road but many heavy trucks.

▲ ▲ ▲

When they arrived at their destination, Victor accompanied Milan to the check-in desk to be registered as a foreign guest.

"How long are you staying?" the clerk asked brusquely. He started to fire off typical questions to verify the purpose of Milan's trip.

"Here is my confirmation, all spelled out in Russian. Here is the form."

After a few minutes Victor interrupted to speak with the clerk.

"You get your room," Victor said as the clerk told Milan to step over to the next counter.

"May I please have your passport?" a different clerk asked in perfect English.

"I'm back in the morning," Victor said after Milan had been shunted from person to person.

A bellboy escorted him to his room located at the end of a hall where an attendant sat on a stool. The elderly woman wearing a flowered headscarf was there to keep tabs on the comings and goings of guests, he supposed. She didn't smile or respond when Milan wished her a good night.

The next morning Milan went to the dining room for a plentiful breakfast and wondered about the shortage of food he'd heard the average Soviet worker faced. He'd read about family members taking turns waiting in long lines outside grocery stores for scarce goods. Although publicity made it sound as if the Soviet Union had a mighty regime, able to industrialize the country in a short time, Milan knew about the purges and mass arrests that took place, as Stalin held absolute control.

▲ ▲ ▲

By October, when Czechoslovakia was divided by the Nazis and two of its provinces were annexed by Germany, refugees began to arrive in Prague in droves. Milan frequented coffeehouses, where he met German- and Austrian-Jewish migrants who talked about their mistreatments, the stripping away of their equality and ability to participate in society. They spoke of the plundering and brutality against the Jewish community, which was becoming widespread, and warned that Hitler would destroy Jewish businesses and synagogues throughout Europe. The threat was drawing close, and Milan felt relieved that he had decided to buy lower-quality skins at the auction in Leningrad. If what these people were saying was true, Milan's customers would spend more cautiously this coming winter.

As the weeks passed, Milan began to worry about his business and his own safety. He liquidated his inventory and began to withdraw money from his Czech bank account. In November, he hid cash inside the headlight compartments of his car and made a road trip to Zurich to open a bank account in Switzerland for safekeeping. He was lucky to get through the border with Germany without any trouble.

▲ ▲ ▲

In March of the following year, Milan awoke one morning, pulled open the curtains, and saw swastika flags flapping in the wind. "Damn it!" he cursed. The refugees had been right. In no time, Germany would begin to take action against the Czech Jews, and Nazi racial laws would apply here, too. Milan knew that although he was an assimilated, nonreligious Jew, he would still be a target of the Nazis. His sole option was to flee.

The hunt for a visa was difficult, with thousands of people frantically turning to foreign embassies in Prague. Foreign visas were required to exit the country, and since few consulates were willing to grant visas to Jews, Milan felt lucky to be able to purchase a visa to Cuba with a heavy bribe.

In London, Milan's brother, Pavel, became aware that the Brits were developing stronger sympathies for the plight of Czech exiles and were providing temporary asylum for endangered refugees. Pavel was able to help Milan obtain a trans-migrant visa directly to England. He made plans to leave right away.

The next day, however, when he went to get a train ticket to get across the border, he found he needed an exit visa to depart Czechoslovakia.

This he'd have to obtain from the Gestapo, the German secret police. His application was immediately denied, as it was noted that he'd visited the Soviet Union the year before and was therefore suspected of being a communist sympathizer.

"They've gone crazy," he said when he called his brother in London.

After a few sleepless nights, Milan had no second thoughts. He had to get out no matter how. He knew that he could not live in Nazi-occupied Prague. He found out a way: There were wilderness guides taking people out of the country for a fee. He hired a young man to take him over the border into Poland, and once there, he'd be able to catch a boat to England to meet his brother.

▲ ▲ ▲

It didn't begin well. The young man, Otto, arrived late, parked his motorcycle in an abandoned shed, and walked up to meet Milan with a cocky attitude.

"*Dobry den*, sorry, I slept in, had a late night after going to a boxing match. Too many beers, you know how it goes."

*A lame excuse*, Milan thought, his anger rising amid his nervousness.

Some time later, as he hiked along a trail in the rolling hills with sweat slowly trickling down his forehead, he forgot about his emotions, concentrating on his physical strength. Milan was slick with sweat when they reached the dense pine forest above, which gave off a scent he would never forget.

They heard running water in the distance, and Otto yelled, "I'll go fill my flask."

When Milan caught up to him, Otto was urinating against a poplar tree; then he lit a cigarette and took off again, continuing to pull ahead. Milan trailed behind, hoping evening would soon come. *Better to lag behind*, Milan thought, *than listen to his bellyaching about the state of the economy and lack of tourists coming to hike.*

The second day in the forest was rainy and cold, and Otto was restless to pull ahead. With the wind whistling on his back, Milan turned up the collar of his jacket, took a deep breath, and picked up his pace. It was slippery along the way; he got drenched. In several places the vegetation was dense, and he moved cautiously. At noon they stopped for a bite. Otto had promised to bring along enough food to last through the trip, but he said he'd only brought a few staples he found in his home, as he hadn't had time to go to the store. Milan's stomach growled, but he remained calm. Otto didn't allow a long break, as they needed to get across a checkpoint by four to avoid getting caught.

Milan was famished and asked for more food, but Otto said, "I told you we must keep to a ration."

*What an opportunistic, callous jerk,* Milan thought to himself. Milan was furious but knew that any attempt at a confrontation might lead to a bad outcome for himself, so he was better off controlling his temper and his hunger.

When they approached a road marking the border, Otto said, "Get down. German soldiers patrol the road here."

Searchlights in the distance illuminated the terrain. "When they turn their backs, we'll dash across and run down the hill."

Milan saw two German soldiers carrying rifles, marching one hundred meters away.

"Now," Otto whispered when the soldiers turned their backs. They ran the long stretch into no-man's-land.

▲ ▲ ▲

Milan awoke the following morning under a beech tree on a patch of soft grass. A mist hung in the air and the sun shone through the foliage. He looked around and spotted a deer, but noticed Otto was gone. He'd disappeared with Milan's backpack filled with clothes and his handgun. Milan got up and began to walk determinedly, following the trail marker that pointed to the next town. When he came to a meadow where poppies were budding, he felt the relief of being in Poland.

Milan traveled with American dollars in his money belt and found someone to give him a ride to Katowice on the back of a motorcycle. There, he bought a train ticket to Warsaw, where he arrived late at night and checked into a small hotel without luggage. As Polish was a similar language to Czech, the next day he had no problem finding his way to the offices of the Pacific Steamship Company where he purchased two first-class tickets, one to London and the other from London to Havana, Cuba.

▲ ▲ ▲

London was gray and it rained constantly, but Milan felt relieved to finally be away from the Nazis. Crossing the border had been risky, and he'd been naïve thinking that he would be able to walk leisurely from one country to the next. If they had gotten caught, he would have been executed on the spot and Otto sent to a concentration camp.

In London, Milan bought clothes for the ship, lightweight garments for the tropics as well as a tuxedo and black patent shoes, to follow the black-tie etiquette expected at dinnertime. He purchased some articles from a drugstore as well as a book to teach himself Spanish. He thought that it would be an easy language to learn, as he'd studied Latin in school.

"Of course, I won't remain in Havana. I'll join the US Army and they'll send me back to Europe to fight," he'd said with great confidence to his brother, Pavel, before he departed to Havana in the middle of May 1939. He had no doubt that six months later, war would be declared in Europe and men would be conscripted into the military.

Milan, ready for his great adventure, boarded the vessel called the *Orduña* in Liverpool, for an eight-day trip across the Atlantic.

When the ship arrived in Havana, Milan tipped his steward,

packed his bags and got ready to go ashore, but Jewish passengers were informed that none of them were allowed to disembark. The Cuban authorities claimed their visas were false.

Panic developed among the passengers. While the steamship company negotiated with the port authorities to allow passengers to stay in port for a few extra days to see whether the immigration problem could be resolved, the Jewish travelers formed a committee and telegraphed Jewish organizations in New York, asking for help. Would they get involved with the authorities in Havana or secure immigration permits to the United States? The committee's efforts failed, and the next thing Milan knew, the ship with its passengers was en route to Valparaiso, Chile. The Pacific Steamship Company was responsible for the passengers' welfare and was obligated to take them back to Europe.

It was music to Milan's ear when Pedro Valdez, the son of the Bolivian consul to Lima, told him he could help.

"Don't worry, man. Trust me, we can get you into my country."

Pedro was heading back to his country of birth after studying in Berlin. He was a bit younger than Milan, but they hit it off right away. They played ping-pong onboard, had good conversations, and, at night, flirted with the single girls.

A few days later the captain advised the Jewish passengers that they would be transferred to their sister ship, the *Orbita*, which was sailing from Valparaiso, Chile, back to Liverpool. Milan consulted with his friend Pedro again.

"It's arranged," Pedro said. "You'll get off in Lima where my father will issue you a permit to travel to Bolivia."

Sure enough, when the ship arrived in Callao, the port a few miles from Lima, the consul came onboard, stamped his passport and gave Milan a visitor's permit to enter Bolivia.

Milan was informed by an officer that he would be allowed to leave the ship right away, although a detective would accompany him, as he didn't have a Peruvian entry permit yet. But he needn't worry, as they were working on getting a temporary permit as soon as they could.

Milan was taken by the detective to meet the chief of police at a fancy restaurant, where he was invited to lunch with him. Although he didn't speak much Spanish, he was astounded by the man's generosity. The chief of police must have thought that Milan was a very important guest to have bestowed this gesture on him.

After lunch, the detective took Milan to a hotel and, using a few English and Spanish words, suggested he rest and wait until he obtained the approval to legally remain in Peru in transit. At around eight, there still was no permission granted for Milan to remain, so the detective returned to let him know that he would have to be escorted back to the ship, which would be sailing at ten o'clock.

▲ ▲ ▲

Milan was shown to the same cabin he had before, where the attentive steward offered him help to unpack. He changed and went to dinner quite late, wearing his tuxedo. As soon as he sat at the table, Milan ordered a drink. He noticed a few girls laughing at a nearby table and asked the best-looking one to dance.

On the beautifully polished wooden dance floor, he suddenly had a flashback of himself at age fourteen when his mother would drag him to dance classes. In the dance hall, mothers and daughters sat on chairs placed against the wall on one side of the room, while the boys and their mothers sat across from them. That's how he'd learned the foxtrot he was now moving to. As he smiled at the girl in his arms, he thought of the teacher raising her voice, repeating, "quick, quick; slow, slow." The girl pulled away, saying, "I feel seasick." A storm kicking up high winds and twenty-foot waves had started to pound on the ship en route to Chile.

Early the next morning, their ship met its sister ship the *Orbita* on its way back to England, and all of the Jewish passengers were asked to take their baggage and meet at the aft promenade deck. Lifeboats were lowered and filled with the travelers' belongings. Milan looked at the haggard faces of his fellow terrified passengers as all sixty-two of them were tendered to the *Orbita* to be swiftly transferred and delivered by the polite crew.

▲ ▲ ▲

A few days later, as the *Orbita* sailed back to Europe, Milan lay on his bed during the afternoon lull, anguishing over his future. Suddenly, there was a forceful knock on the door of his dark cabin, and the steward stepped inside.

"So sorry to disturb you, sir. I am here to inform you that a telegram has arrived authorizing you to disembark. The ship will sail close to port in a few hours and you'll be transported to shore."

Milan couldn't believe it. Suddenly he was in Chimbote, Peru, 250 miles north of Lima, in a small, poor northern fishing port. The day was warm, the sky blue; there was desert scenery with tranquil shorelines and plentiful beaches. People lived in windowless shacks with no radios and no international news.

What was to have been eight days of sailing actually took three weeks, but Milan was adaptable, and he was in the Americas—happy to be far from Europe.

# CHAPTER 7

## Lima, Peru;
## La Paz, Bolivia, 1939

At the Bolivian consulate in Lima, Milan waited for Sr. Valdez to arrive. He saw a poster of a large lake that read "Titicaca" and a number of totora reed boats at the edge of the barren shores. What did Milan know about Bolivia? Nothing at all. Most European immigrants couldn't care less about Latin America; one country was the same as another. They were underdeveloped, ruled by corrupt dictators keeping the population subjugated and in poverty. *But aren't we lucky to be there at this time?* Milan thought.

When Sr. Valdez, the Bolivian consul, appeared in the waiting room, Milan stood to greet him. They walked back to his office, where Sr. Valdez asked, "Have you had a good stay?"

"The hotel is first class," Milan said.

"My president has been persuaded, by a certain wealthy German Jewish entrepreneur living in my country, to issue thousands of visas to Jewish people escaping from Europe. And since you're already here, I recommend you get in touch with him. I am at your service;

my secretary can type your letters or, even better, we can send cables requesting a permit to let you in."

"Thank you so very much," Milan said.

"We are here to help Tuesday to Friday, from nine in the morning until noon."

▲ ▲ ▲

When Milan returned to the consulate two weeks later—after allowing time for a response from the wealthy entrepreneur's office—Consul Valdez was holding a map of Latin America in his hands, ready to unfold in front of Milan.

"It's all set. We got all the permits. You can make plans to depart."

"I am so appreciative."

"I recommend you first go by bus from Lima, south to the border with Chile, to the city of Tacna, about a thousand kilometers away. From there you will cross to Arica, another sixty kilometers farther south. Arica, here you see in northern Chile, is where you'll board the train to our capital, La Paz. This is the best way to get there."

"I see," Milan replied.

"Here is your transit visa," Sr. Valdez said. "It will allow you to stay in Chile for as long as you need, since the train doesn't operate on a regular schedule and you might have to wait a few days."

▲ ▲ ▲

Next thing Milan knew he was on the Jewish Express, *El Expreso Judío*, a train that took refugees from Arica to La Paz, Bolivia. A landlocked country, Bolivia had lost its coastline in the last century, after a war over mineral rights with its neighbors. The railway line had been built to take the minerals to the coast. The train was difficult to operate, having to climb from sea level to 14,500 feet. The advice Milan got before he left was to travel with an empty stomach to avoid getting sick as they climbed. Milan started his day with only a single cup of coffee.

Throughout the journey Milan felt that he was in unknown territory, a very different land from anywhere he'd ever been. He was surrounded by rocky desert in a desolate, daunting terrain. As the train reached the steep inclines, it needed a third cog rail for traction. Majestic mountains with snowy peaks began to appear in the background. When Milan looked out the window, he saw only a few skinny men herding a llama. Up ahead, the train came to a full stop and dozens of Indigenous women wearing brightly woven puffy skirts and bowler hats, some with babies swinging on their backs, emerged from small mud huts. They showed the passengers baskets of food and beckoned them to step down. Some intrigued Europeans looked out the window but remained in their seats, while Bolivian passengers hurried out. Milan was hungry and descended to buy a couple of bananas and a drink.

Local children gathered to stare at the railroad crew tinkering with the locomotive. Suddenly, a chorus of young voices started to holler a rhyme: *Arica La Paz, La Paz, La Paz, tres pasos pa tras, pa tras, pa tras*— from Arica to La Paz, La Paz, La Paz, three steps back, back, back. The engineer blew his whistle and soon the train started to move, while shoeless children ran alongside the track. Waving their knitted woolen hats, they shouted *adios* as the train gathered speed.

It was getting cold as they continued to climb, and Milan felt his ears pop and his breathing suddenly become forced. He heard other passengers begin to complain that they were having difficulty catching their breaths as well.

"*Soroche*," the man sitting next to him said. "The air is getting thin. Altitude sickness. Watch out that you don't get a headache. The best treatment is coca. Come, let's go to the dining wagon and get some coca leaf tea. I'm Gunther Blatt, by the way."

"How do you know so much about the local customs?" Milan asked when they were seated at a table in the dining car.

"By reading," Gunther said and laughed. "Did you notice the women back there with their distended cheeks and black teeth? They were chewing coca leaves. Not only does it help against altitude sickness, but it gives them energy. It's a mild stimulant and suppresses hunger and pain."

"Ideal!" Milan said. Then he realized he was not well informed about the people of the region. He didn't know what to expect and had a lot to learn.

"So, how did you obtain a visa to come here?" Milan asked.

"I come from a small town in Austria. My father was taken to Dachau; luckily, after four months, he was released. A scary experience, being imprisoned in a concentration camp. They did it to drive us away. After that, we knew we had to leave. The Bolivian consul in Vienna, one of Mr. Roland Finkel's network of agents, helped us. But, of course, it cost us an arm and a leg."

▲ ▲ ▲

Roland Finkel, also known as Don Rolando, owned a tremendous amount of land in South America. He had built up an outstanding business in the mineral industry and was known as one of the tin barons of Bolivia. He had come from Germany in the 1920s and, as the industry grew, he became an influential businessman. In 1938 he began to lobby the government to ensure that they would issue visas to save the lives of people fleeing from Nazi Europe. He argued that newcomers could contribute to the Bolivian workforce, in both industry and agriculture, and vowed to pay for the refugees' travel and housing expenses, as well as have jobs waiting for them when they arrived. Milan would be one of them and given employment in his company.

The train arrived in La Paz and slowly pulled up to the terminal station. Milan was amazed to see a building designed by Gustave Eiffel, the French engineer and architect. An airy building, with modern lines, reminded him of the Eiffel Tower he'd visited with his mother as a child. Outside the station, groupings of men prepared to sling passengers' bundles and suitcases on their backs and walk with them to their hotels. Milan went over to take on one of them.

▲ ▲ ▲

After staying at a hotel for a night, Milan found a room in a boarding house with a wooden frame bed, a bathroom down the hall, and two meals a day served in the family dining room. Lunch was served at work. There was an abundance of food, but not much to his taste. Milan was happy to be in the land of potatoes, but avocado, papaya, pineapple, mango—they were all new to him and he'd have to acquire a taste for them before telling whether he liked them or not.

In Bolivia, mining was king. The country had gold, silver, lead, zinc and rich deposits of tin. Easy to exploit and found underground, the hard-rock tin was bagged and exported. Mines were located at great altitude, offering harsh working conditions with appalling living accommodations and meager pay for the miners. Most of the foreign workers, who were employed as engineers and technicians, lived in separate compounds, many at the lower elevations where living was easier.

Right away, Milan got a position at one of the many offices of Mr. Finkel's mining operations in the capital city of La Paz. He was fortunate and, like so many of the recent immigrants, didn't have to live in a provincial town where there would be no entertainment to pass his free time. La Paz was small, with a well-kept downtown and commercial buildings in Spanish-style architecture built along narrow, winding cobblestone-paved streets. Trams helped people travel over the steep hills and reach neighborhoods pressed into the sides of the mountain. Pedestrians walked slowly, due to the lack of oxygen.

Plaza Murillo, the park in the heart of the city, was where the imposing nineteenth-century presidential palace in neoclassical style, the parliament, and the cathedral were located. Milan's office building, just a few blocks away, was a five-story walk-up brick building.

▲ ▲ ▲

Milan worked six days a week as an export manager and, on his day off, liked to go to the matinee movies at Cinema Tesla. There, he saw Argentinian and Mexican films to learn Spanish and made sure to see the occasional European film. Matinees were cheap, but the trouble was, there were too many noisy kids not interested in the *noticieros*, the newsreels, which Milan thought were the best part of the show, as they allowed him to see what was going on in Europe. He wouldn't spend money to go to the six o'clock show, known as the Vermouth, when the elegant crowd attended, since it was double the price. On Sundays after church, a military band performed at Plaza Murillo at noon. Milan made it a habit to leave the boarding house early to see the band's performance before heading to the movie house. At the plaza he liked to inspect the new souped-up Ford and Chevrolet cars parked on the streets and look at the drivers maneuvering them. He counted the days until he could afford one of them.

▲ ▲ ▲

On September 1, 1939, a sun-washed afternoon, Milan heard church bells ring and sirens go off. Everybody fled the office building into the street to find out what was going on.

"War has been declared in Europe!" someone in the crowd yelled in dismay. This was how news was delivered, as telephones and radios were few and newspapers were expensive.

Most days from then on, Milan started to check his mailbox at the main post office to see if letters had arrived from his brother in London, but none came. He hadn't had any mail from Pavel, or from his cousins in Prague, for months. He speculated that mail delivery would probably become an even greater problem with the countries at war. He feared losing contact with them.

▲ ▲ ▲

Warm days and cold nights with rain during the summer months were to be expected in La Paz, but on a clear, warm Sunday in early January, Milan and some of his Czech bachelor friends were able to play cards in the park. They brought along a folding table and four chairs to enjoy the beautiful view of the Illimani Massif covered in snow in the distance.

▲ ▲ ▲

Victor, a lawyer; Ralph, a dentist; and Ernest, a philosophy teacher, were in their twenties, all well educated. But they held professions they couldn't practice without a Bolivian license.

"I've got a plan," Victor said as soon as he'd unfolded his chair. "I've been thinking of opening a delicatessen. With so many Europeans arriving, one is in great demand. Anyone interested in my proposition?"

Milan and his friends had an optimistic outlook on life since they could only look forward to better times.

"Beggars can't be choosers," Ernest said.

"My dad used to make sausages in our home country and, as a kid, I liked to help. I'll find out how we can obtain meat and the ingredients we'll need. With labor being cheap, we can hire a crew and get the production going right away," Ralph said.

"The detail-oriented doctor," Milan said. "What I would give to have some good homemade dumplings."

"Maybe we'll make some as well." Victor nodded and laughed.

"Look, guys, why don't we try to get a house to share? We'll hire some maids, have a large kitchen, work, live, and play under one roof," Ralph said.

"We'll shop at the market on Sundays and cook for the week," Victor said.

The four positioned their chairs to sit across from each other to play cards. Milan took the pack of thirty-six Italian-suited cards and shuffled them.

"A business will bring us stability," Victor said, picking up his cards.

"Victor, what would we do without you? In the midst of the madness, how did you think to pack your cards?" Ernest said.

"I wouldn't leave without them. Bulka is my game. I knew they were special and I wouldn't be able to find them anywhere else in the world," Victor said.

"I hope the krauts get blasted," said Ernest. "I'll go back to Prague as soon as the war ends."

"You won't want to leave us, we'll have a business to run," Victor said.

"I don't know if I can be a businessman. I am a dreamer, but I'll help you out," Ernest said.

"You'll have to come down to earth. You need to survive," Ralph said.

Victor reached into a bag to get the bottles of beer he'd brought with him. "Not the same as our Pilsner, but it's the best I could find."

"Cheers to our new enterprise," Ralph said.

"I brought some salami," Milan interjected.

"Where did you find such a thing?" Ralph asked, delighted.

"I deal with an American guy from the embassy; he gets it from their commissary."

"You lucky bastard," Ralph said.

"Here's a knife; cut me a piece," Victor said.

They played fast, well into the night, talking about sports, girls, and cars. Milan shared his fantasy about the beautiful steel and chrome machine he would buy when he doubled his capital by investing in their venture.

When they finalized the partnership, Milan let them know he would not be quitting his job but would instead join them as a silent partner.

"That's great. Capital is just as important as manpower," Victor said.

They found an old adobe building with wrought-iron window guards in a central location in town. There were several rooms off a sprawling courtyard and a large kitchen on a side wing. The rambling house had so much space, and they were able to hire live-in help. A room with a window and a door looking out on the street was converted into a grocery store, which they named Europa Deli.

As soon as they signed the lease, Victor and Ralph began to look for suppliers. They found an old-time German farmer from whom they could buy cold-cut meats and cheeses. On the weekends, they shopped at the farmers' market set up by the Aymara and Quechua people who came into the city from the highlands with fresh produce and crafts.

The three business partners began their day-to-day jobs. They hired kitchen and customer service help: two Bolivian ladies to attend to the local customers and a cook. Ralph supervised the kitchen, and Victor and Ernest took care of the European clientele. German, Czech, Polish, and Russian languages began to be heard in the store as word got around that the delicatessen was open for business. After a few months, one of the Bolivian women was speaking German, as this was the prevailing language that served to unify the refugees. She was a great help to Victor and Ernest, who were now free to leave the store to attend to other matters. In La Paz, Jewish religious congregations attracted cultural and social groups, so Victor came up with the idea of catering for their social occasions: circumcisions, bar mitzvahs, and weddings.

The working partners were so involved in their business that even when they relaxed in the evenings at home, they only talked about work. Ralph was detail-oriented and efficient, and Milan felt sure that Victor could be trusted to persevere and make the deli profitable.

In his free time, Milan liked to go to the British Council library to read foreign newspapers. Even though the news was a few weeks old, it gave him a fresh perspective of current events. As he still had trouble reading complex sentences in Spanish, the British papers and the *New York Times* offered him a deeper understanding of the events that were developing in a world at war.

One evening Milan entered the library and in a quiet voice asked the librarian for the *Times*. He found an empty chair at a round table and remained standing while looking at the headlines on the front page. A photo caught his eye—Berlin's Brandenburg Gate laid out with swastika flags while Adolf Hitler aroused a crowd from his podium. *An unbelievable mob*, he thought. How he loathed the little jerk giving his hand salute. Milan could not look away and took a seat to read the article describing the blitzkrieg shattering lives as German troops advanced towards the Soviet Union. He felt sick and took a deep breath to calm himself down. Overwhelmed by remorse, he thought about the loved ones he'd left behind who would be suffering.

▲ ▲ ▲

Uncertainty of the future and homesickness, Milan told his friends, were among the reasons why he wouldn't date. Also, at times, he wondered how long he'd remain in Bolivia. He didn't want to commit to a relationship—then he met Soledad Figueroa and things changed.

The beautiful, dark-skinned Soledad had taken the lead on the day she'd flirted with him—a shy, lanky, blond foreigner who spoke with accented Spanish. She'd gone to the delicatessen to buy some imported chocolates on a day Milan was stocking the shelves. They started a conversation about the best brands of chocolate in the store, as she wanted to buy a good product for her mother.

Soledad began to send messages to Milan inside perfumed enve-
lopes, with her household help. One day she wrote that she would like
to see him. After messages back and forth, they agreed to meet at the
store and go for a drink.

He would prefer if they met on Sundays, but this was Soledad's
family day when they would gather with her uncles and aunts, and
at times potential suitors for the girls. One Sunday however, Soledad
asked if Milan would meet her for church services at the Cathedral at
eleven a.m. so they could spend an hour together before lunch. They
would meet at the back and make their way to the pews on the side
aisles behind heavy baroque columns, where they would not be visible
to her relatives. She would be wearing a hat with a veil that would partially cover her face—one of the fashionable ones every young woman
was sporting at the time.

During the next months there were times when Soledad missed a
few of their dates. Then she would beg Milan for forgiveness, explaining she hadn't been able to leave the house as her mother was keeping a
close eye on her, fearing she was becoming too independent for a lady
of her social class.

When they were together, they would escape to out-of-the-way
places—walks in the cemetery or to the national stadium—where she
could avoid people she knew.

Soledad relied on Maria for help. "Maria, our maid, is my friend.
She's always been with me; she raised me and cares for me; she won't
let me down," Soledad explained. "She likes you. She thinks you're
*muy simpatico* and doesn't care that you are a refugee or wherever you
came from."

For Milan, it was difficult to set dates during his lunch break, but
once in a while, when there was a lull at work, he escaped from the
office to meet her at his place.

"Why don't I meet your parents once and for all and we can stop
playing games. I'm a respectable suitor, don't you think? Then we'll be

able to see each other after work, go to a movie or out to a bar without having to sneak away," Milan said.

"I'm supposed to see boys of my own class," she answered, lazily lifting herself from his bed.

He admired her long legs.

Milan got the message—her parents were prejudiced, having formed an opinion without ever having met a Czech or Jewish person.

▲ ▲ ▲

In the kitchen, something was always cooking on the six-burner gas stove—a roast, schnitzels, beets, potatoes—and many times the cook would be rolling out pastry for apple strudel. Milan got a whiff of the smells, looked at his watch and said, "I better rush back to the office. Let's go eat. It smells so good."

Milan combed his hair, pulled up his pants, and took Soledad by the hand, guiding her down the hall.

"What can we offer you?" Lidia, the cook, asked. She was stirring a pot when she saw Milan with Soledad at the kitchen door. "I got spaghetti a la Bolognese. Let me dish some for you." Before doing so, Lidia took a taste with a wooden spoon then said, "*Delicioso.*"

"I'm in a rush," Milan said, finding a place to sit at a side table. Soledad, embarrassed, stood under the doorframe and waved goodbye to Milan.

Ralph came into the kitchen and found Milan gobbling down his food. Ralph was five-foot-eight with a muscular chest and arms. He was particular about his looks but since he'd begun tasting every dish prepared, he'd become slightly pudgy.

"You're fattening up, I see," Ralph said, tucking in his stomach, squaring his shoulders, and winking at Milan. "Listen to me," he continued. "Soledad will appreciate having something to grab onto."

Milan shrugged, finished his dish, and left.

▲ ▲ ▲

The four friends enjoyed attending fútbol games, and on this particular Sunday they decided to see The Strongest, a club from La
Paz, playing against Club Aurora from Cochabamba at the National
Stadium in the early afternoon. The Strongest, founded in 1908, was
favored to win. People flocked into the stands and the fellows found
their seats. They had dressed warmly on this sunny day in late spring,
taking along their hats, coats, and alpaca-wool scarves. As had become
customary among them, Victor collected the slips of paper on which
each man had recorded his favorite team. They would wager money on
their teams, and the losers would pay for their drinks after the game.

Once the players entered the pitch with the game about to start,
everyone quieted down. The only audible voices were from the ven-
dors moving up and down the aisles, selling beer and potato chips.

The game began strongly on both sides; players showed confidence moving the ball, making long passes trying to score. Milan got
absorbed in the excitement of the players' footwork. Players for The
Strongest exhibited better control of the ball, but he booed along with
the crowd and rose when the ball bounced in Aurora's midfielder's
face. Sighs of relief were heard when the player retrieved the ball and,
dribbling it, made his way forward into an open space. Blasting the
ball straight ahead, he tried to put a shot on the net, but it bounced on
the pole and the goalkeeper kept Aurora from scoring. Fans chanted
and cheered. The game was scoreless at the half. Thirty minutes into
the second half, when the referee called a foul and The Strongest got a
penalty kick, Aurora's goalkeeper threw himself on the ground, trying
but failing to make a save. Milan was thrilled and he along with others
were brought to their feet. At the end The Strongest won 1–0 leading
to the home crowd's euphoria.

Fans rushed down to the field to congratulate the team as children tugged at the player's shirts. As the winning team gathered to

be photographed, flashbulbs popped. Newsreel cameras started to roll when the coach made a few remarks to a reporter, and one of the players perched Gaston Marin on his shoulders to parade him around the field. Milan and the others clapped to support the teams.

Ernest and Ralph had bet on Aurora winning the game, so they had to take Milan and Victor out to dinner. The winners decided they would like to eat at the Fuente Suiza, a casual Swiss restaurant where the interior design was brought straight from the Alps, with quaint painted furniture and cuckoo clocks. When they entered, they found noisy patrons singing along with the weekend entertainer playing the accordion, clad in traditional Swiss garb. A smiling waitress wearing a black dress with a white starched embroidered apron came to show them to a table. With their beer mugs in hand, they joined in the yodeling while they waited for their pig knuckles and sauerkraut. *Ah*, Milan thought, *a little familiar food.*

# CHAPTER 8

## La Paz, Bolivia,
## 1940s–1950s

M ilan liked his routine. In the morning he awoke at six when he heard the hooves of the horse on the cobblestone road. It was the milkman, delivering their order to the front door. When he left the house at eight, he stepped out carefully, avoiding the lumps of horse manure the animal might have left behind. He walked to work, always taking the same route so to be behind his desk half an hour later. He wanted to set an example for his staff. Most employees arrived late and were eager to leave before closing time. In the land of *mañana* he pushed others hard, for these days the processing and export department was hectic, as business was booming; minerals were in great demand for the war effort in Europe.

In December 1942, when miners went on strike demanding higher wages, laying down their tools to protest their appalling working conditions, a massacre by army troops took place. Worker-employer relations had become too tense. Indigenous miners worked in dangerous surroundings, with no basic safety rules, in over ninety degrees Fahrenheit heat and high humidity. They lived in substandard conditions with little access to nourishing food, and their energy boost during the day came from chewing on salt pills or sipping a weak tea with sugar cubes. Bloodcurdling accidents were prevalent and not given proper medical attention; there were no compensations or family benefits for miners who were injured or killed.

Milan thought it inexcusable that foreign employees were provided nice, furnished houses with electricity and fuel for their fireplaces, got paid well and received bonuses to boot, while the men doing the heavy work lingered in poverty. He understood how contempt for foreign employees was on the rise and that the enormous discrepancy in wages would bring about consequences.

Don Rolando Finkel, the owner of the firm, lived in La Paz and publicly displayed little social conscience. He was always traveling, visiting his mines, which were spread throughout South America. Mr. Finkel was forced to take note when miners began to express discontent for their extreme poverty, when they started to mobilize and demonstrate on the streets. Once the local and international newspapers challenged the interests of the wealthy mine owners, the government began to act, and it came to a head when foreign nations threatened to suspend negotiations for the sale of Bolivian minerals. When the United States stopped technical and economic cooperation, a few regulations were put in place to try to quell the rising social unrest.

The period during World War II brought much instability to the country; presidents were elected and then gotten rid of. The president who'd allowed the refugees permission to settle in 1938 committed suicide shortly after Milan arrived, and the ones that followed were rapidly overthrown by coups d'état. Refugees were suspicious of the local elite, as many had stories to share about being duped by Bolivian diplomats before they departed Europe. Most refugees agreed that they'd been charged outrageous amounts of cash to obtain landing documents to enter the country, and the only way they could get ahead economically was to grease someone's hand. But they were stuck in Bolivia for the time being.

Since Europeans conducted themselves differently from Bolivian nationals, the groups rarely socialized. The Bolivians struck the new-comers as impenetrable, unable to figure out what was going on in their heads. It was rare to see the foreigners interacting with the locals as they conformed to their own culture, artistic tastes, religious beliefs and tra-ditions, and saw Bolivians as unsophisticated and lusterless. Language barriers were an additional hurdle, as the majority of the local popula-tion spoke the Aymara or Quechua languages, which the immigrants didn't even attempt to learn. "Spanish was the best they could do," they whispered disapprovingly.

Some of the newcomers made it known that they were appalled by the poverty that surrounded them, voicing their disgust at lack of access to basic necessities and the numerous gaunt, vagrant children who wandered the streets. They objected to the unjust practices of poor families who kept their children from attending school to work alongside the parents on grueling jobs.

A great deal of hospitality was shown among Jewish refugees to members of their own community, but there was social pressure to con-form to their cultural norms. The women, in particular, appeared to be broadly aware of other people's conduct and were quick to spread rumors about those who transgressed. Milan was not one to follow blindly or to be bothered by group pressure. He was his own man and couldn't care less about the gossip he heard.

Some people defined themselves by who they had been in the old country, their family's standing, their past occupation and prior wealth. One evening, when the four friends sat around in their living room on their scruffy secondhand couches on a frayed rug, each holding a stein of beer as they waited for the Voice of America news to come on the shortwave radio, Victor began to tell them about one of his regular customers, who was driving him crazy.

"So, it's Mrs. Dittman again?" Ralph asked.

"I told her that I would cut off her line of credit by the end of the month if she didn't pay up, and can you believe it she started to cry. She said she had no money, but that one day soon she'll be able to pay me back with interest," Victor said.

"When will that be?" Ernest asked.

"When the war is over, and she gets back her property. She likes to talk about her family who was knighted by the Emperor," Victor said, raising his eyebrows and extending his arm in a salutation gesture.

"When was that?" Milan asked.

"What is she talking about, she's nuts—families lost their titles in the early part of the century," Ernest said.

"She tells me her grandfather was a Baron and she ought to be called 'Van Dittman.' Should I care?" Victor said.

"I've seen her walking into the deli, wearing her fur coats but unable to pay her bills. Something's wrong! Why doesn't she sell one of her furs?" Ralph said.

"What a snob! Doesn't she get it that we're all poor trying to make a living?" Ernest said.

The men fell silent when the news began, and they stayed glued to the radio to the end of the broadcast.

"I hate to say it, but it looks like the Germans are winning. Hitler has the upper hand," Milan said.

"Just wait, the tide will turn. Hitler will be defeated in the end," Victor said.

"Always the optimist," Ernest said. "We are in for a long wait."

"Let's turn to Radio Berlin," Ralph said.

"Let's not, it's only propaganda. I've heard enough of them," Milan said, getting up and walking away.

▲ ▲ ▲

In August 1944, Rolando Finkel was arrested and sentenced to death. Then, he was released only to be kidnapped, along with his general manager, a few weeks later. Police cars swarmed the streets of La Paz, while plain-clothes policemen went house to house searching for him. Everyone thought he'd been killed until his wife reported she had received a call asking for a hefty ransom for his release. He'd been confined to a closet for two weeks, forced to sleep on the floor and given no food. A photo of the magnate revealed him drawn and unshaven, declaring he was outraged by the events and would leave Bolivia immediately.

▲ ▲ ▲

At the end of the war there was jubilation in the world, but Milan only envisioned the devastation that had taken place in his country of birth. When he found out he had lost much of his extended family, he felt assured he'd never return to Europe. At the movies he now liked to watch the scenes where the Nazi soldiers got killed and the high command got their due punishments.

A few months after the end of the war, Milan started to complain to his friends about his company's inefficient management. Something had changed after Mr. Finkel's departure, and as the country's political volatility continued, there was great instability in the economy. Ongoing rumblings from the military made the state of affairs tense. In July 1946 there was an antigovernment riot against the current leader, a military man with fascist tendencies. When the president was assassinated, and his body hurled from the balcony of the Presidential Palace to the square below, the crowds hung him from a lamppost. This made Milan think he would be better off if he left Bolivia.

He wasn't the type who had problems parting with things, and he didn't feel tied down to anything. Even though his relationship with Soledad continued, he remained guarded and didn't mention he was considering leaving the country for the US until the very end. He knew deep in his heart that their relationship couldn't continue without her parents' approval, and he also knew they would never be thrilled with their daughter marrying a foreigner. Above all things, she worried that her family would disown her.

In his position as an export manager, Milan had befriended an American broker, Mr. Shapiro, who lived in New York City and visited La Paz frequently. Milan had a knack for navigating through life, pushing his way into worlds that opened to him. He began to exchange letters with Mr. Shapiro to raise the subject of immigrating to the United States.

# CHAPTER 9

## Niagara Falls, New York, 1951–1958

In the spring of 1951, Milan boarded a Pan American Airways flight from La Paz to New York, wearing his stylish charcoal woolen suit and a soft felt wide-brim hat. After a few days in the big city, he traveled to Niagara, a place known for its factories and electrical plants, as well as for being a honeymoon destination. Not only did Niagara have the great waterfalls but also eight motion picture theaters and an abundance of restaurants. Milan felt he'd made the right move, since it was just a few months before the next president of Bolivia was about to nationalize the mining industry.

As Milan settled into his new location, he decided to change his name and filed a petition before obtaining a social security number and a driver's license. From then on, he would be known as "Miles Gold," a name he considered more desirable in his new, English-speaking world.

Shortly after, he found a good job at a petrochemical company and started to play tennis and build a social life. He missed his buddies in La Paz and his sweetheart, Soledad, but she'd been clear when she told him that it would be impossible for her to make a life with him. Her parents had expectations that she felt she had to comply with, and she'd never be able to forgive herself if she broke contact with them. She had to carry on their values and their faith, bringing up her children in their lifestyle. He also knew that he would feel smothered and an outsider in that world. He could never be one of them.

▲ ▲ ▲

In 1956, when Miles was thirty-nine years old, he asked an American girl to marry him. They bought a three-level split house with a sprawling backyard on a suburban tract development.

June Kates also came from a family of immigrants. She was eleven when she came to the States from Vienna before the war. After the war, her mother found out that most of her family had perished during the Holocaust, and she was beside herself. June's mother started to show signs of a deep depression, lingering in bed most of the day and losing interest in her daily activities. In her second year of college, June became worried about her parents and quit school to help. With her plans for a meaningful career no longer viable, she took night courses to become a stenographer. She quickly found work as an executive secretary and was able to provide her parents with financial assistance. She held onto her job until Miles proposed when she was twenty-eight, when she left to marry and raise her own family.

▲ ▲ ▲

In 1958, on a windy day in April, while there were still signs of late snow on the side of the roads, Miles sat behind the wheel of his brand-new Chevrolet, smoking a cigarette. He was listening to the latest activity of the New York Stock Exchange on the radio, with June in the passenger seat. They were driving out to the airport to pick up Pavel, Miles's brother who now called himself Paul, and his wife, Alice. Paul and Alice had decided to leave England for good to settle close to family.

Miles parked the car, saying, "I better hurry, we are late." Leaving June behind, he set off at a brisk pace.

He quickened his step when he noticed Paul standing next to the baggage carousel. It'd been seventeen years since they'd last seen each other. Paul's bespectacled eyes glinted happily when he saw Miles, and he waved. As soon as they were together, the brothers lingered in each other's arms, then stepped away to examine one another. They were two years apart and hadn't been close growing up, but this was a new stage in their lives. Miles had not met Alice, a tall, svelte woman who stood erect as she removed her black leather gloves and then extended her arm to shake his hand.

"We've come with two suitcases. The rest was shipped and should arrive in due time," Paul said when he noticed Miles looking around.

"How was your flight?" Miles asked, then turned to help Alice who was struggling with her bag.

"Very good," she answered in her British accent as she straightened her posture, tugged at her waistline-defining white jacket and pulled down her narrow black pencil skirt.

The heavily pregnant June waddled in and stood next to Miles, arching her back.

"Hello, how do you do? Congratulations," Alice said, extending her hand and looking at June's protruding stomach.

"We are looking forward to our new baby," June said.

"Isn't it nice to be here to welcome a new member to our family?" Paul asked, giving June a light kiss on her cheek.

June found a bathroom and had returned to Miles's side by the time they were ready to head back to the parking lot.

▲ ▲ ▲

Once they were home, Paul and Alice were shown to the guest bedroom on the lower floor. June had painted the walls a radiant lilac and made a floral bedcover to match. June opened the closet door to show Alice the space she'd cleared for them.

"When you're refreshed, come up to join us for lunch," June said.

Being pregnant was not a subject for open discussion. At home, June would have preferred to change into one of her comfortable smocks, but she was expected to look proper when visitors were around. Anxious to please, she would keep the allure of elegance Miles liked. She remained in her finest pregnancy outfit, which she'd ordered from the Lane Bryant catalogue, and designed to conceal her bulk.

After lunch, they went into their sunken living room furnished with light-colored wood and clean, Scandinavian lines, which gave the room a feel of spaciousness. *House Beautiful* magazines lay on the coffee table, as June was researching liquor cabinets. After the baby was born, she was hoping to meet other young parents in the neighborhood and entertain. Home bars were the newest craze, and she wondered if she'd be able to talk Miles into financing her project. She'd have to tread carefully, since he would demand a detailed accounting of what she had in mind.

There were many stories for the brothers to share about the events during the time they'd lived separately. Miles had received a number of letters from Paul when there still was communication between Europe and Latin America before the war, and letters after the end of the war when Paul wrote about the horrors of the air raids and the destruction. Miles needed to fill in the gaps and learn how his brother had managed during the time when it was impossible to communicate.

"At the beginning of the war, Alice was living in Italy, working for a British firm, and with Mussolini in power, she became an enemy alien," Paul said. "She was placed under house arrest for many months until Italy and Britain agreed to a transfer of their foreign residents."

"We sailed to Lisbon on an Italian ship," Alice said, picking up the thread of the conversation about her earlier life. "It was a rough voyage, as the captain tried to avoid mined areas and enemy ships. They didn't treat us well. Once we arrived in Portugal we were transferred to a British vessel, where we were given fine food and wine."

"What a time you had," June said, listening attentively as she knitted a white woolen blanket.

"You are so lucky to have survived unscathed," Miles said.

Paul told them about the number of Czechs who arrived in Britain, seeking refuge from Nazi persecution after Germany took parts of Czechoslovakia. Among these refugees was their cousin, Anna.

"Did you have contact with her?" Miles asked.

"I used to meet her once in a while. Anna would have been able to become a permanent resident, but when she met Joe and they got married, they decided to go back to Czechoslovakia soon after the war. I really can't understand why they'd want to leave Britain when Prague was under Soviet influence," Paul said.

"You know he was a hard-core communist and wanted to get back to work for the regime," Alice said.

"How come you decided to leave London now?" June asked. "With the war long forgotten, is this the time to uproot?"

"Oh, June, I wish you could see London. The legacy of the war is still palpable. There are vacant bomb sites in our neighborhood; the unrepaired houses . . . When we take a ride out to the countryside, we see the abandoned military bases. It all brings back bad memories. Reminders of what went on are everywhere," Alice said, letting out a long sigh.

"We still faced austerity and government controls. There are so many regulations and high taxes to pay. Even with a good salary we had little money to spend and not much left to save. The city was becoming too overcrowded," Paul said.

"Butter, tea, meat, coal—they are all still rationed. We did have a refrigerator, but small appliances are very expensive," Alice said.

"Alice had a parcel of land in our community garden where she grew all of our vegetables, but she was kept so busy in summer and fall, canning and freezing, that she had no time for anything else."

"We wanted to move out of the city but couldn't find housing we liked," Alice said.

"Well, I'm glad you are here with a good job for Paul. The next step is to find you a suitable home," Miles said.

"Yes, we needed a change," Alice agreed.

"You wrote that you wanted to get away from pollution, how you were concerned a few years ago when London had such a bad smog problem that a number of people suffered from lung conditions. But I have sad news for you: We've found that Niagara isn't the cleanest. From here, at times, we can see foul-smelling smokestacks that pollute our air. It depends on the winds, but the chemical companies are polluting our air as well," Miles said.

"Perhaps you should start by looking at real estate a bit further removed from town," June said.

# CHAPTER 10

## Niagara Falls, New York, 1960s

The times when his uncle Paul visited were special for young Jerry Gold, since his dad seemed more relaxed. Jerry would come out of his room to hang around with the adults and listen to their stories. One day Paul brought along a coffee table book with photos of Prague, and Miles asked Jerry to join them in the living room.

Paul motioned to Jerry to sit on the couch between him and Miles.

"Our house was large, just like this one—three stories high," Paul said, pointing to one of the photographs. "The basement was where our father had his warehouse full of furs. On the first floor he had his offices, and the two upstairs floors were our family's living space."

"It was in the old town, smack in the city center, a few blocks from our favorite clock," Miles said.

"The famous Prague Orloj, here it is. Jerry, look at this beauty. It's an astronomical medieval clock on the tower of the Old Town Hall. There are a series of dials recording the movements of the sun and moon in the sky, as well as the time of the day. When we were kids, we would sneak out of the house to watch the figures of the twelve apostles surrounding the clock parading every hour on the hour," Paul said.

"During Napoleonic times the house was a police station," Miles said.

"A police station!" Jerry said.

"Have you heard of Napoleon?" Paul asked.

Jerry shook his head.

"He was a French military leader who built a large empire a long time ago," Paul said.

"When was that?" Jerry asked.

"Before I was born," Miles said.

"That's olden times. And he lived in your house?"

"He himself didn't, but some of his men did," Paul said. "And in the basement, they had dungeons where prisoners were kept—under the watchful eyes of the guards." Paul made a serious face. "That's where your dad and I used to play."

"Will you play prisoner with me?" Jerry asked his uncle. "My dad always makes excuses about how he has too much work or tells me he has too much on his mind to play silly games."

Jerry's mother, June, appeared in the room, carrying a basket of folded clothes. "Jerry, you shouldn't talk about your father in a rude manner."

Jerry looked down, embarrassed.

"Come on," Paul said as he got up from the couch. Catching Jerry by surprise, he pulled the boy up and held his hands behind his back. He tied his wrists with a white cotton handkerchief and told him to remain still.

Jerry bent over, pretending to struggle, trying to bust out of his shackles. His legs trembled when Paul dragged him out of the house into the backyard.

Paul whistled. "Don't let this crook get away," he yelled as Jerry ran fast towards a tree where a branch brushed against his head.

"Ouch!" Jerry screamed. The game was over. Jerry had blood dripping down his face from a cut on his forehead.

▲ ▲ ▲

Jerry loved the family picnics in the park. June would lay a blanket under an oak tree draped in moss, and the women would sit on folding chairs, allowing the children to play freely in the field. Jerry had a sister named Marie, three years younger, who liked to be with him. She was shy and frail and Jerry thought he might hurt her, so he was afraid to play rough games with her.

Miles and Paul would go deep into the woods to gather small brushwood and make a fire to roast hot dogs for lunch. Paul, a chemist, was a good cook, and he would bring his favorite potato salad and apple strudel along. Sometimes, in the later afternoon, they would drive a little further over to the river and look across to Canada. Jerry would be given a coin to put into a binocular to take a closer look at the waterfalls.

▲ ▲ ▲

Jerry was a perceptive child and knew that in spite of the few fun stories he heard there were some deep secrets his parents kept. As the years went by, he started to question them and was told that, out of respect for his elders, the past was best left unspoken. Most kids in his school came from large families and talked about celebrating holidays with their uncles, grandparents, and aunts, so why didn't he have any relatives? A few years later, he learned from his mother that many family members had been executed in gas chambers under the Third Reich, and he began to understand some of his family history.

As a father, Miles was emotionally distant, just like his father had been, and often felt irritated by his kids. When June tentatively reproached her husband, suggesting that he should be giving Jerry more affection, Miles would shrug, swallow hard, and tell her that sentimentality was not part of his makeup.

"A man can't lose himself in emotions, he needs to be in control. Feelings and coddling may be all right for Marie, but not for my boy." The world of emotions was foreign to Miles.

▲ ▲ ▲

When Jerry became a teenager, Miles started to involve him in conversations. They were mostly about current events, when Miles often compared the present with the past, without getting personal. In those instances, Jerry noticed that Miles seemed trapped in regret and felt guilty about having abandoned loved ones in Europe when he left. Jerry also took note that his father would always give a reason for having to leave abruptly.

As he aged, Miles became more judgmental, and if he was busy, he handled disruptions poorly, claiming that Jerry provoked him into making outrageous statements. By then, Jerry no longer held back, and as soon as he saw the look of irritation on his father's face—the clenched jaw and furrowed forehead—he'd disappear from view. First, he'd go to the kitchen to grab some food, then rush up to his bedroom, lock the door, and play music to drown out his own bad mood. There were times when Jerry found refuge in the toolshed he'd built. He had discovered his love for woodworking at school when a teacher pointed out his talent. In his shed, he would build intricate structures and get lost in his art.

He started to read about angst and explore the work of various philosophers. He disliked the dishonesty he sensed in his home and tried to find answers to existential questions.

When he learned from his mother that his grandmother had committed suicide and his grandfather had died from a heart attack shortly after, he became troubled. Trying to figure out more of his personal history, where he'd come from and who he was, he began to question his personal values. He thought about how Miles was consumed by moving ahead in a materialistic and competitive world, and that those aspirations were not what he would strive for. He was convinced that his dad was out of step with the new generation and questioned the myths and stereotypes that prevailed in his father's mindset.

Jerry began to look at the writers of the Beat Generation for answers and became excited by the concept of liberation. He challenged himself to feel emotions that came his way and began to talk with his teachers and close friends about issues affecting him.

He listened to rhythm and blues, folk music and rock and roll, quickly learning the lyrics he found meaningful. As the counterculture movement got strong and this new phenomenon became a force to be acknowledged, Jerry continued to examine the values and traditions his parents embraced. The gulf between Miles and Jerry broadened at every turn.

When his mother finally told him that she and his father thought Jerry was going through an angry phase, he mistook her concern for an accusation. "Is it my looks you object to?" he asked. He had let his hair grow long and wore low-rise, flared bell-bottom jeans with long collared shirts, all of which bothered Miles.

"Not only that," his mother said. "It's your attitude."

Then, he really stayed away from his parents' company. He was intent on ridding himself of the many feelings he'd taken on, which he realized he had adopted from his father and weren't his own. But he was too young to understand, and it would be years before he could reshape his patterns of thinking to create a different reality for himself and not be troubled by his parents' demons.

▲ ▲ ▲

Niagara Falls was a boomtown in the first half of the twentieth century, attracting paper, rubber, plastic, and petrochemical industries. It was a place where people joked that if you quit a job in the morning you could find another one in the afternoon.

As the population expanded, the school district needed land to build new schools and, in 1955, the Niagara school board built two schools where chemical waste had been buried. A document was signed whereby the school board assumed all risks and liabilities for any future claims, suits, or actions made for injury, death, loss, or damages due to the presence of industrial waste. The area in question had been covered with a clay seal to prevent leakage, and vegetation had settled and was growing. But when a twenty-foot area crumbled during a rainstorm, exposing drums containing chemical waste, children began to play in the toxic water. The people understood little about the harmful effects of chemicals in the environment.

But Jerry's mother complained about her backyard trees turning black, with one dying outright. Neighbors became concerned that a number of children started coming down with epilepsy, asthma, and burns on their faces and hands. Prosperity ended in Niagara in the late 1960s as aging industrial plants started to move to less expensive locations and people began to talk about the dangers of living by the Love Canal. Jerry's parents remained in the area after June was diagnosed with cancer. She endured chemotherapy and radiation, treatments that turned out to be worse than the disease itself.

In the late 1970s the state department of health launched an intensive soil, air, and groundwater sampling to determine the level of contamination and carcinogens. As an adult, Jerry found out that one of the chemical companies knew their products were causing cancer in laboratory animals due to high levels of contaminants and carcinogens, but by then his mother had passed away and Miles had only a few more years left to live.

# CHAPTER 11

## Lima, Peru, 2008

After the fall of the autocrat Peruvian president Alberto Fujimori in 2001, subsequent presidents moved towards upholding democratic principles. With an agenda for improving the economy, they pushed to increase productive capacity as well as address ways they could rectify the conditions that had placed people in harm's way. In 2006 a trust fund was set up for the benefit of victims of crimes from both sides of the conflict. The government ruled that a voluntary contribution of three percent net profit from mining companies would go to the government, and part of the funds would go towards paying reparations for those who had suffered injustices. Monies recovered from former government officials accused of embezzling from the state would also go into the compensation coffers. It was then that Otilia and Salvador began to look closely at the guidelines they needed to follow to apply for indemnification for their losses. When the regulation for filing the Protocol for the Identification of Victims was made known, Otilia immediately filled out the forms.

▲ ▲ ▲

Otilia was in bed at six o'clock in the morning when the alarm woke her up. She pulled the sheets over her eyes. She hadn't slept well and felt exhausted with so much on her mind. She sat up, rushed to the shower, and got dressed to make her appointment in time.

Otilia pushed open the wrought-iron gate and walked through the courtyard filled with potted philodendrons and rubber plants to reach the foyer. A few years had passed since Otilia had seen Sr. Ernesto Malfi, their lawyer, and now she felt concerned and a little nervous. His office brought on unpleasant reminders of her painful past—the wickedness and the lack of fairness she faced. She was holding these grim thoughts as she walked up the spiral staircase and heard footsteps approaching from behind. She looked back.

"I thought I'd be late," Salvador said, leaping up the steps. He planted a kiss on his mother's cheek.

She reached out to touch his shoulder and kissed him back, happy to see him.

"You worked all night. How often do you have a night shift?" she asked.

They walked into the office and took a seat in the waiting room. After a few words, Otilia reached for the magazine lying on the empty chair next to hers. She turned the page and saw a heading that perturbed her—*Grand Design Fails*, she read silently.

Turning to Salvador, she read aloud: "They found hundreds of videos showing Fujimori's cronies extorting influential members of Congress. A Swiss banker came across a viral tape showing a man offering Mr. Serrano cash for voting in favor of a bill. It was then that the banker recognized that the Peruvian he'd helped make a large deposit in his Swiss bank account was not the wealthy fisherman he pretended to be, but the President's chief advisor and head of the National Intelligence Service."

Sr. Malfi, wearing crumpled black-cuffed pants and a short-sleeved white shirt, appeared at the door and Otilia put the magazine away.

"Please come in. How have you been?" Sr. Malfi said in his formal tone of voice as he extended his arm to greet them one at a time.

Otilia still had the article she'd partly read in her mind. Why had her life been made more difficult than it should have been when her government was stealing millions while her family was robbed of their assets? What she endured was not something she would easily shrug off.

Sr. Malfi took his seat behind his desk and lit a cigarette. While exhaling, he looked at Otilia and said, "Let's go over your case and clarify your situation. You are here due to the fact that under Peruvian and international law you, as a displaced person, are entitled to compensation and therefore have received the request for a face-to-face meeting with the Office of Reparations. Now, I want you to understand some of the statistics the country is facing. There were 430,000 people displaced, all people who ran away from the places they lived to find safety. Some went into hiding, others fought against the subversive activities they faced and some, like yourself, sought asylum out of the country. We are talking large numbers."

Otilia nodded.

"We all have a case," Salvador said.

"As a point of reference, let's recall that the Truth and Reconciliation Commission made it clear that displaced persons had to leave everything behind and have grounds to seek reparations. Also remember that a displaced person is now protected under Peruvian and International Law, so you have the right to a claim. But I do want to be realistic and inform you that despite the economic dynamism the country is experiencing, there appears to be a lack of political will to move forward in this respect."

"I thought progress had been made," Otilia said.

"At this time, the commission and the government favor collective reparations: allocating money to build public infrastructure, schools, hospitals, and so forth; preparing future leaders in small communities; and preserving cultural heritage in the Indigenous communities. Determining which individuals should and should not receive monetary damages appears to be complicated," Sr. Malfi said, raising his bushy eyebrows.

Sr. Malfi's secretary stepped into the office quietly, carrying three coffee mugs on a tray. She offered each one *un cafecito* and the lawyer cleared some of his papers from the desk. The phone rang and the secretary apologized for the interruption, dashing out of the room to attend to it.

"We would like to recover our property; however, I'm not so sure the government will consider our case," Salvador said.

"We abandoned our place because we had no other choice," Otilia said, looking at Sr. Malfi's balding spot as he bent his head to look for a paper that he seemed to have misplaced.

"But we'll have to deal with the outcome," Salvador said.

"Let's talk about that. It appears that there was a falsification of documents regarding your property, Otilia, after you left," Sr. Malfi said. "Fraud involves using deception in order to make a personal gain, so your brother, Tomás, would be such a person. We could establish a civil claim; however, first we will have to prove his intention."

Otilia and Salvador remained quiet as Sr. Malfi leaned back.

"It would appear that Tomás's aim was to misappropriate your property; therefore, his conduct could come under the penal code," Sr. Malfi said, scratching his beard. "We must find some of the staff at the municipality and the land registry office who might have helped him. I will find out if one of those people is still around."

"Thank you," Otilia said.

"We'll have to show intent beyond a reasonable doubt," Sr. Malfi said, making a note on his writing pad.

"With Tomás sitting in jail, it should be easy to learn the identity of the people who lent him a hand," Salvador said.

"Don't be so sure," Otilia said.

"It'll just cost a bit of money, but he'll squeal," Salvador said.

"We need to keep in mind that the registry recognizing and protecting land property was just established recently. At the time when Tomás appropriated your ownership, property was transacted much more informally. Sometimes a handshake was sufficient. Why don't you leave all the information with me and I'll take a closer look?"

"I made some notes as you suggested. Here's the information I have," Salvador said, handing Sr. Malfi his folder.

"In the meantime, I would like you to consider why Tomás—who is your brother, Otilia, and the uncle who raised you, Salvador—was intent on committing fraud."

"That won't be hard to do," Salvador remarked.

"Written statements to establish his motive will be helpful to determine the chain of events that took place," Sr. Malfi said.

"Now, as far as my appointment at the Reparation Council goes, how do I explain that I don't have a deed to my property?" Otilia asked.

"Just state that fact; always provide factual information. Don't cover anything up. They know how the bedlam of the time affected people's lives. Of course, you walked out of your house to search for your husband and child and wouldn't have carried the deed to your property. The conversation will then move to another crucial aspect of your case, which is Manuel's disappearance. Disappearance is a grave human rights violation, and your case should focus on him. And be sure you mention the loss of your personal assets and your animals."

"Our mental scars have to be considered as well," Salvador said.

"What if they want to know why I abandoned the land?" Otilia asked, worried.

"A desperate situation led you to take a desperate measure," Salvador said, reaching out to touch his mother's hand.

"It has become clear, that during that period there was a great degree of violence against women, and that abuses were carried out even when women inquired about relatives who'd disappeared. So, don't worry, you did the right thing; the way you proceeded saved you from greater harm," Sr. Malfi said.

"In peaceful times you could have handled a bad apple in the family your own way, but the situation gave Tomás an advantage. He belongs in jail for absconding with our holdings," Salvador said.

"All he ever was good for was to harass people," Otilia murmured under her breath.

"Conditions were fraught with opportunities to cause damage. We will see how this plays out and take it one step at a time," Sr. Malfi said as he rose from his seat.

▲ ▲ ▲

Salvador had to rush back to his office, but Otilia wasn't ready to go back to her son's apartment to spend the afternoon by herself. It was a disheartening business that they were going through, and getting a guilty verdict wasn't a guarantee. It was not certain what they'd be able to achieve.

Nervous about wandering the streets of Lima, Otilia decided to stay in the downtown core. She'd heard about the Spanish entrepreneur and architect who'd come to Lima a few years ago to buy abandoned buildings downtown to refurbish and rent out. Now they were renovated and exquisitely restored. She walked by some that served as government offices, insurance headquarters, and the main branch of a bank.

Otilia strolled past a woman balancing her baby on her hip under a shady tree and placed a coin on the mother's outstretched hand. She wondered why, in the midst of a bustling internal economic boom—with the infusion of foreign capital pouring in and shantytowns metamorphosing into suburbia with new shopping centers, casinos, and plastic surgery clinics—there was still plenty of poverty around.

Otilia looked up at the historical mansion with its enclosed, newly painted, Moorish wooden balconies shining brightly in the sun and thought how beautiful this area was. The wide boulevard opening to a plaza at either end of the street was as stylish as those in a European capital. As she passed by a noisy group of people enjoying the good life at a café, she realized she was at a peculiar point in time. She was trying to come to terms with what had happened twenty years ago while, on the surface, it appeared that the country had forgotten those times.

She stopped to contemplate a saleslady standing behind the window of a small boutique, preparing a display. Silky layers of soft garments hung on a stepladder next to the half-naked mannequin being clothed. Otilia noticed how elegant the stiff figure became as a muted beige dress was draped with a brilliant colored scarf, highlighting the mannequin's face.

"*Mirando*—just looking," Otilia mouthed when the saleslady noticed her and smiled, beckoning for her to come inside.

Feeling unrestrained, Otilia breezed in, enthused over the mannequin's irresistible transformation. She'd been wearing plain outfits to work for too long, buying them at the discount malls, having no need to follow the newest trending fashion. For once, she didn't stop herself from going inside the boutique and trying on some finer clothing.

"This is made from our best pima cotton, excellent quality. Let me get your size," the saleslady said.

When Otilia came out of the dressing room and looked at herself in the full-length mirror, the saleslady's flattering comments convinced her to purchase the same dress she'd seen on the mannequin.

"You look ten years younger! The men will surely look twice at you," the saleslady said.

Sexual attention was far from her mind. Otilia laughed as the young woman proceeded to find a silk shawl to tie around her neck, describing the different ways she could fasten it. As she looked at herself in the mirror again, she thought of the stranger who'd made conversation on the plane. If he called, maybe she'd wear the dress.

Otilia went back to the change room to remove the bills she'd tucked into the inside pocket of her money belt. She would buy the clothes from the gift she'd received from her employer to mark her promotion before she left. With her shopping bag tucked under her arm, she looked for a café to have a bite.

Sr. Malfi had instructed them to prepare statements about Tomás's character, and thinking about this as she sipped a cappuccino made her forget the delicious fleeting moments of enjoyment she'd experienced while shopping. Now she became stressed. Her shoulders stiffened when she thought of her brother's opportunistic behavior and how she'd have to attest to his moral character. She'd rather let the lawyer do the work. But, of course, she would be sure to let them know how Tomás took advantage of them when they were business partners. She would just have to face the task with a great deal of dedication. No rest for her during her stay in Peru.

She removed paper and pencil from her purse and started to write down some words: "integrity," "honesty," "loyalty," and "sound moral compass." Those were the values her family held. How did her brother go so wrong? Was it his surroundings that taught him to cheat, deceive, and steal? Even as a young boy, he'd taken advantage of every opportunity to augment his own means without thinking of others. Since he was a teenager he operated outside the law.

She'd have to recall the many specific circumstances when he'd proven deceitful and would enumerate them to collect the body of evidence Sr. Malfi wanted. Had Tomás ever shown remorse? Had he always failed to act in others' best interests? She recalled that when he was a young boy, her parents had told him not to pick fruit from the neighbors' yard. But many a time he was found up on their apple tree, taking one bite from each of several apples and then throwing the ruined fruit to the ground. At his first job in a restaurant when he was sixteen, he took money from the till and boasted that the owner didn't suspect him. No regrets. Over time, her family had stopped relying on him and her parents were profoundly hurt. And then, when she was in hiding at the mining camp in the Andes, feeling so powerless and distraught, she'd written to him. She sent a letter and a telegram, desperately trying to make contact with him, but he never responded. I guess this was the way he planned it, she thought. So why had the family coddled him so?

By the time she caught a bus back to her son's apartment building, it was late and most of the stores close to her bus stop had rolled down their metal grilles.

▲ ▲ ▲

That evening, Salvador told Otilia that he would begin his own investigation into how his parents' property had landed in his uncle's possession. "I talked to Gonzalo at work, and he promised to obtain a roster of employees at the land registry in Cajamarca. He'll also look into those who were there in the late 1980s. I will talk to Malfi to see who should contact them. I'm aware that clerks will hesitate to get involved, and if any are still in their jobs, they'll be approaching retirement age and won't want to jeopardize their meager pensions."

Accepting gifts and small courtesies was common among public servants and, besides, the penal code didn't criminalize the use of discreet payments to expedite paperwork. Otilia felt that confronting the clerks might not be the route to take. "I think you should leave that up to our lawyer," she said before going to bed.

Salvador frowned.

▲ ▲ ▲

Otilia found her days long. Salvador left the house early in the morning and Carmen, who worked for a nongovernmental organization helping abused women remake their life, got going soon after. Otilia wanted to be helpful around the home, so she walked to the market to do the shopping, prepared meals, scrubbed the toilet and bathtub, and mended their clothes. One day she played tourist and went to a gallery to see an exhibit of Mario Testino's photography. Testino was the Peruvian who hadn't fit into society and had become well-known for his fashion and celebrity photographs. That day, she thought of the gringo, Jerry. What would he think of this artist who, freeing himself from conventions, had left the country at twenty-two to live in London? Would Jerry appreciate his striking portraitures?

▲ ▲ ▲

The afternoon Sr. Malfi called to report back, he said that the protection of property rights had indeed been very weak at the time Otilia left Peru. "Ownership transactions in the northern part of the country were very informal. We lived in a society where unreported transactions for buying and selling property were not out of the ordinary. Many transactions were conducted by the interested parties on their own, at times with just a handshake, as registering property was terribly complicated. I also found out that property registration dockets were poorly compiled, and many folks didn't bother recording their property with the public records office at all. Dealings were conveyed daily, with buyers and sellers going by their own rules. They called them 'informal land sales,' an acceptable practice then. So it would have been easy for your brother to find a notary willing to take on a deal without the proper backup documents."

"Will we be able to go ahead and press charges?" Otilia asked.

"I'm afraid that the law today clearly states that if there is a fraudulent sale, the original owner cannot get the property back even if it has been sold under false pretenses. In a well-ordered society, theft of private property is treated as a criminal act, but not here, not right now," he said.

The other night, Salvador had mentioned that resolving disputes could lead to high legal costs, since the courts were slow and overburdened. "Let's face it, with no proper documents, we don't have much of a case, do we?" Otilia said.

"We will get names, see where it goes," Sr. Malfi said before he hung up.

Otilia felt frustrated and angry—two very familiar emotions.

# CHAPTER 12

## Lima, Peru, 2008

Salvador was seated at the dining room table when Carmen came home. His back was to her, and she put her arms around him, squeezing his shoulders gently. Otilia came in quietly, looking over the records she'd prepared, each with a proper account about how and when Tomás had betrayed them. Carmen poured tea and sat in silence, as she knew that Salvador and his mother had a lot to work through.

Salvador remembered the day he tracked down Tomás months after his father ran with him in his arms into hiding. He'd spent the night alone in the woods, and when his father did not return, he went to find shelter at an old woman's humble hut. The woman asked her grandson to take him into Cajamarca the following day, straight to the police station for help. But the boy left him halfway, pointing to the path Salvador should take. Salvador found his way to the Plaza de Armas, the town square, where he was befriended by several homeless kids. They became his companions for a time. With them he panhandled at the food market during the day and spent nights sleeping amongst the graves at the cemetery on the outskirts of town.

One day Salvador met a taxi driver waiting for passengers leaving the market with heavy bags and asked if he knew a driver by the name of Tomás Campos. The man gave him the name of a mechanic he knew by that name and Salvador went to see him right away. However, he was not the person he was looking for. He searched every area of town, doggedly trying to track his uncle down, at times getting awfully discouraged as he thought he'd hit a dead end, before he was able to find him.

"Where should we begin?" Otilia asked, pulling him back to the present.

"Right now I'm thinking of the day I found Tomás," Salvador said.

"You were a bright kid to recall that Tomás drove a cab. But you liked cars, especially taxis, and would count how many would be roaming around when we went into town," Otilia said.

"He took me in, sent me to school, but never talked about you or my dad. I remember so well the day he told me we needed to move away from Cajamarca. It was *un golpe fatal*, a fatal blow for a child. I was distraught, thinking I would lose track of you and Papá. I knew it would be so much harder for you to find me if we left his house. I was sure Tomás wanted me to forget all of my memories of anything that might remind me of my roots. He didn't want me to bump into acquaintances who might know where you were. As I grew older, I was eager to find out what happened to you, and although I begged him to take me back to El Milagro, he kept stalling, making excuses about the dangers of the trip."

"Is all of this in your notes?" Carmen asked gingerly, her light-brown eyes wide.

Salvador nodded.

"Such a liar," Otilia said.

"He kept reminding me how lucky I was to be with him, since I was safe," Salvador continued. "That I should be grateful for my new clothes. I had good food to eat and a school to go to. I guess it was better than living on the streets, yet I always felt like an intruder in his home."

"No amount of food or clothes could smooth out all the uncertainty and homesickness you must have felt," Carmen said.

"He was telling you lies! In the meantime, he was snatching our property behind our backs. Bribery, embezzlement—he lived in a world that was loaded with bribery," Otilia said.

"The war-torn country was his oyster, chaos worked in his favor," Carmen said.

"I always wondered what happened after I left. Our personal belongings were gone—our furniture, the kitchen appliances, our clothes. Who took the old sepia photos and colored prints? The memorabilia to trace our family? Our documents, certificates? Who cleared the house from its goods? Was it Tomás?" Otilia asked.

"I don't think I ever saw any of our stuff. Knowing him, he probably sold it."

"I was deprived of my rightful ownership, and now I find myself in a position where I'm unable to prove it. The property was in your father's name, but it would have passed on to you when he died."

"All this information is very important, and surely it will count towards a proper compensation," Carmen said.

"My, my, Tomás"—Otilia sighed—"he's still a thorn in our side."

"Think of how he is stewing in his own juice. He claims he's a legitimate family member and we're being disloyal to him. Just the other day he told me he took steps to guard the security of our property, such a farce. He claims that by the time he took hold of the land, the cattle and horses were stolen, and since you hadn't returned, he wanted to make sure the place wasn't abandoned or invaded. He was scared that thieves would break in, or hoodlums set fires just for kicks. He also feared that if the house was deserted, it would be confiscated.

He argued that he thought you'd be happy he was taking good care of me," Salvador grumbled.

"Now he's the martyr?" Carmen chuckled.

"He liked to have things his way," Otilia said, shaking her head.

Otilia could see how Tomás would have played his own game, sowing confusion among the people he dealt with, paying some off, charming others, passing information to some behind the backs of higher-ups.

"I'm sure Tomás could have easily made up a sad story about how his nephew's parents had to flee from the brutal Shining Path guerillas, leaving their only child behind, eliciting sympathy," Otilia said.

"Sure, in troubled times there's real danger. A fake affidavit and cash would have sufficed to make his case," Carmen said. "What about Otilia's financial potential and means? All was lost." Carmen turned to look at her husband.

He nodded.

"The government believes most of the violence took place in southern communities, and since it's set the criteria to remunerate them, it won't be likely they'll take responsibility for our single case. Especially when they hear that one of our own family members was to blame," Salvador said, scratching his head.

The more Otilia dwelled on her story, the more she was convinced that she should inform the officials who dealt with the *búsqueda de justicia*—redress—how her circumstances had played out. Both her brother and the government had contributed to the flagrant transgressions of her fundamental rights. "I'll tell them my story as I see it," Otilia said, giving Salvador a pleading look.

"I suppose you should," Salvador said.

▲ ▲ ▲

A week later, Otilia and Salvador traveled to the center of town to see their lawyer again. In the lobby of his office building, they were approached by a security guard who looked them over, hesitated, then asked who they were there to see. The guard checked their names on a roster, nodded, and motioned Salvador towards the staircase. Salvador ran up two stairs at a time, anxious to give Sr. Malfi the information he'd obtained from examining Tomás's papers thoroughly. Otilia took her time trailing behind.

Salvador reached for one of the folders in his scuffed leather briefcase and waited for Sr. Malfi to take a seat. "I have more names for you," he said.

"Let's see," Sr. Malfi said, looking down at his desk and not allowing Salvador to speak. "As you know, I engaged an independent investigator to look into the titling history of your land. He was told that those documents were destroyed in a fire. Questionable. He did find out that there was a head clerk at the time, a person who worked his way up the ranks to become manager in 1985, who was known to have broken the rules. He's since retired but accused of bilking the system: charging high fees for favors and taking cuts from his subordinates."

"What in the world!" Salvador said.

"And his name was . . . " Sr. Malfi picked up a sheet of paper and brought it close to his eyes. "Cristian Guerrero. Have you heard of him?" he asked, directing the question at Otilia.

"No," she said.

"I have," Salvador said. "Guerrero is one of the names that appears in Tomás's papers." He was looking down at the file.

"How old would he be today?" Salvador wondered out loud. "I hope he's still alive."

"My source informs me that nobody is too keen to talk or take responsibility for shielding the corrupt practices of the past. I can subpoena the current department head and see if I can get further information about what the office knows now about what went on then."

"Do you think that should be the next step?" Salvador asked.

"It's still premature; let's see what else we can find. We've got a name. That's a good start."

It was a reassuring thought. It was hot in the room, and Sr. Malfi had drops of sweat on his forehead, which he dabbed with his wrinkled cotton handkerchief.

"I would like to discuss another issue," Salvador said.

"Go ahead."

"I found this notarized record of Tomás's claim where he declares that my mother and father made him my guardian. It's dated January 1988."

Salvador picked up a sheet, pointed to a sentence, and read, "If for some reason the parents leave and do not return due to unexpected circumstances within a reasonable period of time, or if there ever is a financial need to do so, the parents authorize Tomás Campos to sell the property on their behalf. Funds would then suffice to provide for the child's education and upkeep until he has reached adulthood."

"I would *never* have prepared such a document," Otilia said, raising her voice.

"Excellent!" Sr. Malfi exclaimed. "This will be proof that negotiations were initiated in bad faith."

"My mother left in February, 1989. At the time, she was not on speaking terms with Tomás. There is strong evidence that he lied."

"Otilia, before you return to the United States, we must prepare an affidavit where you deny the validity of this signature," Sr. Malfi said. "We must prepare both your and Salvador's accounts of what went on. We must clearly lay out the facts we want to present to the court. It will be done in the form of a sworn affidavit, whereby we state that Tomás perjured himself and did not try to locate you."

"The lack of basic information about my parents' whereabouts hurt me greatly. I had no sense of them and, of course, I felt abandoned. So lost. For years I worried that losing them was my fault, that I should have waited for my father at the spot where he'd left me. Later, during my teens, I wasn't distressed, nor depressed, but angry. My anger became an obsession as I tried to figure out what happened to them and where they could be," Salvador said, with a rising intonation.

"We will try to make it right," Sr. Malfi said, speaking softly, looking straight into his eyes.

▲ ▲ ▲

The day Gerald Gold arrived back in Lima from Chile, he called Otilia
to ask her to meet for coffee at the elegant Larcomar shopping center,
perched high on the edge of the hard rock seaside cliffs. Otilia decided
to put on her new beige dress and get there early to spend time at the
Love Park, a small green space named after a piece of art. She took
a stroll down the well-maintained flat path planted with violet and
pink petunias along its borders, to take a look at the larger-than-life
sculpture of an embracing couple known as *El Beso—The Kiss*. It was a
clear, warm afternoon, and all the surrounding benches were taken. As
soon as she noticed a couple standing, she rushed to the free mosaic
tile bench. Looking out at the surf in the distance, taking in a few
deep, fresh, salty breaths, she lost herself for some moments in the
blue Pacific Ocean. Feeling the warmth of the sun on her shoulders,
she saw a sole Hare Krishna playing his bells, then spotted surfboards
making their way on the waves. A bit before five o'clock she got up,
working up the courage to meet Gerald Gold.

"How was Santiago de Chile?" she asked, after they were shown to
a table by the host.

Gerald pulled out a chair for Otilia and remained standing behind
until she brought the chair close to the table. "It was a good trip."

"Thank you," she said, enjoying his courteousness. "First time in
Santiago?"

"No, I've been there before," he said, dragging his chair closer to hers.
He rummaged through his backpack and pulled out a camera to show
her some photos.

She fidgeted with a spoon.

"The plans for the museum have been drafted by the Brazilian architects. A simple modern structure with a beam, an elevated airy space for

the exhibits, and a base. There'll be a ramp to take visitors to a garden patio," he explained as he pointed out each section. "The first stone was laid at the site by the Chilean president, who, as you may know, was a victim of torture."

Otilia rested her elbow on the table with her face on her palm and listened to him talk about his meetings with a designer and the junior architect. She was sitting across from a couple raising their glasses of wine. *Maybe I need a drink,* she thought to herself.

"It's a museum meant to remember the human rights abuses committed under the brutal Pinochet Dictatorship," Gerald said, putting his camera away.

"I decided to stop back in Lima for only forty-eight hours to interview a photographer who has been using photography to raise awareness of the conflict between your government forces and the Shining Path. She's done an excellent job and I can learn a lot from her. But I'm so glad I could see you. How have you been?"

He looked straight at her and she straightened up.

"All right."

"I must tell you about this photographer, I have an appointment to see her tomorrow. She has documented people's destinies—exactly what the Chileans are looking for. She witnessed events as she moved through the streets and was able to capture people's pain during the conflict. In Chile, people are interested in understanding how to portray a society's recovery from acts of violence so they can move forward. Reconciliation can be well understood through art forms, and in Chile they intend to exhibit hundreds of photographs."

"I see," Otilia said.

"A photo allows us to see, hear, and feel what others experienced."

"But how can they change people's minds?" Otilia asked.

"By providing all points of view, having all sides tell the story. Lifelike images are more powerful than reality described in words."

"That's so true."

"Photographs are meant to raise people's awareness of situations and influence opinion. But enough of that. How has it been going for you?" he asked.

"Complicated," she said. "We are in conversations with a lawyer."

"I would guess that things don't move fast enough. I find that's a big barrier for me here in South America—a cultural difference, I guess."

Otilia nodded. "When we live in the north, we develop a need for speedy outcomes."

"So right, I get impatient, especially during protracted meetings. Here things take longer, there are usually more discussions than necessary."

An awkward silence emerged.

"You said you were in Peru before. What did you think of the country back then?" she finally asked.

He smiled. "I remember so clearly that people were consumed by the Miss Peru contest. She would have been the first Afro-Peruvian to represent the country at a world contest like Miss Universe. The big news wasn't about her beauty, but that after her coronation her crown was stolen. Two robbers had entered her home and taken off with her suitcases full of trophies, jewelry and clothes. She lived in a poor neighborhood, her father was a taxi driver, and the stolen goods were on loan. They were worried about not being able to return them. Her father went on the radio asking for help to identify the thieves, but the family began to be accosted by journalists and it all changed for them. Afterwards, I learned that the break-in was staged. Nasty comments made in the press about the family made the poor parents wish they had never encouraged their daughter to participate in beauty contests."

"I heard about that story on a Spanish TV channel. The girl received so many flowers, expressions of sympathy, that one day her mother was approached by one of the neighbors who asked her if someone had passed away."

Jerry laughed.

They sat for a while nursing their second cup of coffee and sharing a chocolate cake. He seemed nice enough—spontaneous, curious,
passionate about his work. But she'd have to figure out what he really
was like.

▲ ▲ ▲

Night was beginning to fall when they exchanged phone numbers and
home addresses in California. Gerald walked her to a cab and said, "I
hope we can get together in the Bay Area soon. And, please, from now
on call me Jerry."

# CHAPTER 13

# Washington, DC, 2008

In early September, Jerry waited for Dario Alvarez to pull up in front of the Hyatt hotel at Washington, DC, national airport. It was a humid Sunday morning and Jerry was starting to sweat when, at precisely ten o'clock, Dario arrived. Jerry climbed into the air-conditioned BMW with a smile.

"My half-brother, how about that! This is life-changing," Jerry said, sitting back.

Dario, still a muscular man with a full head of white hair, wearing tan pants and a polo shirt, raised his eyebrows and said, "It's so good to meet you."

Jerry reached over to give him a hug and, as he lowered his arms, Dario grabbed Jerry's hand, holding it for a few moments. When he let go, Dario placed both hands on the steering wheel and said, "A reunion fifty years in the making."

They sat silently looking at each other.

"How is the pregnancy going?" Jerry asked suddenly. Dario turned the ignition.

"Very well. We are so relieved. We were very concerned that Madelaine might carry the autosomal recessive gene and the baby would have a higher chance of developing symptoms. But we found out there is no risk of inherited retinal disease. We are happy to know that the baby's genes are working properly," Dario responded in his rich, deep voice. "In other words, there are no gene variants, no changes in the DNA sequence. We had excellent genetic counseling and support to help us understand the risks. Thank you for being there for us."

"A baby girl, then," Jerry said, looking straight ahead, grappling with his tumultuous thoughts, feelings, and flashes of memory.

▲ ▲ ▲

Once they were on the highway, Dario warned that it would take a little more than an hour to get to his home and he wanted to stop along the way to show Jerry some of the new construction cropping up.

"The communities are changing. There's been a lot of gentrification in the inner city, forcing some of the population to move our way. Charles County used to be considered country, but it isn't in the country anymore. Washington's urban core is expanding rapidly."

"How long have you lived in your home?" Jerry asked.

"We've been there a couple of years. When I retired, we thought it would be nice to live in a rural area, a peaceful place, and since we wouldn't be commuting, distance wasn't a concern. We found a nice place with plenty of trees for privacy. We have a large vegetable garden and fruit trees, and we enjoy spending time outdoors."

"You're in great shape," Jerry said, turning to look at him.

"It's the exercise, proper nutrition, and rest."

The first detour Dario took was to the Gaylord National Resort which had opened a few months before. The site along the Potomac River was to be known as National Harbor, a multiuse waterfront development. "This area used to be known as the Salubria Plantation, and when the plantation house burned down it was offered for sale. Environmentalists like myself were upset, as we wanted to preserve the Heritage Trail. So far we've been promised that one day there'll be access to the trailhead."

Dario parked. "What do you say we walk a few blocks and stretch our legs?"

"Great idea."

Jerry walked rapidly to look at the construction equipment up ahead, then waited for Dario. "I must admit you look so much like Miles. The way you move, your facial expressions, uncanny."

"You're saying this because we have proof that we are related." Dario laughed.

"I don't think so, you have his coloring and the same blue eyes."

"Czech stock! Who would have thought," Dario said.

"Don't forget I'm fifty percent Jewish too."

"Since I found out I wasn't Osvaldo's son, I wondered how my life would have been if I grew up with a father from an Eastern European cultural background instead."

"And I've thought about what it would have been like for Miles if he had stayed in Bolivia. Would he have married Soledad? Would he have integrated into her society?"

"We would be altogether different people," Dario said seriously.

"Do you think my dad ever knew your mother was pregnant?" Jerry asked.

"No, she was ashamed when she found out she was carrying a baby. She broke up the relationship and felt forced to marry Osvaldo right away."

"She never told him she was pregnant with another man's child?"

"She never did."

Jerry continued to walk, thinking about how times had changed. How back then it was considered acceptable to cover up a pregnancy and come up with a clever plan.

"I'd like to learn more about him," Dario said.

"He was an introvert, didn't make friends easily. He had a sarcastic sense of humor; he liked to joke that he was a kindergarten dropout. He never liked school but, don't get me wrong, he read the newspapers like they were textbooks. He analyzed the source of the news, asked questions, always wanting to dig deeper. He didn't only read one paper, he read many across the political spectrum. He liked to debate and had a highly competitive nature. He was sharp. For him emotions didn't count, it was all about trusting concrete information. No hunches were valid for the man!"

"He sounds like quite a character . . . Ah, here we are back at the car."

When they were buckled in their seats, Dario asked, "Are you a seafood lover?" Dario turned towards the south roadway, classical music playing softly in the background. "I would like to take you to one of my favorite spots for lunch."

"That would be great," Jerry said. "I'm starting to feel hungry."

Dario turned onto a narrow country road and, when they were passing a few one-story clapboard frame houses, said, "These are the remnants of a historical village known as Port Tobacco."

He made a left turn and drove to an open-air restaurant on the water's edge. Dario parked in a crowded, unpaved lot and they walked to the entrance; the hostess seated them on a spacious back terrace overlooking the river.

"We don't have soft-shell crabs this late in the summer. They're only in season for six to eight weeks, but the ones they are serving right now are sweet and delicious," Dario said.

Dario ordered a tray full of crabs, then turned to Jerry and said, "I'm anxious to know more about my father's background. His being Jewish."

"What would you like to know?"

"I was raised Catholic, with our Latin American prejudices. I went to a parochial school where we were taught that Jesus was killed by the Jews. I married a Catholic girl, never paid attention to the life Jewish families led. Ethnicity became a sensitive topic at the time my daughter decided to marry a Jewish man. Had I known that I was half Jewish, I would have been more tolerant and accepted Peter right away. At the beginning of their relationship, I gave them a hard time."

Jerry reached for a crab and Dario took one for himself. "Position your knife in the middle of each of the two large claws and hit the handle with your mallet, like this. When you open the shell with your fingers, you'll find the best meat inside," Dario said.

"My dad was an atheist," Jerry picked up the thread of their conversation. "He didn't believe in organized religion and never participated in religious events. If he was dragged by my mother to a High Holiday meal, that was as much as he could take. But he was a real believer and supporter of the State of Israel. He was convinced that the Jewish people needed a country to call their own, as there'd been centuries of discrimination and persecution against them. He realized how lucky he'd been to escape Czechoslovakia."

"I understood why my mother was ashamed to admit that she had become pregnant out of wedlock. It was a cause for deep shame, but she didn't seem to mind that my father was a Jewish immigrant. I wish I had known the truth sooner. She carried that secret with her for so long. I could've asked her so many questions had I known before. She told me she never shared any of this with Osvaldo. He died several years before she passed. Osvaldo was told that I was a *sietemesino*."

"Premature? I guess that's what they all said at the time," Jerry said.

"My grandmother made sure Soledad married the fellow the family selected for her right away." Dario twisted one of the crab's legs. "Osvaldo was a good man, but he raised me at a time when fathers were not involved with their children. Other than Sundays, when we attended church and my parents entertained family members and friends, we didn't spend much time together. Still, I grew up content."

"You did better than me. I was a rebel."

"How so? Please tell me what type of father Milan, or Miles, was," Dario said as he reached for his beer.

"I didn't know Milan. Miles was my dad."

"I knew neither."

"I'm sorry," Jerry said.

Jerry sat up and looked at the fishing boats on the river, then he told Dario how he'd experienced his father.

"Now I have a personal connection to the Jewish people and the plight of the refugees. Perhaps I'll get some insight into my own makeup," Dario said, wiping his fingers on multiple paper napkins.

The fact that Dario and Jerry were half-brothers weighed on them, and they had to find out if they could find ways to form a bond. They continued to talk about their lives to understand each other and find common threads. They recognized why Milan and Soledad hadn't shared more of their story, but they also discovered their biological father wasn't the person either of them had believed him to be. The disconnect bothered them both.

"Milan . . . Miles—we will figure it out one day," Jerry said.

"Did your father ever talk about his life in La Paz?" Dario asked.

"Not much. It seemed that the past was gone and he wanted to move on."

"The reason I ask is that my mother told me the story of how they met. She became infatuated with him after meeting him at a European delicatessen."

"I don't remember my father ever talking about meeting a girl at a deli. He mentioned that he went into business with these four Czech guys who opened a delicatessen. But all I remember him saying was that he made a profit when he sold his share of the business to them before leaving for the US."

"I had hoped you could tell me more about their relationship and how serious it was," Dario murmured, then became silent for the next ten minutes of the trip.

▲ ▲ ▲

The Alvarez's post and beam house had beautiful grounds, lush foliage, and a manicured lawn with colorful flower beds. "You keep your grounds in impeccable shape," Jerry said.

When they entered the house, Jerry was taken by the large windows offering an expansive view of the Potomac River. In the background, a radio played Astor Piazzolla's tango music, a tune Jerry was fond of. Oil paintings on the walls, lush carpets, and plants in earthenware pots gave the room a warm feel. The stone fireplace in the living room rose up to the wood plank ceiling, and Jerry commented on its beautiful craftsmanship. After spotting a heron flying by over the river, he asked Dario if he could take a few photographs.

Dario suggested they sit outside on the screened porch and opened the sliding glass doors. Mary Margaret, a tall, blonde, heavyset woman wearing a flowing summer dress appeared, carrying a pitcher of sangria with both hands.

"Our daughter and son-in-law are on their way," Mary Margaret announced. She placed the sangria on the patio table and turned to Jerry.

"Let me give you a hug. We are so grateful to you, and we welcome you to our family."

"Thanks," Jerry said, hugging her gently in return.

"I'm so happy to have you here," Dario said, slapping Jerry on the back.

After a few minutes of chatting, Jerry got up and walked over to the hallway where he retrieved his small backpack and removed a package for his hosts.

"I put together a photo book. Here are the best photos I found of my dad and the family," he said.

"How very thoughtful of you," Dario said.

Dario looked at the front cover of a bound book with the photograph of a young man dressed in a spiffy suit on the deck of a ship. He opened the book and quickly flipped through the pages with photos from different periods of his father's life.

"I will really appreciate looking at every small detail," Dario said and smiled, his eyes glowing.

▲ ▲ ▲

Madelaine and Peter arrived at dusk when shadows stretched long over the lawn. Mary Margaret suggested they move inside to the dining room table for the meal she had prepared. The delicious, Southern-style dinner consisting of fried chicken, okra, corn, and scalloped potatoes was already laid out on the table. The young couple said they were anxious to hear stories about Jerry's childhood, so he shared some of his memories with them. After a couple of glasses of wine, both Jerry and Dario summoned the courage to speak openly.

Dario got up from his chair and marched out of the room and returned with a manila envelope for Jerry. All eyes were on Jerry when he opened it. Two dozen Christmas cards spilled on the table.

"I never imagined my father sending cards. It seems so out of character," Jerry said.

Jerry picked up one of the cards and recognized his father's handwriting but was reluctant to read the words. He looked at the hosts then read silently, while Dario looked intently at Jerry to see the reaction on his face.

Dario went to stand behind Jerry's chair and said, "This was the first one he mailed, dated 1952. It's postmarked New York State. Here, he asked my mother how she was, and I think he expected a response."

Jerry picked up the cards one by one and put them back inside the envelope. *This isn't the place to find out about my dad's relationship,* he thought.

Mary Margaret, Madelaine, and Peter looked at Jerry expectantly until Mary Margaret realized this was making Jerry uncomfortable. "I think we are ready for some dessert—will it be apple or peach pie for you, Jerry?" she asked quickly.

During dessert, Mary Margaret asked about Miles's later years.

"He was afraid of death. He started to talk about dying once he lost his independence. Chemotherapy and radiation left him with aches and pain, and he would sit on his easy chair for hours at a time. He was no longer able to drive and get around, although he was of sound mind. He did not believe in the afterlife but worried about what he would find on 'the other side.' At the end, he became agitated and asked to be released from life."

In the silence that followed, Jerry knew it was time to go.

"I am ready to call for a taxi," Jerry said. "It's been so nice to finally meet and spend time together. Thank you for the delicious supper and your pie—superb." He hugged Mary Margaret goodbye.

Dario protested and said he would be happy to drive Jerry back to his hotel.

"Sorry, Daddy, but there's no way you can drive after so much wine. We can take you, Jerry," Madelaine said.

"Don't put yourself out, I know that's a two-hour round trip for you," Jerry said.

Once Jerry was in the taxi, he realized that it was clear they would remain in touch. He now had an extended family, of sorts, in the making. And he was sure he'd soon come to terms with this legacy.

Before going to bed, he looked at Soledad's Christmas cards. Jerry laughed when he saw the picture of Dick and Jane playing next to a snowman, the same characters that appeared in the basal reader when he was in first grade. He inspected Soledad's perfect cursive

handwriting and read every word. He wanted to find words of affection, something intimate, but no sentiments were expressed. He would
ask Dario to send photos of his mother. He was upset he hadn't asked
when they were together. He'd wait for Dario's next email.

# CHAPTER 14

## Lima, Peru, 2009

The first business day after the New Year celebrations, Carmen drove Otilia to the Reparation Council's office on her way to work. Carmen's curly black hair was up in a ponytail and her oblong earrings dangled as she looked over her shoulder to check for cars. A number of waste collection workers were out on the streets, gathering wrappers and firework casings left behind by yesterday's revelers. Impatient drivers honked, creeping along in the chaotic traffic, and at the upcoming transit circle, a female police officer in a pressed dark-green uniform whistled, giving a garbage truck the right of way. Suddenly a car came up close and passed. "That son of a bitch, he could have easily hit us," Carmen said, raising her voice.

"Watch out!" Otilia yelled suddenly. A woman dragging children on either side of her jumped off the pavement in front of their car, making a mad dash across.

Carmen came to a full stop. Her thin silver bracelets jingled as she raised her left hand to cover her mouth in shock. "I hope we won't be late."

"We have plenty of time, just take it easy," Otilia said. "I see so many female police, how come?"

"They are the newest addition to the force. Someone came up with the idea that women are less corruptible than men, so they hired a bunch of them."

"Is that so?"

"They say women are more honest, more disciplined, more trust-worthy than the men. Taxi drivers seem to like them. They claim that you can't bribe a policewoman and they aren't being harassed as much as before," Carmen said.

"I suppose it's good if they can get *la coima* cleaned-up."

Carmen pulled up at the curb and Otilia got out of the car, step-ping over a half-burned large effigy along with some party hats. Trash of the past year would soon disappear, signaling the start of a new one. It had been twenty years since Otilia had spent New Year's Eve in her country of birth.

"Have a good meeting," Carmen said, rolling down the passenger window and blowing her mother-in-law a kiss.

▲ ▲ ▲

Carmen continued on her drive cautiously and parked near her office in a quieter neighborhood. She was scheduled to meet with a few women activists speaking out on behalf of mothers who'd been caught in the sterilization program initiated during Alberto Fujimori's presi-dency. His perverse political campaign had praised sterilization as a way of reducing poverty. Starting in 1990, it lasted until the president was overthrown in 2000. Instead of receiving access to birth control, women were forcibly sterilized. Healthcare workers were pressured to meet quotas and doctors carried out orders. Women and a few men, especially those with large families, were rounded up and forced to undergo procedures they knew nothing about.

After decades of seeking justice for the physical and emotional pain families had endured, only those who'd lost their partners as a result of complications from the surgery received compensation. Mandatory sterilization was considered a crime against humanity under International Law, and Peru was finally ready to carry out a preliminary criminal investigation. In her professional life, Carmen had listened to many grim stories, but this was one of the most painful ones. She'd done her homework and was ready to go to bat for the women.

▲ ▲ ▲

Otilia entered the Reparation office building and took the elevator up to the third floor. After checking in with a clerk at the front desk, she was told to wait. Ten minutes later, a clean-shaven young man asked her to follow him to one of the cubicles. "Jaime is my name, and I am here to assist you," he said.

He offered Otilia a chair at a small rectangular table and went to sit across from her. Otilia placed her purse on the floor, folded her hands on her lap, and realized how tense she was.

"Can I have your identification card please—I need to verify the information on your application."

He checked her full name and the number on the card.

"As you well know, the laws of a country are meant to organize communities to live productively and in peace. Unfortunately, those who were in power during the time of conflict violated them. You and your family experienced much hurt. We are here to see if reparations are viable for those who were affected by the lack of civil liberties. I would like to review your claim so we can move forward with it, but first, why don't you tell me what brings you here today."

Otilia thought this man had memorized some lines from a handbook and chuckled to herself. Sr. Malfi had counseled her to tell the truth and be candid, so Otilia was ready to do as he recommended.

"I'm here to register my husband's disappearance. I also need help to obtain copies of several important missing documents." She needed birth certificates for herself and her husband Manuel as well as their marriage license. She'd left her home in a hurry, never to return again, and now that she was making claims, she lacked the supporting documentary evidence.

"When I submitted my application, I didn't know that my brother Tomás had misappropriated my house. I have since learned that he stole our property and then sold it. He did not have my consent. I lost my animals and my personal belongings. I never saw a cent. Everything is gone. As you can see, the laws at the time didn't protect me. Had we been living in peace, this never would have occurred. I've been trying to find out what happened to my husband but, to this day, I don't have an answer," Otilia said.

"So, let me get the story straight. When you left your village, your brother became your son's guardian, and you are telling me that he thought it was right for him to take possession of your property?"

"We've just heard that's what happened. I didn't appoint him as my son's guardian. My son was left alone and became lost. Eventually he found his uncle, who took him in. As for my home, he and my child never lived there," Otilia explained. She spent a few more minutes answering questions about her situation.

"He felt entitled to the family assets to care for your child," the man repeated back to her as he scribbled information on her form. "And you believe that he bribed an official at the land registry. Once the transaction was closed, your brother placed the house on the market."

"That's right," Otilia said.

"Do you know who bought the house?"

"It belongs to a church now."

The Evangelical Charismatic movement became strong at a time when social contracts were breaking down. When the dark-horse presidential candidate Alberto Fujimori ran for office, he received the support of the Pentecostal and other Evangelical groups. Once in office, the president offered these churches taxation benefits similar to those that were in place for the Catholic Church. And in her village of El Milagro, the *evangélicos*, hoping to get a foot in the door, rushed to obtain a sweet deal from Tomás, who was eager to divest himself of the land.

"I also need help to obtain bank statements. I've requested those for some time, but I've had no response. As I have stated here on my application, my financial institution has not been willing to communicate. There were funds in my account when I left, but the last time I had a word with them, they claimed my account was inoperative."

At the beginning of her displacement, when Otilia was in hiding at the mining camp, she'd been able to use some of her savings, but over time as more money went out than went in, she ran out of checks. As the bank did not have branches where she lived, she couldn't make any deposits in that account. By the time she left the country, there was still a small amount of money left. She requested her statements be sent to the address in the United States, but she never received them. Years later, after asking again that funds be transferred to her US account, they responded they couldn't comply with her request because they had no proof that her letter was valid, even when she'd had it notarized.

"Those funds certainly belong to you," Sr. Malfi had claimed. Funds from an inactive account would have been sent to the State and would be refundable. Refusing to send funds overseas was a ploy, her lawyer advised.

"You must understand that displaced-persons reparations are not a priority relative to other forms of victimization right now. But the Office of Reparations will review your eligibility, to process your case in due time," the young man said, leaning back in his chair.

"And my lost husband? Suddenly he was gone. We suffered a tragedy . . ." She looked away.

"Yes, I understand and sympathize with you; however, his body has yet to be found."

*An unnecessary comment*, Otilia thought. *Should I feel ashamed?* She recalled what Sr. Malfi had said—that the burden of proof rested with the State and her family would be claiming benefits. Otilia took a deep breath and felt somewhat empowered again. She remained silent while the young man entered the information Otilia had given him into the computer.

"If there is anything else you want to tell us, please don't hesitate to come back. Thank you for your application; have a good day," he said, shaking her hand before leading her out of his office.

▲ ▲ ▲

That evening when Salvador and Carmen returned from work, they invited her out to eat. "But I cooked something for you," Otilia complained. It was her last night with them. She would be flying back to California the next afternoon after being in Lima for three weeks. They insisted they wanted to take her out for a bite and they would have the supper she'd prepared the next evening.

They went to a recently opened neighborhood restaurant that featured northern Peruvian food. The establishment's motto was "*come cómo en casa, sin tener que lavar platos*"—"like eating at home without having to wash dishes." It was a small place with a cement floor and a dozen tables covered with checkered tablecloths. The scent of spices and coffee was pungent, and the music enhanced the pleasing ambiance.

Salvador ordered a pitcher of beer to share and ceviche for starters, followed by two orders of *seco de cabrito*. Otilia ordered the sea bass prepared in a lemon sauce and served in a corn husk.

Once the waitress had left, Salvador wanted to know how Otilia's meeting with the reparation office had gone. He was expecting to be called up next and wanted to be prepared.

"It seems clear that they are making a distinction between those who suffered imprisonment or torture and those who were displaced. I am not sure how they'll view my case. For you it's different, you were left all alone—orphaned," Otilia said.

"How do you feel?" Carmen asked.

"Upset. A bit betrayed. The clerk had the nerve to suggest that since Manuel's body was never recovered, he might simply be missing abroad."

"Oh no, not again," Carmen said. "I thought these people were taught to show respect."

"He was polite, but I was hoping for more," Otilia replied.

"So, they're ignoring people's sufferings?" Salvador asked.

"I think they're using a narrow lens. They forget the fact that Otilia's security was taken from her. Her daily life became a deadly threat, and when she moved away from El Milagro, she faced an unfamiliar environment. Nothing was stable anymore, and her protective support was gone. She was facing a crisis and had moved to a place where she felt oppressed and humiliated," Carmen said.

The waitress returned with their order. "*Algo mas?*"

"All good." Carmen looked at her with a smile.

"I doubt I will get compensation," Otilia said.

"We will continue to press on with Sr. Malfi," Salvador said.

"How's your goat?" Otilia asked after Carmen and Salvador had a few bites of their meals.

"Delicious," they both replied in agreement.

"Where I once felt invulnerable, the next thing I knew I was out of the house, running to find you and dad," Otilia said, looking at Salvador after a few moments of silent thought.

"This is all wrong. This exercise is not about letting those who suffer forget the past; it is about explaining the truth and compensating for damages. If they don't accept your explanation, then this whole process becomes a charade," Salvador said.

"They should be aware of each person's pain," Carmen said.

Otilia gave a long sigh as she rose from the table. She was with her family, feeling their care, and with this came reassurance.

"Mother, will you be all right?" Salvador asked as they left.

"Yes, *mijito*, I will be." Otilia had lived by herself for two decades.

# CHAPTER 15

# The East Bay,
# California, 2009

The postcard sent from the Galapagos Islands told Otilia that Jerry was thinking of her. True to his word, he was letting her know he'd be home on the first of July, signing it, *un abrazo—Geraldo*, his Spanish name. Otilia turned over the card to look at the photo collage. There were two small penguins facing each other, a turquoise marine iguana sunning on a rock, and a giant turtle with its stretched-out neck. Jerry had been out of town for a while. That was how he worked: one project could take him away for a few months. During the past year they'd met for coffee when they found time, and she was feeling more comfortable talking to him. Although conversations had become more natural and felt good, they hadn't shared any intimate thoughts. No promises were made. Nevertheless, she was starting to miss his attention after his long absence and was excited to reconnect.

▲ ▲ ▲

On the second day of July, after dinner, the phone rang. "How was your trip?" Otilia asked.

After a brief conversation about the wonders of nature and the myriad birds and animals on the Galapagos, Jerry said, "Let me pick you up tomorrow and bring you to my studio."

Otilia agreed.

In an older low-rise apartment set back from the road, the top floor had been converted to a living-working space.

"Welcome," Jerry said after he opened the door.

The first thing she noticed was the exposed brick and the intense amount of light filling the room. Next to a well-stocked bookcase, a large bulletin board filled with notes, pictures, and sketches hung on the wall. Storage bins held an assortment of well-organized tools, and two computers were on an L-shaped desk.

Otilia remarked on an upright piano in a corner of the room.

"I bought it about a year ago," Jerry said. "It's always been my dream to own one. I played as a child and I want to get started again."

"Stop thinking and end your problems," she read aloud, squinting to read the plaque on the wall as a bar of sunlight crossed over it. Turning to face him, she asked, "How does this aphorism resonate with you? You're a deep thinker."

"It all depends what kind of thoughts a person has. I try not to worry about banalities. Lao Tzu's phrase keeps me centered."

On the opposite wall was another inspirational phrase: "Awakening begins when a man realizes he is going nowhere and does not know where to go"—Gurdjieff.

"Who was Gurdjieff?" she asked.

"George Gurdjieff was a Russian philosopher, a spiritual teacher in the first half of the last century who drew from Zen, Buddhism, Sufi Islam, and the occult. He taught self-awareness and the importance of

knowing who we really are. Most people don't have much knowledge
of themselves; they live in a dream. He came up with methods to foster
inner growth, develop consciousness, and become fully awake. When
I was growing up, I was hostile and struggled with my upbringing. I
rebelled against my parents, went my own way, moved far away from
my heritage. I longed to be set free, but I couldn't do so until I was
forced to face my demons. Many teachings have shown me the way to
an authentic existence. Gurdjieff is one of them. He made me aware of
the importance of being grateful for the opportunities we meet. And
look at me, you've come into my life!"

She smiled and brushed his comment away. Otilia wanted to let
him know that she had trouble with quotes. "Quotations can strike the
right chord, but they are short-lived. I exist in a disconnected world,
and I've come across too many selfish people who are only out for
themselves. My world has been one full of danger and hardship. I've
had to put up with predators, deceivers, people who have wished me
and my family harm—serious stuff. No quotation can put my mind
right." Her voice rose as she became agitated.

"I fully agree, please don't get me wrong. You have to go beyond the
phrases and delve into the philosophy. Lao Tzu tells us to be aware of the
places our minds go and the thoughts we hold when we are not paying
attention. He says we need to know how we water our dreams. Water
them with worry and fear, and you will produce weeds that choke the
life from you; water them with optimism and solutions, and you will
cultivate success. Be on the lookout for ways to turn a problem into an
opportunity; be on the lookout for ways to nurture your dreams. There
are pains that don't go away. Healing doesn't mean the damage never
existed; it means the damage no longer controls our lives."

Otilia sighed.

"One more of Lao Tzu's wisest ideas is to watch one's thoughts.
Thoughts become words, words become actions, and actions become
habits," Jerry said.

Otilia continued to move around the room until she stopped to look at a series of photographs illustrating upheavals around the world.

"These were taken when I went to the Eastern Bloc countries after the collapse of the Soviet Union," Jerry said. "These here are from artists of the former Yugoslavia. I'm interested in exploring uprising and unrest and how these issues are interpreted in art."

Walking to a different part of the room, he told her about the renderings of his current work. Models were spread out on a table, and a larger one stood on the floor. Then she looked at the photograph of people posing next to the Chilean president at an empty site.

"You enlarged the photo you showed me in Lima," she said.

"Yes, that's right. This guy here is the curator, the person who will decide which pieces are a go and which are not. He will select what will be offered to the public. Later, I'll be working with the artists to map out the exhibits themselves."

"Will you go back to Santiago?"

"I'll go back to set up the installations. Many ideas will be explored and then we'll have to test them out. We have to find the right balance between catching the visitor's attention and communicating an exciting and meaningful experience. We'll have to figure out how to make the exhibit work. In Chile, we are working with culturally sensitive material, and we have artists and technology specialists to advise us."

"A lot of thought goes into your work," Otilia said.

"It's all about communicating a message to jar the viewer's consciousness."

"How will you transport the pieces?" she asked.

"I will attempt to make the models here in my studio, and once it's decided which pieces are a go, the finals will actually be built on site."

He led her upstairs to show her his living space, and they went to sit on a couch.

Some time later, clearing his throat and with some hesitation, he asked, "I was wondering if you'd like to go on a picnic tomorrow? I'll put a basket together and we can go on a hike to Canyon Trail Park."

▲ ▲ ▲

As agreed, the next day Jerry knocked lightly on Otilia's door and came through with a big smile. He embraced her with warmth, seeming thrilled to see her.

"Are you sure you don't want me to bring anything along?" Otilia asked.

"Why don't you grab a blanket? We might not find a table. I expect it will be busy since it's a holiday, and we might have to sit on the grass."

"Do we eat first or go for a walk?" he asked once they arrived.

"Let's eat, then we don't have to worry about the food spoiling."

He had picked up sandwiches from a delicatessen close to his home and fruit from the farmer's market. Later, after he filled her in about his time in the Galapagos, he fed her strawberries with his hands.

He reached for his backpack and removed two small gift-wrapped packages with curled bows of satin ribbon. "These are for you."

She unwrapped a small copper vase with figures of ancient Inca icons overlaid with small encrusted pieces of jade. "Thank you, it is beautiful," she said. She was moved.

"The other one is another knickknack, I'm afraid," he said.

The glass llama covered with a thin sheath of silver on its face and tail was delicate and elegant. "I love it," Otilia said, overjoyed.

She was not one for memorabilia. She had avoided purchasing artisan crafts since she'd left Peru, but these pieces were different. They came with a special thought.

She told him about the T-shirt she'd spotted at a store with three llama faces on the top pocket and the embroidered words "¿cómo te llamas?"—"what's your name?"

"Nothing says Latin American like a llama," he said, and they had a little laugh.

When she lay back to contemplate the clouds in the sky, he gently placed his sinewy arm around her shoulders. "As a child I would make up stories of dragons and butterflies as the constantly changing puffy formations floated along," Otilia said.

"I love your imagination," he said, giving her upper arm a squeeze.

After a while, Jerry said, "Time for a forest bath, the best way to enjoy the day. Let's go for our walk." He pulled her up.

"I don't escape into nature often enough," she said.

Walking through the trails, she felt young and giddy and a bit scared. Somehow, she knew the rapport was right, and she had nothing to lose by being with him. But she felt a flicker of bashfulness when she considered a romantic relationship at her age.

▲ ▲ ▲

The next day she stayed at home to catch up with housework.

"Si No Te Hubieras Ido," the favorite song of 2008 in Peru, "If You Hadn't Left Me," played in the background as Otilia ironed her clothes and hummed along. It was a sad song, and she felt a tear running down her cheek. Manuel had been the love of her life. *Stop!* She told herself. *Focus on the present, you can't think of Manuel for the rest of your days. You've found somebody who is understanding and considerate, and you should give Jerry a chance. You needed more happiness in your life.*

Once Manuel disappeared, she never chased the idea of love, and the few times she felt a connection with a man, it was short-lived, as she soon realized he wasn't like Manuel. But Jerry was different.

Otilia left Peru when the chaos around her veered out of control and, due to the unfortunate circumstances that followed, she'd become vigilant. The dislocation and the unknown had disrupted all of her past relationships, and new ones became difficult to sustain. She'd yearned to live in an orderly world where norms were predictable, but it wasn't meant to be. And once she was in the US, her identity became that of a refugee, a citizen living on the periphery. Even though in California she'd experienced social support, she'd kept most people at arm's length. She'd been lucky to reunite with her son and could now dedicate time to her career, her family, and her few friends. Feeling the need to let healing take place, she struggled to figure out where she best fit. Was it Peru or the United States? She didn't need to make a quick decision, since these days she could easily reach her son and daughter-in-law digitally. But a new partner? That hadn't entered her mind. Anyways, it was too soon to commit.

Thinking about her relationship with her country of birth, Otilia asked herself if she should return. Returning was not the same as going home.

A person went home when there was a place for them: a house, a network of people to rely on, a sense of belonging. But none were available to her. In California she interacted with people who came from all over the world, and she liked the idea of being a global citizen. Her son and daughter-in-law lived in Lima, but she couldn't rely just on them to ease her way back into society. And then there were some Peruvians who believed that since she'd been uprooted, she didn't belong, because she didn't know what it meant to have lived through terrorism. But as Peru changed, would she be able to feel more serene? That was still a big question, as in Latin America there always was uncertainty.

She would have to think hard about what was truly most beneficial for her. She'd have to decide which homeland to choose. In her heart, she knew she could visit Peru and enjoy it, but to return to live there from exile was another question. Living in Peru was complicated. After years of living abroad, carrying a great deal of hurt, her memories of the past were entangled in an intricate web. She'd left after feeling trapped, pushed up against the wall by an autocratic government. She'd had no choice. But at times she wondered if she should've remained, to stand up to the intimidation she faced. Had departing been an act of cowardice? But it was not about a lack of bravery, since she'd continued her search in a new land, looking for her loved ones from afar.

Which country was hers? Where did she belong? Peru was a mixture of longing, nostalgia, and bitterness where she would have to live with the demons she knew. Her future might be here, in the US, where she could move on.

Otilia steered her attention back to ironing and noticed there weren't any more clothes left to press. Her sheets and pillowcases were neatly folded on the top of her dresser and her ironing board put away. Where had the time gone? She shook her head at her own absentmindedness.

# CHAPTER 16

## Lima, Peru, 2011

The story Salvador told himself about his past was important to him, as he felt it was part of his country's history. The problem was that his disquiet followed him too closely whenever he decamped for work. The early trauma brought on by the war that separated him from his parents caused him a severe amount of pain and was rekindled every time he went out to dig for evidence. Investigating disgraceful crimes was onerous. As a child, Salvador believed that if his parents were "disappeared," he could one day vanish as well, and presently in his posts in the field he verified how ruthless the enemy had been. The term "disappeared" was synonymous with "rebel sympathizer," and he questioned if his father could have been one of them. When he asked his mother, she'd been offended, saying she didn't understand people's sketchy grasp of history, because his father would never have been in favor of the far-leftist ideology. Salvador knew exhumations provided a moving testament to what had occurred and pointed to terrible human rights abuses.

In childhood, living on his own, Salvador had been disoriented, perplexed, and bewildered, but as he grew older, he overcame his limitations and his actions kindled new strengths. Over the years, he came to terms with his abandonment and his hurts, accepting the fact that his experiences in life were the upshot of his circumstances. His life experiences didn't impede him from moving on; on the contrary, they gave him self-confidence as he learned to face fears and bring his insecurities under control. He hadn't become an angry radical teenager with rigid views; instead, as soon as he was able to, he sought ways to discover his parents' fate. He was proud to have risen from a murky childhood to become the person he was today, with a wife and a job in the forensic department of the capital city's police force. There he'd developed a passion for uncovering truths.

Recently, extra funding had been made available to increase exhumations, as the number of reported disappeared persons was growing to bloodcurdling heights. Figures ranged from 6,400 graves approximated in 2003 to more than 13,000 in 2008 and up to 15,731 today. The goal was to find all who had vanished during the war; still, some people claimed that they were going too slowly. If they continued to excavate at this pace, it would take seventy years to conclude.

Salvador toiled in the midst of those who had been victims of crimes, recovering the remains of faceless adults and children from concealed graves. He sifted and sorted, looking for shards and stray threads, analyzing for injuries, as well as for clues to identify those who could have been responsible for inflicting the offences. All of the exhumations bore indications of the savagery that had taken place. With each exhumation, deep in his heart Salvador hoped there would be a chance that his absent father's remnants would one day emerge. While he had given up hope that his father was alive, finding his body would bring him peace of mind.

Salvador thought of his father again and again but couldn't remember him well. Could it be that his mind had totally blurred his last images of him, and now Salvador was in the dark? All he recalled from his last hours with his father was playing superhero games to quell his unease before he was put in a hiding place. He had clearer images of himself all alone as a seven-year-old sitting in one spot in the great outdoors, listening to the blustery wind making tree branches creak, scaring him out of his wits. Still with him were visions of himself nestled tightly through the night until dawn when he ventured down to wash off in the icy cold waters of the creek. He would never forget his hunger pangs as he ran after a cow grazing in the pasture to draw milk from its tit for nourishment. And, through it all, the longing for his father ripped through his heart and remained 'til this day.

Always attentive to rumors and news of people who'd disappeared and reappeared, Salvador would dash to the source to confirm the possibility of his father's identity. After reuniting with his mother and obtaining information from her, he paid a visit to each of her acquaintances and relatives. He met with anyone who might be willing to help. He looked around ravines, up on the hills, and in all the hiding places Otilia could recall, surmising one may be where his father had hidden him. He stopped by nearby soldier's barracks, police stations, and jails, but nobody could provide him with further information. He contacted the Red Cross and multiple other organizations with no results.

Although some government officials spoke about reconciliation and the need for evaluating past events, the great majority of young people weren't aware that thousands had succumbed to atrocities. This was a war nearly forgotten since the tragedy had gone unreported for so long. Salvador was afraid that without making people aware, the nasty events would fade further away, then be erased. Victims had waited decades for the truth to be known and to see injustices rectified. It was time to give the forgotten dead a greater and lasting remembrance. But did justice mean recovering bodies, or attributing blame, or both?

Recovery in the aftermath of devastating violence was complicated, and it was difficult to account for those who should be responsible for an individual's death. Besides, often the legal system was not able to point to the perpetrators under investigation for crimes. Once when Salvador inspected shell casings found in close proximity to a grave and expended bullets that were in the earth neighboring the skeletal remains, he thought this was proof of what had occurred. However, the judge did not consider it sufficient evidence as to who was responsible for the person's death. In another instance, a young man's death was deemed to be caused by alcohol and cocaine rather than by the signs of torture and wounds found on his remains.

▲ ▲ ▲

Salvador was taking an afternoon nap on his living room couch, after having returned from working around the clock in a remote location, when a phone call woke him. It was the Forensic Medicine Institute. It had been three years since Salvador had given a sample of his own blood for a genetic match in case the remains of his father ever showed up.

"We have performed a forensic examination on recovered human remains, and a match has been made with your family," a voice on the line said.

"We are calling to make an appointment so you can identify your relative before we can return the remains to your family. When are you available to come to the morgue to meet with one of our officers?" the soft-spoken woman asked.

Salvador tried to grapple with the information he'd just heard.

"Yes, of course I can come—when is your next available appointment?" he asked.

▲ ▲ ▲

When Salvador told Carmen he'd received a phone call, she became upset. "If they have the DNA information, why do they need a visual identification? It'll be an awful moment," his wife said, her face tightening, trying to hold back the tears that were streaming down her cheeks.

"Carmen, calm down—it's protocol to make it official. Don't worry, I'll go. They simply need a person to see the remains. I won't be looking at a rotting corpse, he's been dead for too long. There'll only be bones. I must comply with the government's request."

Salvador had waited so long for this moment, but now that his father's remains had been located, he was perturbed about having to face the inevitable grief. He felt as if his intense longing for his missing father would no longer be valid and he'd be forced to face his frozen regrets. It hit him hard, the truth that his dad would never return.

The few memories he carried came flooding back. As his heart pounded, his thoughts went to his father's character and the values he'd held. He had loved him so much.

"Could his loss have been avoided?" he asked, without expecting a reply from his wife, who sat next to him, rubbing his back. It was so painful to think of him dead.

▲ ▲ ▲

Salvador and Carmen were told to put on a mask before they were escorted down a long, dark, forbidding corridor to the room where human remains were kept. The forensic expert standing by the door, dressed in a white gown, extended his hand to offer his condolences. "Please follow me," he said, leading them to a coffin resting on a stainless-steel table under strong fluorescent lights.

"Please gather around," the officer said.

Standing in front of the coffin, the box seemed small. Shouldn't the bones rest in a bigger space? Salvador was alarmed. A strong smell of disinfectant arose while they stood on the industrial tile floor of the high-ceilinged room.

"I'm very sorry but before I can turn the coffin over to you, I need you to see the remains."

Carmen, unnerved, stiffened and blurted out, "He has a name, his name is Manuel." Trembling, she reached over to grab Salvador's arm, squeezing it hard.

They watched silently as the expert opened the lid slowly. The human remains had decomposed to a skeletal state, and its elements were perfectly arranged. Salvador caught sight of something unusual; the right hand was mummified. "How did this occur?" he asked. Salvador had never come across anything like it before.

"There must have been some antimicrobial factor that protected his hand from decay," the officer replied, closing the coffin.

The officer handed Salvador the post-mortem report of the exhumed remains. "Laboratory work was carried out and here is the information we obtained."

Salvador skimmed the report with quivering hands. The remains had been found in a remote place not so far from the family home, a place Salvador had been to on one of his forensic explorations. The area was mapped, with a star indicating the exact location where the body had been disposed of. Salvador shifted his weight from one foot to the other, reading about the soil condition where the body had lain. The report stated that the bones had been discovered by a shepherd who notified the authorities, who in turn contacted the head forensic officer working on an exhumation of a mass grave fifteen kilometers away. Salvador looked at the date and the place where his father's body was recovered and turned to his wife. "Where was I on that day?" he asked quietly.

There was no definitive cause or manner of death. No bullets were found. A blow to his head? Had his father been caught in a crossfire? Had his death been swift? Had he been at peace? No obvious signs of any fatal illness, as his organs were long gone. Attached to the report were a few photographs providing further evidence of the place he was found, as well as the DNA sequencing information.

"We will now transport the coffin to a waiting room where you will be able to recover it once you've made burial arrangements," the officer said.

Salvador looked over at the coffin once more before walking out of the room. He swallowed hard and reached for Carmen's hand as they entered a room where a dozen white coffins lay on a long wooden table, each one labeled with the victim's name. Fresh flowers had been placed on top of each coffin, and a lit candelabra on a marble tabletop was under a large crucifix. This is where his father would rest until Otilia could come down and arrange for a proper solemn burial.

"He died with no family with him," Salvador said. The horror of it all was hard to absorb.

Where would the family bury him? Salvador didn't know; he would leave the decision to his mother. The one thing he was certain of was that his father would no longer be referred to as an "unknown." He'd been a "disappeared," which in the minds of some equaled a political transgressor, deserving to be a forgotten person. But it would no longer be so, as it was clear that his father had been a victim of the state. Now that the truth about the circumstances in which his missing father was killed were known, he deserved to be honored in the proper way. The next step for the family was to obtain a certificate of death, as finding the body was the only source of legitimation for the state. Remains attested to the identity of the deceased and the survivors as victims. After a formal funeral, reparation proceedings could begin in earnest.

# CHAPTER 17

## The East Bay, California, 2011

Otilia lay back in the velvety brown La-Z-Boy chair close to a window and stared at the blustery day. She'd been living in Michael Sweeney's apartment in Lake Merritt since she learned that Michael had passed away and willed the two-bedroom condo to her. They'd met at a mining camp in the Andes when she was running away. At the time, he was in Peru for six months on a short-term contract after retiring from a large, international mining company. It was Michael who helped her make up her mind to leave for the United States, offering her shelter at his sister's home in Oakland. It'd been hard for Otilia to accept the extent of his generosity, and she took her time before moving in from her rental bungalow. Owning a property without the burden of a mortgage was a tremendous economic benefit. She still had monthly homeowners bills to pay, but they were manageable.

Michael had been more than a friend, mentoring her to improve her life every step of the way, and if this was what he wanted for her, she would honor his wish.

When Salvador first met Michael, he was suspicious of him, wondering if Michael wanted something in return. "Why does he offer so much assistance?" he had asked. Salvador thought that Michael's real intentions were to entrap her, but she'd known Michael for a long time, and he'd never been the deceitful type. "I've never doubted his intentions," she said, assuring her son that he was a good man. "Michael is a real humanitarian."

While her rented bungalow had been sparse, the apartment blended her furniture with Michael's. Now she possessed an eclectic mix of old and new that Otilia felt gave it character. She'd kept his paintings and ornaments and the treasures he'd brought from his travels around the world as a way to remember him. It was Michael who encouraged her to read novels by great American writers, and they were all there on the bookshelf.

Jerry preferred to spend time together at his place, an airy, modern, and minimalist loft, as he found "the apartment," as he referred to it, too cluttered. It bothered him that she wasn't keen to dispose of some of Michael's things. But when she explained that the apartment was special to her, Jerry didn't object.

"It's charming and cozy and reminds me of the one person who stood by my side when life got difficult," she said. "Besides, I like the neighborhood, I'm walking distance to the shops and the lake."

▲ ▲ ▲

It was beginning to get dark, and she remained in the chair for a while, thinking about the wonderful news she'd had a few weeks ago. Carmen was pregnant! She just had one hope for the child: to live in peaceful times. Otilia worried that Salvador's own childhood experiences might affect him as a dad. It weighed on her that the critical bonds of family had ruptured for Salvador when he was seven years old. He'd been isolated, living without parents until his uncle took him, but Tomás hadn't shown him love. Denied a normal upbringing might hinder his fatherhood. Fathers occupied a critical role in a child's life. Would Salvador be able to provide the new baby with a sense of security in the world? Would the baby face an overprotective parent who'd create anxiety? Otilia fretted.

Too bad she wasn't comfortable discussing these issues with Salvador, but she was mindful not to infringe upon his personal boundaries. As she met him when he was an adult, she was hesitant to ask personal questions. So, she mostly listened to him and acknowledged what he said. Both of them felt the hurt of abandonment, yet they barely touched on the pain they'd both experienced during their separation. They hadn't had much opportunity to spend long periods alone together, and now, perhaps, that he had a child on the way, she could expect a stronger relationship between them. She looked forward to playing an important role in the baby's life. And as for Salvador, she wouldn't worry about him for now, as she knew that Carmen was there if and when he needed help. Carmen stood on solid ground and would ensure the baby would have a stable start.

Otilia stood to look out the window to check if the rain had stopped and saw the graffiti on the garage wall opposite hers. She'd have to give the city a call to have the slurs removed. Graffiti brought on tragically charged memories. She understood how it had become a popular means of expression, but she objected to messages intended to agitate. Orange and red paint especially offended her, as they represented the colors of the authoritarian movement known as "fujimorismo." Those were the followers of Alberto Fujimori, the president and the one responsible for human rights crimes led by his military death squad.

She pulled the heavy woven-cotton curtains closed and went to turn on her iPad.

At eight o'clock, she heard a ring and Salvador's and Carmen's faces appeared on the screen. Salvador wanted to show his mother his beautiful wife walking down the hall and asked, "Do you notice anything different?"

"I'm not sure," Otilia said.

"Look at her closely."

"Yes, I see her belly!" Otilia exclaimed, even though when Carmen placed her arms around her newly protruding tummy so Otilia could appreciate its firmness and shape, she couldn't tell much difference.

"I'm so happy," Otilia said, feeling elated.

▲ ▲ ▲

Later that night Jerry called to ask if she would like to go to a concert to share in his love of classical music.

"Ode to Joy,' in Beethoven's Ninth Symphony. It's not only a beautiful piece but a powerful one, a masterpiece about peace and unity. It's now the official anthem of the European Community. There'll be a full orchestra, a chorus and vocal soloists—you'll enjoy it," Jerry said.

After they picked up the tickets from the box office, they entered the concert hall where the musicians were already on stage making dissonant sounds with their instruments. "They're warming up," Jerry said.

They found their seats and she had time to read the program notes to learn about the conductor and the vocalists. The first violinist made an entrance, and all became quiet. "When the concertmaster comes on stage, his job is to tune the orchestra," Jerry explained quietly.

Two featured sopranos in glitzy, long evening gowns followed by the two baritones in tight-fitting tuxedos walked to their chairs in the front of the stage and stood tall as the high-spirited conductor entered the hall. Otilia was surprised when members of a large choir rose at the back of the stage. The lights were dimmed and, shortly after, the music whirled her into a current of emotions. Dramatic and forceful cadences engrossed her.

"What do you think?" Jerry was anxious to know when there was a pause.

"I feel like I'm in a cathedral."

"The soaring voices are beautiful," he whispered.

At the end of the concert, Otilia and Jerry joined the audience in giving the performers several ovations with abundant applause.

When they walked out of the theater, Jerry asked if Otilia wanted a nightcap. Taking her hand, he guided her inside a small restaurant he sometimes frequented after a performance. They each ordered a glass of prosecco and a piece of cheesecake to share.

"I was reading about 'Ode to Joy' and found out that during Pinochet's regime in Chile, women would sing 'Himno a la Alegría' outside the prison gates to give hope to their incarcerated loved ones," Jerry said.

"It is beautiful. We should look for the recording, I'd like to hear it again."

"We will—nothing better than music to direct our emotions to a place of hope, when one day all men will be brothers again."

"Talking about new days and a new life, I will become a grandmother. And peace is my one wish for the child."

"Isn't it wonderful? Congratulations! Though you're too young to be an *abuela*," he said, raising his glass.

"It's about time, they've been married for a while." Otilia raised her glass to click his. "I don't like that word, '*abuela*.' I'll be known as nana."

"You'll be a great nana," he said.

"I'll try to make up for my lost years as a mother," she said.

Jerry reached for her hand and planted a kiss.

# CHAPTER 18

## The East Bay, California, 2011

That night Otilia and Jerry remained awake in bed talking about old times. It surprised Otilia how easily she could engage with Jerry in conversations, and she began to talk about Manuel's death. She shook her head wearily and said, "The thought of Manuel's bones buried under some rocks in a desolate part of the country really upsets me."

Her thoughts pulled her back to when she and Manuel first parted. She'd tried to piece together what might have happened the day Manuel took Salvador into hiding while she waited alone in their home. She made up possible scenarios but hadn't expected Manuel's body to be found one hundred miles away from their place. After telling Jerry the details of her days full of worry, she noticed the sound of her voice going from a faint quiver to a strong pitch. "There was a rumor that he was last seen in a car that veered off the road and burst into flames. But investigators found no signs of charred body parts."

Jerry flinched. "Now you know it was hearsay." He propped himself up on one elbow. "You have to take comfort knowing he's been found.

This should give you some degree of ease." He reached out to caress her face.

The next morning when Otilia rose from bed to open the blackout curtains, she felt a pounding headache. She took a few steps back and let herself sink back down onto the bed.

"Let me get you some coffee," Jerry said.

"I really need caffeine," Otilia agreed, pressing her fingers on both sides of her head.

"Are you okay?" Jerry said, alarmed by her looks when he entered the bedroom, holding two mugs.

"I have a terrible headache," she said, turning over on her stomach, looking away from him.

"You carry too much tension," Jerry said, crouching down by the bed. He began to massage Otilia's back, applying a light pressure from her waist to her head. Extending his fingers, he massaged her scalp. Making circular motions, he moved across her shoulders and down her arms.

"How I wish everything would go back to ordinary times," she said, her eyes still closed.

"Can you please turn over?" he said, then cupped Otilia's cheeks in his palms and gave a gentle squeeze. "What is ordinary?" He worked his fingers down to the top of her chest.

"Nothing has been ordinary for a couple of decades," she said, abruptly sitting up.

"I want you to see my acupuncturist. He'll be able to help you balance your body," Jerry said.

She lay back again.

Slowly, as he rubbed her legs and her toes, she felt her anxiety lessen. She got up with his help and placed her head on his shoulder. Holding him tightly, she told herself there was little to gain from reliving past pain.

It was Saturday morning, and they had no obligations. They could spend the whole day at home. So, after a warm bath, Otilia lounged around in her sweats. Jerry emerged from the shower, dressed, then went to prepare breakfast.

When they sat down at the dining room table he said, "You remind me of my mother."

"How so?" she asked as she buttered a piece of toast.

"The dark circles under your eyes. I'm sorry you are troubled."

Otilia was silent and spread a teaspoonful of jam on the toast.

He reached out to stroke her face

"She was kind and attentive. She was sweet, but in her last days of life she suffered. I remember her with a great deal of love. I wanted to do everything to keep her comfortable."

"Tell me about her. June was her name?" she asked.

"Yes. She was a woman caught in the tyranny of the time. First as a child refugee who had to care for her traumatized parents, then trapped by her husband whom she was expected to please. She kept a nice home. She was the ultimate caregiver, relinquishing her own needs for others, but the end came too soon, and she then needed a great deal of help."

"It must have been tough." Otilia filled her coffee mug.

"She was the worrying type who needed to control her environment and minimize the unknowns. I wondered who she really was. A few times she would play the martyr card to get some attention, but most of the time it seemed to me she was in control."

"I'm not sure I understand."

"She would make statements about the sacrifices she'd made or tell us we were awful children and give us the silent treatment."

"Were you a terrible child?"

"At times," Jerry said and smiled.

"When did you lose her?" Otilia asked, picking up a grape.

"She died in 1978, at fifty-five."

"Were you living at home then?"

"No, I had left for college. Her death hit me hard. I was confused. I felt a lot of unwarranted guilt. It was then that I turned to drugs, for a short while, until I realized I had to let go, for I wasn't to blame for her unhappiness. And I didn't have any control over my screwed-up family and what they went through during the war." Jerry looked at Otilia and she reached for his hand to assure him he was fine.

"It's hard to accept," she said sympathetically. "Did her wounds ever heal?" Otilia asked.

"I don't think so." Jerry said. "Looking back, I believe she felt continuously threatened. And I'm sure she passed on some of those anxieties to me. In her childhood there was not enough stability in her everyday life to make her feel secure. Then she met my father who was not one to look into the emotional side of things. She endured humiliations, chaos, shame, threats, persecution, and loss. Her biggest hurt was that she lost all of her extended family in the Holocaust."

"I understand. I too have felt the strain of being concerned for those we love. It's bad when they're in danger and we have no news of them. We always carry our family in our heart."

"Events that lead us to emotional instability create a negative impact. They leave us with a high price to pay," Jerry said.

When Otilia asked Jerry about his relationship with his father, he had lots to confide.

"There were conflicting interactions at times. He was an older father and twice a foreigner, which made it challenging for me."

"What do you mean?"

"I mean he went from Europe to Bolivia, and after a few years he left South America for the USA. He had to adapt to a few cultural differences, customs, and attitudes. To begin with, in Bolivia he faced different norms from the European ways he was accustomed to. My dad used the term 'strangeness.' Strangeness about living in the highlands among Indigenous people where he saw a lot of injustices. This troubled him. It was madness for him to go from a cultured city like Prague to a place of extreme poverty. He said he faced intense depravations, culturally and biologically—even *soroche*, a lack of oxygen."

She laughed.

"Once he said that he'd rather have become a partisan fighting in the woods against the Nazis or have joined the American army and gone to war than live in Bolivia. He understood he was a lucky man to have gotten away from Europe, but also robbed of his opportunity to excel. Once he immigrated, he was never his own boss again, and he disliked being an underling. Although the family was comfortable, it bothered him that he never made the income he had in mind. This affected his self-worth and he perceived himself as weak."

"But he formed a family of his own and provided well."

"Sure, but he tended to dwell on the negative."

"Did you stay close?"

"By the time I went to college, I felt my dad was out of step with the new generation. He lacked patience. To me he always seemed troubled and impatient. My mother claimed it was his nerves. I remember I just needed to look at the muscles on his face, how they would compress, and suddenly all I could see was his severe irritation. That was enough to make me run away."

"What bothered him?"

"Noise, our playfulness, if he did not like what we said or we did. At times he would apologize for his gruffness and blame his behavior on the ups and downs of the financial markets, but when I grew up I thought that was a lame excuse. He was consumed by finance; he would listen to the stock market report every morning and night. Would his money last him a lifetime? Would there be a financial collapse? How could he stay ahead of the market? Those were important issues for him. He took no advice from anyone—he was a very stubborn kind of guy. But enough of that!"

"Did you forgive them?" Otilia asked as she began to remove the dishes from the table.

"A long time ago, but I didn't forget I still have scars. A certain loneliness, dissatisfaction."

"That's natural," Otilia said.

"Did you know that scientists are studying the possibility that emotional trauma can trigger biological changes in our cells that can be passed down from one generation to the next?" Jerry asked.

"That's scary," Otilia said, removing the dishes from the table to take to the sink.

▲ ▲ ▲

Awash with a certain contentment beneath her pain, Otilia was slowly opening herself up to Jerry. There was no posturing in their relationship; they were able to speak their minds without inhibition. Jerry had not asked Otilia much about her past life, waiting years until she was ready to tell him about her loss and time in exile. He admired her attitude in overcoming the hardships she'd faced and rebuild her life. Otilia liked to hear how much he appreciated her, her strengths and her vulnerabilities, which allowed them to connect at a deep emotional level. When they clung together physically, she took pleasure in his endearments and warmth.

"You bring me peace," he would say. She liked hearing those words, as she'd been so distant from intimacy for such a long time.

She'd grappled with thoughts of whether she was able to form a new bond with a man while reluctantly giving of herself for fear of losing her loyalty towards her husband. But having proof that she was an actual widow made things different—a little easier, as the hole left by Manuel's absence was slowly closing. She would give herself wholly to Jerry, spend more time together and make the most of their differences. It was a marvelous feeling to desire someone. She felt joy thinking about the good times that lay ahead. She was content.

▲ ▲ ▲

Otilia noticed that they started to laugh a lot more, talking about each other's quirks, attributing them mostly to their age, and joking about their wrinkled bodies, their laugh lines, their hair turning gray. She welcomed their quiet times, when she could engross herself in her knitting and her reading, while he occupied himself in his art. She felt grateful for their relationship and committed to him.

# CHAPTER 19

## Lima, Peru, 2011

In the early hours of the morning, Otilia stepped off the flight from San Francisco to Lima and headed towards passport control where, for a change, she had no interaction with the immigration officer. Instead, he took a quick look at her passport and beckoned her to go through. After passing through customs, she continued down the hall, claimed her bags, and found a porter eager to help. At the exit, a security guard stopped her to scrutinize the luggage tags. Otilia spotted Carmen and Salvador standing to one side of a crowd and asked the porter to follow her. As soon as she met them, Otilia hugged Salvador, lingering for a moment in his arms.

"Mother, what do you have in your bags?" Salvador asked as he lifted her heavy suitcases from the cart.

"Gifts for my grandchild," she said with a smile. "I couldn't resist."

Otilia embraced Carmen and kissed her on the cheek. "You shine," she said, noticing the pregnancy glow on Carmen's face.

On the ride to their home, they drove along the seaside road where new high-rises were being built facing the beach. After a sharp turn Otilia noticed the many new businesses: Scotia Bank, Radio Shack, Golden Gym, and Atlantic City Casino. She couldn't believe how things had changed and the streets were so clean. Hanging baskets on lampposts and decorative planters brightened the pedestrian walkways.

Otilia was thrilled by the spacious townhouse her children had purchased a few months ago. With the new baby on its way, they wanted more indoor space and a yard. Carmen had decorated it with exquisite taste. Otilia had been able to contribute towards the down payment and, in return, they had offered her a room of her own.

▲ ▲ ▲

A heavy mood hung over the home the morning after Otilia arrived. It was the day of the funeral. She'd had trouble sleeping the previous night as a knot of dread filled her gut. Manuel's loss had been a devastating blow, and he carried with him distressing secrets that they would never be privy to.

Carmen and Salvador called Otilia to join them for breakfast once they'd put out a few items of food on the counter. The three of them sat down silently and they barely ate. Otilia's lower lip started to quiver before she could finally speak, though she felt inarticulate. "I shouldn't have let him go."

"Mother, not now," Salvador said.

"Please have something to eat. We have a long morning ahead and have a lot of healing to do," Carmen said, giving Salvador a sideways glance.

"You did what you could," Salvador said, nodding his head as he acknowledged his wife's fleeting look of disapproval over the harshness of his comment.

"There's no point feeling bitterness. Do not replay the scenes in your mind. Breathe and accept it. That's all a person can do," Carmen said.

"We have nothing to take with us to the burial. No objects of his, no photographs, no memorabilia. Nothing to remember him by," Otilia said, feeling her loneliness as anger rose inside of her.

Before departing for the cemetery, Otilia, Carmen, and Salvador formed a circle to pray, embracing each other. They wanted to have a few private words to share and give voice to some of the memories they retained.

"Manuel, you were my best friend. I imagined spending all my life with you. I'm so sorry I couldn't be next to you the day you departed. I'm sad you had to spend so much time alone. I pray that our ancestors were there to guide you and remain at your side on your journey," Otilia said, while tears slid down her face.

Salvador called out his grandparents' names and asked them to take good care of his dad. "I remember you, Daddy, and when you said goodbye, you left me believing I was the superhero in our game, ready to overcome the enemy when they showed up. This gave me great confidence," Salvador said.

"Did I ever tell you the story of your grandma Carina the day she was caught with a bundle of wood tied to her back as she collected fuel for her stove? She was found trespassing on her landlord's estate," Otilia said.

When Salvador shook his head, she went on. "She was taken in by the guard for questioning. She explained that she had five children at home and her youngest Manuel hadn't eaten for a day. It was theft, the guard claimed, and she would have to be penalized for it. The guard took her in to see the chief who decided she would be let go but would have to return in a week's time to serve two days in jail. How would her children survive if she was in the *calabozo*? she asked. She returned the following week after making arrangements with a neighbor to look after the kids. But instead of sitting in a small cell, one of the guards took her to his house where she had to scrub walls and the floors. He fed her well and let her go that first night."

"Let's say a prayer for grandmother Carina, who was strong," Carmen said, bowing her head. "I'm sure she is at Manuel's side."

"Farewell, *papito*," Salvador said as he quietly wept. "We love you very much. I hope *abuela* keeps on taking care of you."

Carmen swallowed and found it hard to speak. "I wish I could have met you," she mumbled. She took a look at her watch and carefully moved away from their embrace. "I think it is time to go, the car will be here to take us to the cemetery any time," Carmen said softly when she went to stand by the entrance.

▲ ▲ ▲

They'd had a discussion about where they would bury Manuel, whether at the cemetery in El Milagro or right here in Lima, and they concluded that it was pointless to go back to their village when it was no longer the community they had known. They decided that Manuel should rest close to family in Lima, where he could be visited frequently.

Salvador found a priest who would conduct a graveside service since Otilia had expressed her wish for a simple ceremony. The burial was scheduled for eleven o'clock and arrangements to have a car and a driver pick them up an hour before had been made. Carmen ordered a funeral wreath to adorn the coffin, and she hoped it would be delivered on time. There wouldn't be any mourners to pay their condolences other than a few of Salvador's colleagues.

The driver dropped the family off at the entrance to the cemetery, and Otilia eased her body out of the car. Carmen and Salvador came to Otilia's side to link arms and walk down the path to where the priest was waiting for them. Otilia stopped midway and took a deep breath as she looked up at the sky. It was a peaceful place, the tombs surrounded with pines.

The elderly priest stood next to a pile of gravelly, sandy dirt and offered his condolences. He bestowed a benediction on each of them. Salvador's two friends arrived on a motorcycle, and the priest said he would wait before starting the service so they could join in. The men walked briskly down to the gravesite to greet the family, then set down their helmets on a grassy spot.

"We are gathered here at the gravesite of this innocent man killed by terrorism to restore his dignity. Justice is rendered to the victim and the family. We bestow this man, a much-loved husband and father, to his final resting place," the priest said, then recited a prayer.

Continuing with a flattened voice as he read from Scriptures, he lowered his head and explained, "Our Christian hope in eternal life will ensure Manuel's return to God. Brothers and sisters, let the sadness of death give way to the bright promise of immortality. Dearly beloved, do not live in the past; you must know that this good man's soul rests next to the Lord and He will watch over him for eternity."

The priest sprinkled the coffin with holy water and blessed Manuel's final resting place. "I commend these remains to you, Lord," he said. He motioned to Salvador and his pallbearers to come forth. Otilia stepped up and opened the coffin to slip in an envelope with a note she'd prepared for Manuel. With the help of a gravedigger, Salvador and his two friends lowered the coffin to the ground. The priest threw a handful of earth onto the casket and asked all present to follow suit.

Otilia sobbed bitterly. Carmen placed one arm around her shoulders and held her tightly. Before the ceremony was over, the priest invited the family to celebrate a mass for Manuel on the one-month anniversary date at his parish church.

Otilia knew that by then she'd be gone from Peru, and she didn't need mass or a church to remember Manuel. She recalled listening to a widow who went to church daily to pray for her beloved husband after he passed away, and a middle-aged man who stopped by his son's grave every day on the way to work, yet she preferred to grieve privately.

Otilia tried to compose herself, staying behind at the grave site momentarily and bowing her head. She'd been fortunate to have married a caring man who was serious and determined to get ahead—someone who intended to make the world a better place. A decisive, hard-working person who took his responsibilities seriously, he stood up for his friends and people in need. She prayed for his soul and bade him farewell.

Otilia felt the tension in her shoulders release when Salvador put his arms around her and kissed her cheek. "My beautiful mother, come along."

▲ ▲ ▲

Before she returned to California, Otilia and Salvador made an appointment to see Sr. Malfi again. He'd called Salvador to tell him he was frustrated with the bureaucracy. "At the municipality they're dragging their feet, sitting on their asses, and giving me crap, having me chase from one person to the next, with no one willing to take responsibility for our case. Years have passed and now they're telling me there might be a statute of limitation. We must act fast. I'm glad I can see you before your mother leaves."

Sr. Malfi closed the door of his office and said, "They've wasted our time. The department head sent a report denying any knowledge of employees aiding and abetting influence peddling, illicit enrichment, or bribery. I thought they might name a scapegoat, a token junior man responsible for conspiracy to defraud, but they are outright denying our claim. It is futile for us to go through the proper channels. I talked to a colleague who lives there and told me the department is in an organizational nightmare."

"First, they tell us the documents were destroyed in a fire, now that all of the employees were above board. I placed my faith in the legal system," Salvador said.

"Again, I heard the excuse that since Tomás is family, it was logical that nobody would have questioned a transaction like yours. They think they can get away with this excuse." Sr. Malfi smirked. "I've been thinking that since Congress will be passing a bill to amend the constitution with respect to the anticorruption bill and has specified different corruption offenses establishing sanctions for each one of them, we should give it one more try in a few months. In the meantime, I will look into the possibility of enlisting the help of the current owners of the property to see if they would be willing to press charges against Tomás."

"Why would you do that?" Salvador asked, surprised.

"We need to have their cooperation to prove their purchase stemmed from a legal sale based on proper documentation. If they agree to help, we can support them and claim they received fraudulent services and therefore are entitled to compensation."

Sr. Malfi scratched his cheek. "Let me see what action we should take next; I'll consult with others, do my best."

He looked at his watch and continued, "Now, Otilia, on the matter of reparations: Since you are living out of the country and you've had the ability to support yourself, I'm afraid you will not be able to obtain a government supplement."

"Since we have found my father's body, won't my mother be able to collect a pension?" Salvador asked.

"Unfortunately, these funds have been earmarked for spouses who lost their partners and had young children at home."

"I was a kid, for heaven's sake," Salvador said.

"But your mom didn't take care of you. At this time there are two types of benefits, one is symbolic and the other meant for people with little means. Collective reparations have been made a priority, as I mentioned to you before."

Otilia sighed. Although her heritage and sense of place was stripped away, what could she do now? Perhaps it wasn't worth the money and time to continue fighting for her rights.

# CHAPTER 20

## Prague, Czech Republic, 2011

From the air, Prague appeared stunning, precisely as Jerry had imagined it to be. A staff member of the recently opened International Somerset School of Architecture was at the airport to pick him up. Jerry felt relieved to see the stranger holding a sign with his name, as he wasn't sure he would be able to communicate. He'd been leery about grappling with the difficult language his father had never pushed on him. Luckily, the man, in a neat shirt and pants, spoke English.

Jerry had accepted the offer to teach a two-week studio workshop to international students, partially to learn more about his own family history. He was sorry that his trip had been scheduled at a time when Otilia would be flying down to Peru for Manuel's funeral, but after talking matters over, they both decided it would be best for Jerry to go ahead with his trip after months of planning and negotiations.

Jerry was delivered to a bed-and-breakfast a few blocks from the architecture school, where the main floor housed a contemporary art gallery. At the entrance to the building, a slim suited man welcomed him and showed him to a studio apartment on an upper floor.

Jerry had done quite a bit of research in preparation for his trip. He'd studied the map of the city and the transportation hubs. Since there was still some daylight left, he deposited his bag and went for a stroll to take in the grand architectural styles of the historical buildings. As he walked, he took note of the many renovations he would explore in the weeks to come. Premises that had been left intact during the war, and had become run down during the Soviet era, were being redone. He was in awe of the magnificent city in front of him and, determined to fight jet lag, he continued to walk towards the Prague Castle, located on the opposite side of the Vltava River.

At the Charles Bridge, which connected the castle with the Old Town, he stopped to contemplate the Old Town Tower's sandstone gateway. It had been built in the fourteenth century. He would come back another day to climb its 138 steps to the viewing gallery. His eyes drifted to the two rows of baroque-style statues of saints that decorated the entire span of the bridge.

▲ ▲ ▲

His first night in Prague was restless, and he rose early the next morning to have breakfast but found the breakfast room closed. He went down the stairwell onto the street and walked several blocks before he was able to find an open café. After reading his emails and the news on his cell phone, while waiting for his food to be served, he studied the few customers sitting across from him. He chuckled, amused by their perfect table manners, just like his parents' own, he thought. A waitress brought him a coffee as well as a plate with two pieces of rye bread, rolled up cheese and a few thin slices of folded ham. When he was done, he placed his knife and fork parallel on the right side of the plate as he'd been taught back in his childhood.

After breakfast Jerry walked once again to the head of the bridge where, on the pedestrian deck, travelers of all sizes and shapes, and street musicians, were starting to gather for the day. He stopped to listen to a group playing new wave music while tourists were swinging wildly. Strolling along, passing by artists displaying their works and by portable pop-up shops with lots of tourists haggling for inexpensive mementos, Jerry went to stand by the guardrail to look at the city view. He soon realized that he was thinking about his father's multifarious existences. He drew a quick breath; he was at the very spot where his dad's life had commenced. In his youth Jerry hadn't been interested in his father's life. What a shame that he hadn't been even mildly curious about the place where Miles was born. Now he realized how much he'd missed by shying away from his father's anecdotes.

Before he accepted this job for the two-week period, Jerry had read up on his family genealogy and Czech history. He wanted to get a sense of how life would have been for a middle-class merchant family in the first half of the twentieth century. He continued exploring the area and climbed up the hill to see the Prague Castle, where he stopped to listen to a wind ensemble playing Mozart.

He returned to the old city by tram and got off at the Grand Café, located right across from the astronomical clock, where a large crowd waited for its hourly show when twelve statues of saints were set in motion at the doorways above the clock. He recalled sitting in his childhood home between his father and uncle when they explained that the astronomical dial, showing the time of day, twelve signs of the zodiac and position of the sun and moon, had been installed in the fifteenth century and was still operating.

At the café, sitting beneath the cut-glass chandeliers suspended from the high ceiling, people sipped coffee while reading newspapers attached to a holding stick. Jerry went up to the counter and couldn't resist ordering a *kolache*, a dense yeast dough bun with a pocket of plum jam, along with an espresso. He found an empty table and remembered how his father fondly recalled Saturdays—when his mother would bake all day for the week ahead. Jerry savored the sweet, bold flavors he remembered from his childhood.

Once outside, he looked at his GPS to guide him to the house where his father had lived, located a few blocks away. On the narrow cobblestone lane on Michalska Street, he found number nine, a freshly painted four-story house. The intercom system by the front door listed a number of apartments and he randomly chose one button to press. When he'd searched for this address on the internet, an ad for an expensive three-bedroom apartment with modern amenities had come up. He thought it too expensive for a single person, but since he was there, he had an urge to see the place. A voice came on, speaking Czech. Jerry explained in English that he wanted to see the apartment for a future date, but a woman's gruff voice responded, in broken English, that it was not possible to show as it was presently occupied.

This house could have been mine, Jerry thought as he traced his way back to his bed-and-breakfast. Back in the 1990s, the government of Czechoslovakia came up with a plan for residents to reclaim properties that had been confiscated by previous regimes. His father had told him that compensation was meant for citizens who presently lived in the country and they wouldn't qualify. Such was life.

▲ ▲ ▲

After teaching his seminar and going out to bars and restaurants with his colleagues, Jerry took a few days to explore the hidden gems of the city and visit his dad's only cousin who was still alive. Before his death, Jerry's uncle, Paul, had worked on the family genealogy and made a list of survivors' names and addresses. Jerry had written to some of them, but only Anna responded. She was the last person left in his dad's generation.

Jerry called Anna and got her son, Franz, on the phone. Franz explained that Anna was hard of hearing, and he didn't speak much English, but they would be glad to meet. He would talk to his mother and decide on a place and get back to him. It would have to be a quiet spot, off from the tourist scene, where it would be easier for his mother to have a conversation.

Anna was short, chubby, bent over. Well over ninety, Jerry assumed. She had snow-white curly hair and wore a tight, ill-fitting light coat. She arrived late and alone. "Franz won't be joining us," she apologized.

When they sat down at the café, Jerry noticed her rheumy, blood-shot eyes. Her voice was strong and she seemed to be in control. When Jerry inquired what she would like to drink, she responded *"slivovice"* in no uncertain terms.

Her plum liquor and Jerry's double espresso, along with two pieces of chocolate cake, were delivered by a beautiful young waitress.

"You must excuse me but my hearing is not so good," Anna said in a rather loud tone. "But that is all that is wrong. Our family has good genes. Most of our ancestors lived long and have been sharp to the end, as long as those dreadful Nazis let them live."

"How did you manage during the war?" Jerry took the opportunity to ask.

"I was in England, saw your uncle Paul quite often—that was between 1939 and 1946—before I returned to Prague. We had good times, Paul and I." She paused to take a sip of her *slivovice*. "I was not treated well by the Brits, but of course it was better than having stayed in Czechoslovakia. You are aware that when the Nazis came into Bohemia-Moravia, we weren't allowed to transfer or sell our proper-ties after 1941, and then the Jews were deported to Terezin."

"Yes, I'm aware. But tell me how come you were unhappy in England and came back?" Jerry asked.

"I had to take odd jobs, mostly cleaning homes. You see, I had no language at first and felt people took advantage of me. Towards the end of the war I got a better paying job at the Lockheed hydraulic brake company. Have you heard of them?"

Jerry shook his head.

"I was assigned to build undercarriages for single-seat Spitfires."

"Oh yes, the fighter aircraft that became the symbol of freedom."

"That's where I met my future husband," she said, with a smile.

"And you had only one son?"

"Yes, 'the son of a traitor,' that's what they called him. Poor Franz had to go through life with that name. He still is not normal, became traumatized—never got over many bad experiences."

"What do you mean?"

She gave a little nervous laugh. "Franz was tormented by other children throughout his school life, couldn't get into university, had a series of uninteresting jobs, many which he lost, all as a result of his father being in the communist prison. Joe was a good man, worked hard for the right cause—communism. He was betrayed by the members of the party, and Franz suffered the consequences. He was belittled. Franz is not very social, doesn't trust people, things in life didn't turn out so well for him."

Anna wanted to know about Jerry's father, her handsome cousin Milan that she remembered from back when she was a child.

"It was a pity we never met again, he didn't stay in London long," she said.

She told him how happy she was that after the Velvet Revolution in 1989, they'd made contact with the family who lived in the West. "So many years of Soviet influence isolated us. Your father was very good to us, sending us money, helped us survive during harsh times."

Jerry wasn't aware that his father had helped his Czech relatives. Miles hadn't told them much.

Anna was pleased that Franz would get to meet a cousin, she said, meaning Jerry.

"Why don't you come to dinner before you return."

▲ ▲ ▲

Jerry walked up to the second floor of a run-down building, a twenty-minute tram ride away from his bed-and-breakfast, carrying a flower bouquet and a bottle of wine. His eyes had to adjust to the darkness when Anna opened the door to welcome him, enthusiastically offering a warm hug. Jerry walked across the room extending his hand, but it took Franz longer than Jerry expected to respond. Franz closed the heavy curtains, then flicked on the lights before going to sit on the couch.

An old square box radio stood on a large rococo console, and a couple of frayed Persian rugs were spread on the wooden floor, one by a sofa and the other under the dining room table. An oil painting of farmers working the fields hung on one of the walls close to a table set with decorative Czech Bohemian glassware and embossed plates.

After a simple supper of meat stew, potatoes, and cabbage salad, Anna went to gather the family photo albums. She opened one of them. "This is my husband, Joseph Bena, when he was young," she said with a smile.

"Joe joined the Young Communist League and, as he showed great promise of becoming a young politician, they sent him to Moscow to train at the Soviet academy for international students. He told the story of how one evening he and two other Czech students went to the movies and before the show began, they watched a reel about events taking place in Spain. The Spanish Civil War was underway. Joe started to think about how the Republicans were at a disadvantage, with no proper army and few weapons.

"How could they possibly fight against the well-supplied opposition led by General Franco?" he asked. And a few months later he decided to leave the Soviet Union for Spain to join the International Brigade.

"This is his last picture in Moscow," Anna said after she turned the page.

"Who made up the International Brigade?" Jerry asked.

"Men from many countries, but even though they were considered a multinational group, the units were arranged according to their nationality with their own leaders. Stalin, of course, backed the Republicans in their fight against fascism, and his intention was to see a communist government take hold in Spain."

"I'm so sorry I interrupted you," Jerry said, as he noticed Anna was anxious to turn the page and show him the next photographs.

"From Moscow Joe travelled by train to the port of Sevastopol, in the Crimea, where he had a passport waiting for him. He was now Martin Novoa, a Spanish citizen. Here he is showing off his new identification," Anna said, pointing to a black-and-white photo dated 1936.

"His new profession was that of a stocker on a commercial Spanish liner. To me this was funny, since Joe couldn't tolerate sailing, as he became extremely seasick. Onboard the ship he spent days bending over the railing retching. Here he is on the ship along the Bosporus on their way to Istanbul. This was the heart of Italo-German espionage activities, and the captain became worried when a small Turkish vessel approached his ship. A few men climbed onboard, claiming they were there to pilot them through the dangerous zone. But the captain thought they were spies, and invited the men for a few drinks, and by the time they returned to their 'pilot boat' they were dead drunk. When they sailed away from Turkish waters, the captain suspected a submarine nearby, and ordered the sailors to disguise the name of the ship by giving it a quick coat of paint and printing a new name. The vessel became the *Merry London* and happily sailed towards the Suez Canal under a British flag. From there, without further problems, they reached the Spanish harbor of Valencia safely."

"What happened to Joe when he arrived in Spain?" Jerry asked.

"He was taken to meet other international recruits and given further training with the Dimitrov Battalion in Madrid. But on their way to the Spanish capital, they were stopped by the captain of a different Russian battalion who needed men. They were losing a great number of soldiers, and he needed to replenish his force. Joe fought many battles, and the battalion experienced heavy losses, but he was lucky to have survived. In October 1938, however, his brigade was demobilized.

Joe left Spain on foot over the Pyrenees to France, only to be interned in a camp until the fall of France. In the summer of 1943, he was able to join the Czechoslovakian Army in exile, in Britain."

"My mother is so happy when she can share the story of our family hero," Franz said. He hadn't said much all evening until then. "I remember my dad talked about how he met the right woman in Britain to be his wife. Independent and most important, capable of making a decision during an emergency."

Jerry was intrigued by Franz's comments. Joe must have had a warrior mindset, with a high resistance to stress. Perhaps he knew he'd be facing insurmountable odds in his life and would have to leave a wife to defend herself on her own.

"I liked him from the start," Anna went on. "His life was attractive, full of adventure, and he was fighting for a good cause. I disliked middle-class habits and boredom. I was a feminist, wanted equal rights for women and more freedom for myself. But I was naïve, didn't think about the consequences or what was in store for me."

"The glorious revolution," Franz said.

Anna turned to the photos of her wedding.

"We returned together to Prague after the war. I was so excited to go back, I dreamed about it for years. But once we were here, I became very sad. Every corner we passed on the street brought memories of relatives and old friends who hadn't returned. There was a lot of emptiness," Anna said.

"My mother came from a German background, and when my parents returned, she was not that fluent in Czech, and that was a real concern," Franz said.

"This proved troublesome for my husband. He was a good communist and followed the party line, and you can imagine how they despised Germany. Joe claimed I was too German. I was German in the eyes of the Czechs, and yet I was Jewish, born right here in Prague. One day we went to the Jewish cemetery to visit my mother's tomb, and being at the grave site was awkward for Joe. He left before anyone could claim they had seen him," Anna said.

"Tell me about life during communism," Jerry said as he watched the expression of disappointment on Anna's face.

"I spent so much time on my own. I lived in fear sometimes bordering on paranoia. I lived in what I called my golden cage, because we had a security guard for both safety and surveillance, night and day. Every word we uttered was promptly passed on to the relevant authorities."

"How did you know?" Jerry asked.

"I'll tell you a story. A childhood friend, a communist who was living in Israel, came to study in Prague. One day, without an invitation, he visited us in our flat. He asked who lived next door, and I told him it was a residence for the Soviet Embassy staff. It was a secret, we had restrictions since we shared a wall. A few days later, I was informed that due to my offence, the student would have to leave the country. How else would they have known about our conversation?" Anna said.

"We searched for listening devices but couldn't find them. But then came the arrests. At the time, in 1951, Joe was Deputy Minister of the Interior. They went after our friends who'd fought in Spain. Joe resigned from his job, but his resignation was not accepted. Soon after, our house was searched and eventually he was picked up by the secret police."

"It was a cruel punishment. He was given a twenty-five-year sentence for espionage. We weren't able to communicate. We had no news from him, and he didn't know how we were coping. Mother was unable to get any work, and I was constantly taunted," Franz said.

"He spent many months in solitary confinement, accused of treason and sabotaging the regime," Anna added.

"It was a sham. He was told he was an enemy of progress, responsible for the lives of good men who died in Spain. He was accused of everything possible, of being an agent of French espionage, of working for the Gestapo and for the British Intelligence Service. Enough crimes to last him a lifetime in jail. Everybody was afraid to be in contact with the family of a traitor, even though the charges had been invented," Franz said.

"When was he freed?" Jerry asked.

"On March 6, 1964."

Joe had been a member of parliament when he was arrested and imprisoned for thirteen years; now they wanted him to stand for parliamentary elections again as part of his rehabilitation. He'd heard that there was a new wave of politicians looking to make radical changes and they needed experienced people like Joe. Joe didn't accept.

"This picture is at Christmas time, the year he came home from prison. He got some compensation and went out shopping. This is the bike he got for Franz. He bought a typewriter, books, and clothes for me. We were so happy."

"What type of work did he get once he was out of jail?"

Anna stopped to take a breath. "He was sent to organize international sports events, although he'd never done anything of the sort. He always said that under socialism, everybody did work they were least trained for. That certainly fit his activities with the sports organization. Then, at the beginning of January 1968, a new first secretary of the communist party took the country by storm. It was a short period known as Prague Spring when reforms were proposed. Joe was named Home Secretary."

"That government didn't last. Why didn't you escape when you had a chance?" Jerry asked.

Anna explained how Joe was a revolutionary and a patriotic man. He had to play to the end, even if the end turned out to be tragic. And Jerry was beginning to understand how Joe valued Anna's ability to think on her own, as he was a man that followed both his party's discipline and his own conscience while speeding full throttle ahead.

"And what about you, Franz, why didn't you leave?" Jerry asked.

"At the time of the Prague Spring when my dad had this high position in government, I went into hiding. I didn't want anybody thinking I would take advantage of his position. Lots of the people who'd shunned me before were now greeting me and treating me kindly."

"But you could all have run away when the Soviets occupied the country before the gates were closed," Jerry said.

"Joe felt people trusted him and he wouldn't abandon them. He felt that if he stayed, he would be able to prevent greater bloodshed. At three o'clock one morning, Joe got a call saying that Soviet soldiers were rushing into the city with their tanks. That day there was no transportation and people walked to work. Farmers took trusses of straw to the airport to plaster the landing strip to prevent planes from landing. Joe was forced to hand in his resignation, and thankfully the Russians did not arrest him."

Anna offered Jerry a coffee and Franz stood up to go to the kitchen to make it.

"Last but not least, let me show you a picture of our *hata*," Anna said.

"A cottage?" Jerry inquired, after Anna found the photo.

"We were able to obtain a small garden with a shed where we could spend the night. It had good soil, and we could get there on the local train. We liked it in the countryside—collected mushrooms and berries, barbecued sausages. Here is a box with my flowers—daffodils, lilies, lupines—to remind me of England."

Anna closed the album and sighed. "Later I got tired of my interesting life. The situation got tough once again. Joe was attacked by all sides—he became both a revolutionary and a counterrevolutionary. One day he was accosted by thugs sent by the party. We moved out to our *hata* in the country where Joe could lead a quiet life."

Franz returned to the table with a pot of coffee and a plate full of packaged cookies.

"April 8, 1973, was a warm day. Joe did not feel well and went to bed. Shortly before midnight I called Franz to tell him his dad had passed away. There were no speeches at his funeral, only music: Spanish songs, a song written and sung by a concentration camp survivor, a Czech folk song. Freedom fighters from Spain were there, and members of the International Brigade stood guard of honor. It was 1973 and not all was rosy. It was still Soviet-style rule. People had heard that the funeral would be held somewhere else and failed to attend. Days later we found Joe's grave was trampled, all flowers cut in small pieces."

"I'm so sorry to hear how difficult things turned out to be. It is sobering to hear how you dealt with the serious blows that you faced," Jerry said. "Can I please take a picture of the two of you? I would like to share your saga with my half-brother. But that is a story for another day."

"We must see you again before you leave," Anna said. "We never talked about you. We want to know about your life, your mother, your sister and father."

"And your half-brother?" Franz asked.

"Dario is his name, my father's child from a Bolivian woman. I'll come back. Is Thursday good for you?" Jerry said before he left.

Walking to catch the tram back to his bed-and-breakfast, Jerry thought about how much the family had been subjected to, the horrendous allegations against Joe, and the people that had turned against Anna and Franz. So many sacrifices for a movement that hadn't supported them. How much pain the family had endured.

# CHAPTER 21

## Lima, Peru, 2011

¿*Dónde está?* Otilia, Carmen, and Salvador thought, back at home after the funeral as they retreated to their rooms, still wondering where Manuel could be. This had been the pressing question they'd asked for years, and now finally there was an answer and a place to honor him. Manuel's resting place would be where the family would take their child to talk about the grandfather he should have had. Manuel would have liked being a grandfather; a celebration of life he would have said, smiling proudly.

How Manuel fell to his death was still hard for the family to grasp. His body was proof of his death, but they would never be able to piece together the true events of his last breath.

▲ ▲ ▲

Otilia came into the living room and eased herself into the couch across from where Carmen and Salvador sat in mourning. It was heart wrenching to see Salvador weep. She too wanted to cry, but instead, she sat stoically. The three of them remained quiet, and when Otilia looked at Salvador and saw the sadness on his face, she recognized she'd failed him. "I'm so sorry," she said. She felt a sense of shame for not safeguarding him, but all she could do was to be present, to be there for him, for them, for their new baby.

"It will pass; you'll find calmness again," Carmen said, turning to her husband and patting his knee.

Salvador had few memories of his early years, and the few he had were painful to verbalize. "Why talk about something so horrible," he'd often say. Not remembering had helped them endure and protect their relationship. They had been left with no family photographs, no family treasures to trigger recollections, so the subject didn't come up very often. That door had been closed the day they both left their house. And since their reunion, mother and son made a point to focus on moving forward, rather than looking back. But now, after sitting with pain in their hearts since they got the call that Manuel's body had been located, grief was taking a toll on them.

Carmen sat with Salvador, holding his hand in silence again. Only one lamp was lit, and it was beginning to grow dark. This was their cross to bear, Otilia thought, hoping that Carmen, with her love and understanding, would find him help.

"You can't let this get to you. So far, you've managed so well. Look at how far you've come," Carmen said, kissing her husband's cheek.

Otilia saw the furrows deepening in his brow when Salvador got up, wiping the tears from his cheeks. "Please excuse me, I'm being selfish; it's been hard on all of us, but I have to go to the gym and flood my brain with endorphins to distract me."

Carmen went over to sit next to Otilia and said, "Exercise improves his mood." She placed her arm around Otilia's shoulder, saying, "I'll get him some counseling before it gets out of hand."

Otilia nodded. "He's been very despondent this week. Thank you for being such a good support."

▲ ▲ ▲

The next day, Salvador went to sit at his desk to stare at photographs of the excavations he'd been involved with. As a forensic officer, he would go on trips to remote sites looking for clandestine graves and exhumated bodies and look for indications of what had occurred. Now he was looking closely at the different graves he had been to, analyzing each of them carefully. He started by spreading the photos out then stacking them, hiding the last one with the next, to pay closer attention to each one individually. He felt a cold sweat as his heart pounded, thinking how this had been his father's twist of fate. For years Salvador had clung to the idea that his father might not have faced the same destiny as those of hundreds of other poor souls he'd exposed, as his father was far from the locations where mass graves had been exhumed. But now he was sure that his father had been caught in the crossfire when he tried to get away. Manuel had been found dead in a ditch, close to one of the many mass graves. Salvador felt sick.

When Salvador took a magnifying glass to take a closer look, he had a better understanding of how his dad had died. "*Hola*. What are you up to?" Carmen said when she came home. Salvador was startled.

She noticed the photos Salvador held in his hands and didn't say a word. She headed down the hall to hang up her coat before returning. "Are you alright?" she asked.

They stared at each other in silence once Salvador peeled his gaze from the photographs. "I keep wondering about him. I need to get a feel for what he went through. I can't believe he ended up like the rest of them," he stammered.

"Why put yourself through such agony? You need to let go; why don't you shave and get out of your pajamas?"

Salvador shook his head. Carmen came closer and threw her arms around his shoulders. "I'm sure your mind is tormenting you, but you're making it worse by taking other situations and linking them to your father's case. You can't read into those photos what your father went through. Each situation is unique."

Reluctantly, he put the photos to one side. "I'm sorry, I feel so helpless," he said. "I think we should have his case investigated for murder."

"What good will that do?" Carmen said, taking a deep breath.

"Men like him shouldn't be dehumanized, left like roadkill. I know by experience that people found in mass graves were considered unworthy. That's what we've been led to believe—it was a myth then but not much has changed. To change attitudes and transform that mentality we must bring on charges. We must make sure that we look at these killings through a different lens. It's about uncovering what is right and wrong, even if the country was in turmoil. Standards of behavior should have prevailed. I want my father recognized."

"I understand, but please consider that your father's case happened to so many. Why would they hunt for his killers when nothing suspicious was reported?"

"Every person deserves an inquiry; we need to do it for the living."

Although the government was pushing their version of history, that the country was now living in a democratic, inclusive society implementing a culture of peace open to ethnic and linguistic diversity, there still was the stigma that those that were caught in the conflict were responsible for their deeds. The ones found on the ground were considered "revolutionaries" regardless of whether they were running away to protect themselves or forced to join in the atrocities. With the rise of democracy there'd been an attempt to overcome stereotypes, but scapegoating was still prevalent.

"The official government death tally is low, and we still have too many unaccounted for. There's a lot of indifference to what went on," Salvador said.

▲ ▲ ▲

It was Otilia's last night in Lima, and at dinnertime Carmen said, "I'm sorry you won't be here for my ultrasound in two weeks. The doctor informed me today that everything is fine, the baby's heartbeat is strong, and all my signs are good."

"Will you send me a picture?"

"I will," Carmen replied.

"Do you want to know its sex?"

"I'm not sure," Carmen said. "How much did Salvador weigh?"

"He was not a big child, regular weight, around seven pounds."

"Where was he born?" Carmen asked.

"Our *matrona* delivered him. It was a home birth, everything went smoothly, it didn't take long. My mother came to help as well."

"When did he smile for the first time?"

"Six weeks. I remember the day when I went to his crib to pick him up and he gave me a sweet smile. I knew he knew who I was."

"And his first step?"

"On his first birthday."

"When did I talk?" Salvador asked.

"It was a few months after your first birthday—maybe you were fifteen months. And do you want to know what his first word was?"

Carmen and Salvador nodded in unison.

"It wasn't 'mamá' or 'papá'—it was '*si*.' You were my little yes boy."

Carmen laughed. "You were born good natured. I hope the baby inherits it. What other memories do you have?"

"His rolling out of the bed at about three months. He was lying in the middle of the bed when I went to fetch something, and when I came back, I found him on the floor."

"Oh no!" Carmen said.

"I didn't expect him to keep rolling. I was shocked."

"I've never asked you those questions," Salvador said.

"Men do not think like we do," Carmen said, giving Otilia a wink.

# CHAPTER 22

## Lima, Cajamarca and El Milagro, Peru, 2012

"You must be Miranda," Salvador said when he met the man sitting at the bar, nursing a drink.

"*Sergeant* Miranda," he said as he stretched out his hand, remaining seated.

He had a bulky build and deep lines on his forehead; his mostly gray hair was cropped short.

"I'm sorry. I'm glad you could come." Salvador settled onto the bar stool next to his and ordered a beer. It was a good place to talk, as it was early afternoon with hardly any customers.

"Sr. Malfi suggested I see you and explain why it is that we need a person we can trust for this job."

"But you're in the police force, you could do it yourself."

"This is not a work-related matter, it's personal and I can't travel and take any more time away from work."

"I can attempt most anything," Sergeant Miranda said, removing a single cigarette from the inside pocket of his overcoat.

"The job's out of town, a fair distance away."

"Is there a place to stay?" Miranda asked, lighting up.

"You'll stay in Cajamarca; there are many options." Salvador gave him a quick rundown of the job.

"It seems pretty straightforward. Seek witnesses from the past who are able to testify about the situation at the Land Registry office twenty years back, find out who was handling matters at the time."

"You got it. Plus, we want names of public servants who were on the payroll."

"Can we bring the witnesses to Lima to identify this man Tomás?" Miranda asked.

"We'll see about that—right now, Tomás is in jail."

Miranda shook his head, pressing the cigarette butt into an ashtray.

▲ ▲ ▲

The alarm woke Sergeant Miranda before sunrise. When he was ready, he walked across the street and slid behind the wheel of a Fiat that they'd lined up for him. During the drive, he stuck to the speed limit and stopped twice to fill up the car with gas and use the restroom. He wished he didn't have to continue to work at his age, but after contributing for thirty years to his retirement plan, his pension was not enough to meet his expenses and afford him the small pleasures he sought in life.

The first thing he did when he got to Cajamarca was to visit the red-light district. He walked the dark streets, avoiding making eye contact with the street walkers or their johns. Instead, he went down to the end of the block to a gloomy, smoke-filled joint with no glitter or sparkle, where young girls walked around dazed and scarcely clothed.

When the girls saw him, a few approached him. A tall one with long legs came up close, brushed her body against his chest, and offered her service. She put her hand on her hip, showing off her curves, and waited.

She stared him down and, once he'd agreed on the price, took him to an empty cubicle in the back. There was a cot with a single stained sheet and some hooks on the wall for his clothes. A single light bulb dangled from the ceiling on a cord. It took him a minute to notice that she had two different-colored eyes, which disturbed him.

He undressed, and when she started to utter some words to incite him, he placed his hand over her mouth and told her to shut up. She rolled her eyes and shook her hips. He turned her around and took her from the back to avoid looking at her sharp facial features and those eyes. He climaxed immediately. It was hot in the narrow compartment, and he felt engulfed in its stuffiness. He stood, removed the sweat from his body with the palm of his hands and got dressed. He left a few bills on the bed and hurried out.

The next morning, Miranda asked for directions from the lady who ran the boarding house and walked to the Land Registry office to check things out. He'd had enough experience with this kind of work to cut to the chase and, when he arrived, asked to speak with the general manager.

"So, what's this about?" the clerk at the front desk asked.

"A private matter," Miranda said, waving his expired detective badge.

"Please take a seat. I'll get Mr. Romero right away."

A young man, dressed in a business suit, greeted him with a friendly smile. "Alberto Romero, head of personnel; follow me to my office, please."

"I'll be straight with you," Sergeant Miranda said after Romero closed the door behind them. Miranda handed him a letter Sr. Malfi had drafted and sealed to make it look highly official, requesting full cooperation with the investigation they were embarking on.

The young department head read every word and then was silent as he fumbled with the loose button on his jacket. "Of course, I'll get on it. I'll see what information I can gather for you right away."

"I'm requesting this be completed today. Otherwise, we will have to prepare a summons for you to appear before a magistrate."

"That won't be necessary," Mr. Romero said.

He was young and naive and Miranda chuckled silently. The young man wasn't aware that in the enormous confusion at the judiciary branch of government, no warrant could be expeditiously obtained, at least not without coming forth with a big *coima*, a bribe.

"Mr. Miranda, why don't you let me know what specific information you require, and in a few hours, let's say by the end of the day, I'll make sure we provide you with what you came here for."

▲ ▲ ▲

Miranda wasn't feeling well. He'd drunk himself sick the night before and felt queasy with a bad headache. He would go back to his room at the pension and sleep for a while.

Midafternoon, Miranda returned to the Land Registry and Mr. Romero came out right away. "Why don't we go back to my office," he said as he gestured the way with his head.

"I spoke to our director, and he informed me that all of our records from the late 1980s to 1995 were burned in a fire during the Shining Path bombing campaign. The blast destroyed our building and everything in it."

He is green but must be aware of the facts. He should know better than to pull this charade. Miranda didn't believe that the records wouldn't have been adjusted. Other jurisdictions, those that had been badly hit, had done so already. They're beating around the bush, thinking I'll get bored, give up, and head back home.

"So, can you suggest how we can trace the names of the employees that worked in this department at the time?" Miranda asked.

"I'm afraid I don't have those answers. You can request a meeting with the director whose office you will find in the building next door."

How convenient for these bastards to be evasive, to use past wrong-doings as their excuse. The present federal government was intent on setting up a functioning stable bureaucracy to create public trust and restore normalcy. These employees would have recreated their log-books as best they could. But maybe in this municipality they haven't cleaned out all of their oldest employees. Perhaps there were still some who were implicated in past offences. Conflict fueled by scarcity had provided an opportunity for breaking the law, and maybe those with no scruples, and who'd benefited from impunity, were still around. It was clear that they didn't seem to like outsiders asking questions. Were employees trying to protect each other's wrongdoings?

▲ ▲ ▲

When Miranda arrived at the director's office, he was told that the person he wanted to see was out of town, but a subdirector would be happy to talk to him.

"We must follow protocol. First you must open a request for an investigation of our records. As you can understand, what we have are re-creations of the original documents that were lost, and there might be some that aren't exactly correct, but please be aware that we have done our best to be accurate. As for your other request, the release of the names of employees that worked in the department during the years in question is difficult. And frankly, Mr. Miranda, we don't have the funds to carry out this kind of investigation, so there will be a cost to you if you still deem it necessary for us to go ahead," the subdirector said.

*These people need to be locked up*, Miranda thought after he listened to the subdirector's explanations. *All past employees have been removed? Sure they were, since those who were no longer employed cannot be accused of a crime. This whole thing stinks. Did the man really think he would be sucked in? Forget putting on an act for the sake of expediency, a wasted effort*, he told himself. *This is just a delay tactic to cover their asses.*

"We cannot be incriminated when we have done what we can to make things right for the citizens of this province," the subdirector continued. "Times have changed, and we've become fully transparent. We try to do our best for the public."

An increased sense of annoyance unleashed inside of Miranda as he said, "Thank you so much—we will have to think about how to proceed."

Miranda shook the subdirector's hand and walked out of the room in a huff.

▲ ▲ ▲

"What's the good news?" Miranda heard Sr. Malfi ask when he called that evening.

Miranda gave him a quick rundown of his past two days.

"Transparent? For heaven's sake, that's what he calls it when they are bullshitting you?" Sr. Malfi exclaimed.

"They said they had to be careful, as they are abiding by new regulations."

"What on earth! This is public information—we shall not pay a cent for it. You go back, Miranda, and get into the archive. You get the night watchman to let you in. You do what you must to obtain those records. Scrutinize them, get as much detail as you can, take photographs. Convenient or not. Don't screw up."

Miranda appreciated Malfi's strong viewpoint.

He went back to the Land Registry the next day and asked where the archives were located. He inquired about the use of the library and where older records were kept. He charmed one of the young clerks, who offered to show him around, and she took him to a back room where the old documents from before the 1990s were kept. She told him he would need special permission to study them.

The night watchman was doing his rounds when Miranda arrived after dark. He drove up beyond the gate and stopped to eye the guard in the rearview mirror. He observed the watchman who had gone to sit on a chair by the gate, in a makeshift stall under the dim street-lights. The guard took a portable radio from a box while Miranda decided to park, driving up a dirt road off a side street. He walked back, trying to avoid some muddy puddles that had formed by the rain earlier in the day. He was relieved not to see any scrawny teen-agers begging to mind his car. Approaching the gate, he heard the voice of a broadcaster covering a fútbol match. "How's the game?" Miranda asked, casually walking past.

The guard was a friendly man who was easily engaged. Miranda lingered for a while, following the game as well.

"How late do you work?" Miranda asked at the halftime, offering the guard a smoke.

"All night, sir, I don't get home till the crack of dawn."

A police car drove by, honked, and the driver rolled down the window to ask, "Is everything all right?"

"All good," the smiling watchman hollered, and waved as the car kept moving on.

"It's ten o'clock—that's when they make their rounds," he offered.

Miranda remained in place. "What if I get you some coffee?"

The guard smiled, "Thank you, *señor,* that would be great!"

Miranda went off to relieve himself and returned with a drink for the guard.

Miranda took another walk around the block and, when he returned, noticed the guard dipping his head to his chin and snoring away. Miranda hadn't discussed with Malfi the use of a sleeping pill, but he couldn't worry about it. He would get to work immediately.

Miranda unhooked the loop on the guard's belt, which held a bunch of keys, and checked to see which one would unlock the pad-lock securing the gate with the heavy chain. Once it was opened, he ran across the yard and up a few cement steps. He fiddled with the dead bolt at the main entrance and pushed through. Finding his way down the hall with the help of his flashlight, he felt luck was on his side. He discovered the building was not alarmed. As he'd inspected the building a few hours earlier, he was familiar with its layout and walked down the hall, turning the corner to enter the room in the back where rows of boxes lined the floor.

Where to look first? He opened one of the boxes and saw that they had stacks of disorganized papers. He went over to open one of the filing cabinets placed in neat rows and, to his surprise, saw they were systematically labeled in alphabetical order. He opened a few drawers looking for the one labeled 1988. At the letter "P" he lifted several files, turning every page until he found the first one with the name of Perez. When he found Tomás's file, he wondered if he should just pull it and take off. *Nobody would notice it had gone missing*, he thought. He looked at his watch and decided against it, because it might get them into deep trouble. He had time to take a look, as the guard would still be sleeping heavily. He removed the file from its place and took it over to a table to go through it.

He scribbled some notes and took several close-up photographs of the signatures in the notarized documents. He made sure he got all the names he came across.

Miranda hurried out of the building, locking the door behind him, and ran back to check on the security guard. He kneeled to gently place the keys back on his belt. The guard did not move, and Miranda slipped away surreptitiously. He felt triumphant as he found a phone booth.

Malfi was grumpy. "What now?" he asked.

Miranda related the facts and noted a change in Malfi's tone of voice.

"I'll be able to unravel how the property ended up in his hands," Malfi said.

▲ ▲ ▲

Miranda had not only scurried around the land title registry building, but also visited El Milagro to take a look at Otilia's old neighborhood. Before approaching the property, he talked to a couple of neighbors on the block, asking if they knew the Evangelical church. Two women who were sweeping the sidewalk outside their homes said, "We don't belong to the church." But they heard from others that long-ago pastors had carried out evangelistic campaigns and prayer meetings to recruit converts. The women were both in agreement that the church was a good neighbor, a place where honest people congregated.

"They usually have services Saturday afternoon or in the evenings that last until late at night."

Miranda thanked them for their information and continued on his walk to look for the exact address he had written down. Once he arrived, he looked behind the chain-link fence at a man planting a flower bed. He unlatched the gate. He walked over to introduce himself, and the man squinting at the light said he was Pastor Miguel. They started a casual conversation and Miranda could tell the pastor seemed a bit intrigued by his visit. Miranda made up a story about how he had heard about him and said he was thinking of buying some land in the area and wondered if he knew anybody who would be interested in selling a plot.

The pastor responded that he was new to the town and, since he'd just arrived from the south, taking over from the pastor who'd retired, he didn't know many of the congregants. When Miranda asked about ownership of his property, the smile disappeared from the pastor's face. "The church owns this property; any further questions need to be directed to the headquarters in Lima. This is an open-and-shut case that we don't need to discuss further."

Retreating, he walked back towards the house and disappeared from Miranda's sight.

# CHAPTER 23

## Lima, Peru, 2012

The year Manuelito was born, Salvador became depressed, but he didn't want to admit it, as his hurt came on gradually. First Salvador started to feel restless, then he noticed he was having trouble falling asleep but attributed this to the baby's crying fits. At work he felt fatigued, and at night he questioned if he'd made a mistake wishing for a baby.

"What's wrong with you? You've been complaining a lot," Carmen said.

It was true that he had headaches and stomach pains, sometimes so sharp he couldn't recall ever experiencing them this intensely. He'd lost interest in sex and was aware that he was less affectionate. He noticed he became angry at himself after experiencing mood swings, as he saw them as a sign of personal weakness. He only found peace of mind at work, embroiled for unusually long hours in paperwork.

"Are you worried about money?" Carmen asked gently.

Salvador didn't reply.

Over the coming weeks, the more Carmen nagged, the more irritable he became, until he lashed out, saying, "Just leave me alone for God's sake!"

It was then that she cornered him until he broke down and confessed. "I don't know what's wrong with me."

"If it's the baby disrupting your life, just keep in mind that this is just a stage in his development, and it will pass. He'll soon be sleeping through the night, and we'll be able to get more rest."

But there was more than the baby—it was a combination of things, for the pressures had come all at once. The recovery of his father's body had brought on bad memories, and his hearing at the Reparation office had made him remember all the wrongs that had been done. It was too much for him to absorb.

In a flat tone of voice, Salvador confessed to Carmen that he was experiencing the same thoughts over and over again throughout the day. "I've also had recurring dreams before I wake up in a sweat around midnight," he said.

"I think you need help," Carmen said.

"I am reliving the time when my father left me in hiding and feeling guilty about it."

"It certainly wasn't your fault. Try to understand that the baby may have opened old wounds."

He felt there was a big blank in his life—he didn't remember much about his time with his dad. The stories he heard from his mom had appeased him somewhat, but he didn't know the man with whom he'd spent the first seven years of his life. He felt abandoned, carrying confusing ideas that lingered throughout his childhood. He questioned how he could possibly enter into fatherhood when he wasn't sure what role a dad should play. He knew nothing about raising a family and less about an infant boy. It was funny, as over the course of his life, he believed he'd gotten over the ghosts of his past, but now these repressed feelings were raising their nasty heads. How could his strength be failing him? He felt nervous that his son might not be safe with him.

▲ ▲ ▲

Salvador and Carmen had a quarrel at dawn one day after he tried giving Manuelito a bottle and a diaper change. The baby was fussy and refused to suck, and he wailed throughout. Holding the baby in his arms, Salvador marched over to their bedroom and deposited the child on the bed next to Carmen. "I can't cope with this one anymore," he said and walked away.

After sleeping for a few hours, Salvador felt guilty, experiencing a deep discomfort. The sense of disconnection made him want to run away. His mixed emotions led him to become disappointed with himself.

"A high-strung infant is difficult to please, but you have to understand that he is suffering and we have to try to give him some comfort," Carmen explained patiently. "I hired *tía* Luisa, the lady who lives down the street, to come three evenings a week to help. I think we should try to make time for each other and let her deal with the child. Hopefully she can give Manuelito a bath and get him to sleep."

▲ ▲ ▲

"Will you please try to come back from work early tonight?" Carmen said a few weeks later before Salvador left for work. This would be one of the evenings when Luisa was not scheduled to help.

He stiffened and answered, "Of course," stifling an unpleasant response.

"I'd like us to put him to bed together," Carmen said, coming close. "You are critical for the baby's development, so please don't get caught in your past. Let's think about how we can thrive—all three of us.

Manuelito needs to learn from the start that we will provide for him. It's important for him to develop strong bonds."

▲ ▲ ▲

It was ten minutes to nine when Salvador walked through the door to a quiet house. He'd failed her again. He'd missed giving Manuelito a bath.

The house was turned upside down. Dishes cluttered the dining room table, and the baby's dirty clothes had been dropped on the floor. A putrid smell permeated the room. He blamed himself for not giving Carmen some time to pull herself together. He got himself sorted out, removed his shoes, went to pick up the diaper pail, and checked the garbage bin under the kitchen sink. He closed the Venetian blinds and walked over to Manuelito's room where Carmen, now half asleep on the rocker, was gently rocking the baby on her chest.

Salvador stepped out of the room to go to the kitchen to get dinner. He opened the refrigerator door, found a plate of roasted chicken and salad, and smiled. Carmen still had time for him. He poured himself a beer and carried it to the dining room table. Although he felt hunger pangs, the lump in his throat made it difficult for him to swallow. He couldn't stop wondering whether he was fit for fatherhood.

He didn't hear Carmen coming down the hall until she stood in front of him. He straightened up and noticed her paleness and large circles under her eyes. "Go to bed. I'll take care of him if he wakes up," Salvador said after he reached out to kiss her.

"Make sure you cradle him in your arms. If he gets cranky, bounce him around. I did a lot of carrying today, since I read that if a baby is carried during the day it will help him sleep through the night."

He cleared the table as an ambulance drove by, siren blaring. "I hope the baby doesn't wake up," he whispered.

▲ ▲ ▲

"You've been focusing too much on the dead," Carmen said when he mentioned he was scheduled to go out of town on a dig the following week.

"Now you should look at the living—you have a baby at home who needs to attach to you."

Salvador remained silent then said, "I'm terrified to be alone with him. I've brought a child into the world and don't know how to be with him," he mumbled, shaking his head.

"Your own childhood trauma has hit in full force."

"It's hard not to think of my own childhood when I see my son."

"You had a very different experience than the one he will have; we will care for him. I promise you he won't be orphaned. Salvador, you must move forward in your thoughts. We have the power to alter our minds, and you have no alternative. We are unable to change our past. Harping on your experiences is painful, but you can't hold on to that pain," Carmen said.

"I had a traumatic childhood," Salvador said.

"You were strong, you were resilient, and you never gave up. Look at it this way: Tomás provided for you, he clothed you and fed you, sent you to a good school, even though he undermined your parents and your chances of seeing them."

"He never understood who I was. He would never answer my questions about my mom and dad."

"You had needs, but he didn't want to deal with them. He feared that if his deception was detected, it would be the end of him," Carmen said.

"The bastard, my life was at stake and I suffered."

"His thinking was flawed, and it affected you. Your wounds are still deep in your heart, and now they've become a driving force in your life, setting you back."

"Did he really believe that preventing me from visiting El Milagro was a kind act? That it wouldn't have repercussions?"

"Obviously he wanted to prevent you from finding out about your parents," Carmen said.

"I don't have good memories of him."

▲ ▲ ▲

At last, Salvador realized he needed help. Carmen was pleased to hear that he would be open to seeing a counselor to help him snap out of his misery.

"I want to learn the meaning of fatherhood," Salvador said. He needed the skills to pass on a sense of security and stability to his son right away.

Carmen went to the bedroom to get the phone number of a therapist he could see. "He's well respected, has lots of experience. I'm so glad you're game to see him."

Salvador feared that talking about his emotions would be a struggle that he did not really want to face, but distancing himself from his anxieties was not an alternative. He'd have to face his childhood experiences to expunge them from his memory and resolve the unfinished issues that haunted him.

"You need to be released from your pain," Carmen said as she threw her arms around him.

"Maybe he'll refer me to a doctor for pills."

"You should not ask for medication. You don't want to numb your feelings with addictive drugs. I wish you'd consider trying meditation instead."

"At least some sleeping pills? Isn't that how anxiety and depression is controlled? A person needs rest."

"I think this therapist will get through to you by using other methods, focusing on your thoughts and behaviors, rather than meds."

▲ ▲ ▲

When Salvador returned to town from the week spent away working in the field, he felt rested. "How are you holding up?" he asked Carmen. He noticed his wife's smart summer dress and new silver earrings dangling along her long neck and said, "You look lovely."

"Nice of you to say that. The baby's sleep is getting sounder since I started a strict sleep routine. I'm laying him down earlier in the evening, soon after he's eaten and has had his bath. I've noticed an improvement."

"I thought I could spend the next few nights in the guest room and take care of Manuelito by myself," Salvador said.

"That will be heavenly. And you can enjoy our baby who's becoming much more playful and is starting to engage in games. He's going to charm you."

▲ ▲ ▲

The following day, a Saturday, Carmen asked Salvador to come to the kitchen and take a seat. "Now that he is four months old, the doctor suggested we give him solid food to help him sleep through the night," Carmen said.

It would be Manuelito's first taste of rice cereal flakes. The baby was on top of the table on his infant seat, sticking out his tongue and grimacing. "He likes the attention," Salvador said.

Carmen placed the tip of a baby spoon on his lips, and Manuelito wrinkled his nose and pushed the food away with his tongue. On the next trial the baby seemed excited and opened his brown eyes wide. He gurgled and made sounds while shaking his arms and his legs. He swallowed the next few small bites, and Salvador noticed the beginning of a smile. A few spoonfuls later, he had covered his face and his hands with the mush.

Salvador and Carmen had a good laugh when Salvador picked up the leftover cereal and drew a happy face on the back of a black tray.

They placed Manuelito in his crib, and he seemed content. Carmen asked Salvador to rub the child's back to help him fall asleep. But soon after, he started to fuss and let out a cry. Carmen turned Manuelito over to one side and placed a pacifier in his mouth. A few seconds later, the child had calmed down.

"He's a finicky one. I've noticed he's easily affected by touch, light, and loud sounds. I think we have a highly sensitive kid on our hands," Carmen said.

"I'll try a gentler touch next time. He's so adorable," Salvador said, placing his arm around his wife's waist and hugging her hard.

▲ ▲ ▲

Salvador asked for a leave of absence from work for a month to work with the psychotherapist.

"How did your session go today?" Carmen asked when Salvador returned home from his visit to the counselor one late afternoon.

"We discussed how when I was growing up, I couldn't talk about my parents' disappearance with Tomás. He didn't provide me with an emotionally supportive environment. I developed a sense of isolation and feelings of inadequacy about family. Patricio tells me that it's important for me to understand that this wasn't something that was under my control and I had no choice but to remain with Tomás to survive."

"He is helping you free yourself from the self-destructive mentality interfering in your life."

"I have to learn to ignore these inner voices meddling with my mind."

"I'm sure you'll free yourself from this bondage in due time, with a little more help."

# CHAPTER 24

## Lima, Peru, 2013

Otilia headed toward the glass doors to exit the airport as soon as Jerry picked up their bags from the arrival area, oblivious to the crowd that waited outside. She was in a rush to embrace her son and see her little one. After long hugs, she formally introduced Jerry to Carmen and Salvador, since their association so far had only been through Skype. Jerry gave a big smile, shook Carmen's hand, and slapped Salvador on his back. Manuelito giggled when Jerry turned to him, making a funny face. Otilia leaned over to squeeze the baby's round cheeks; secure in his mother's arms, he smiled and waved his hands.

As she sat next to the baby in the backseat of Salvador's car, Otilia studied his reflection in the rearview mirror. He looked tired, his face more drawn than when she'd seen him last, and something was amiss in his eyes. There had been many calls to encourage Salvador to continue with his therapy, to ensure there was progress, and he appeared to be moving forward. It broke her heart to see him so silent while Carmen was doing the talking, telling them about Manuelito's latest accomplishments. Otilia watched the baby, admiring his smooth olive skin as he delighted in singing and following his mother's finger plays.

Otilia, mindful that Salvador required special attention at this time, asked Jerry a few weeks before to accompany her to Lima. "He is making progress but needs a little help as he battles depression," she said.

Otilia wanted to provide support and make it easier for Carmen during Salvador's recovery. Jerry agreed to fly down to watch over her and help her overcome her feelings of responsibility for causing her son pain. Jerry had no trouble understanding how being separated from Salvador against her will weighed heavily on Otilia still.

"Some people are incapable of turning things around by themselves," Jerry said. "They keep their thoughts crawling around in their minds, unable to silence them. But Salvador has help, he'll get over it."

▲ ▲ ▲

Otilia entered the living room in her son's home, feeling refreshed once she'd taken a soothing bath, soaking in Epsom salts. The aches and pains from sitting on the long plane ride had melted away. Wearing a light summer dress, she approached Salvador, who was sitting on the couch, holding his laptop and playing a game of solitaire. She planted a kiss on his forehead and went to take a seat in a chair facing the patio. "You've done a good job in your garden. It's beautiful," she said, looking at the potted pink cyclamen in full bloom.

"The lawn needs mowing," Salvador said. "I meant to do it before you arrived. I neglected my duties."

"Please don't worry about that, *mijito*. We'll be happy to help."

"Frankly, you shouldn't have come. I didn't want to inconvenience you," Salvador said, closing his laptop.

"What do you mean? You're important to me. We are a family. We're here to assist one another. I came out of love and concern."

"I'm so much better; I'm getting over the worst. I'm going back to work full time, and I'll be able to stay at the Lima office for the next six months. I won't be traveling so I can continue with therapy. *Terapia*, Mamá, is a long process. I have been forced to face the experiences of my 'susceptible years,' as Patricio calls them, and understand how they came into play," he said, giving a little chuckle.

"What did you learn?" Otilia asked.

"Until I started therapy, I hadn't thought much about why I suddenly became so depressed. Patricio Morales has helped me see that on the surface, life continued as usual, but reality slowly crept up when I had to adjust to a whole new series of circumstances. I'm slowly coming to terms with who I am and have a deeper sense of what it meant to be misunderstood during my childhood. Patricio has shed light on my thought process after we lost touch, my struggles to keep strong, the bargains I made with myself, and the fantasies I had about finding you and Dad."

*He's open to talking*, Otilia thought, pleased.

Salvador reflected for a moment then said, "But I had a breakdown. I'm upset at my lack of fortitude."

"The important thing is that the worst is over; you've come far."

When Jerry entered the room, Salvador stood to offer him his seat next to his mother, then asked if he and Otilia would like something to drink.

"What do you want to see while you're here?" Salvador asked Jerry when he gave him a glass of mineral water.

"I know Lima quite well—it's not my first time. I'm here to get to know you and Carmen."

"Is that so?"

"If you'll have me," Jerry replied.

"Of course, man. This is my mother's house too, you're most welcome."

"Oh, *mijo*, don't be silly." Otilia laughed.

After parking the stroller by the front door, Carmen walked into the room with Manuelito in her arms.

"Let's go play," Otilia said as she took Manuelito from Carmen.

Carmen went to sit next to Salvador and reached for his hand to hold on her lap. She wore jeans and a short-sleeved shirt with a thin silver necklace around her neck.

Salvador looked at his watch and grinned. "Should I start the barbecue soon?"

"In about half an hour," Carmen said. "I'll go prepare the marinade for the steak."

Otilia and Manuelito sat on a mat in a corner of the dining room where there were toys on the floor. The child crawled to grab a chair and pulled himself up to a standing position. "Bravo!" Otilia laughed, clapping for him. She grabbed a ball and rolled it to him, and Manuelito slowly came down to sitting. Carmen came into the room to give Manuelito his dinner, then put him to bed.

"How are things for you?" Otilia asked when Carmen returned to the kitchen where Otilia was preparing a salad.

"It's been rough, even with Luisa to help. Work and the baby, Salvador's needs. But don't get me wrong, we're very close. I've enrolled our family in a music class on Saturday mornings. Parents and infants—there are times when Salva joins us. You should come with us tomorrow." Carmen reached into a cupboard to get a pamphlet. "Here, this will give you a sense of the program."

"*¿Cómo puede ser para guaguas?* How can that be—music for babies?"

"They love it—the songs, games—you should see how Manuelito follows the rhythm and swings back and forth. The teacher is fantastic; she is a strong maternal woman, nurturing and laid-back; she makes us parents enjoy the class as much as the babies do. Otilia, I want to tell you that it's good of you to bring Jerry along. He can be a companion for Salva."

"It was about time I introduced him to you. Has Salvador expressed any feelings about him?"

"No, he seems to be okay with it."

"I'm so pleased he's facing his troubles," Otilia said.

"He's learned to dial down the demons. I am a bit concerned about how people at work will perceive him."

"For having missed work?"

"The stigma, trapped by his past with scars that didn't heal. Not everybody believes that intense grief is a reason for taking a leave," Carmen said, her shoulders slumping.

They continued to chat while they prepared the meal. "I've asked the therapist to prepare a report to send to the Reparation office. Salvador's problems all stem from the time he was separated, and they better take this information into account when they determine the type of compensation he's entitled to. I hope his report will strengthen the fact that his present condition is due to his history. He was wronged and I don't want them to drag him along, finding excuses, telling him he lived with family and was better off than some," Carmen said as she reached into the refrigerator to retrieve a cake she had bought at the bakery.

Otilia refrained from adding her comments. Her daughter-in-law was an educated, strong woman who would do what she thought was good for them. Otilia went to gather the cutlery to set the table. "Do you have a tablecloth I should use?" she asked.

▲ ▲ ▲

After dinner Otilia and Jerry went for a walk in the neighborhood. Otilia stumbled on a stone that had fallen to the ground from a crumbling wall. She felt the pain on her toe and told Jerry they should cross to the opposite side of the street where the sidewalk was in better repair. "No barricades to indicate danger," she said, shaking her head.

Jerry slipped his arm into hers, and she appreciated his watchful concern. It was a warm, pleasant night with visible bright lights in the sky. They walked for fifteen minutes in one direction, then turned back. They made no conversation until Otilia finally said, "I think my son is moving in the right direction."

"He has a good head."

"I hope he can find proper balance."

"It's a hiccup. He'll be fine in the long run."

"If only he'd had the love and support growing up and he'd come into contact with a different world. It was like moving to a foreign country for him. His life with Tomás must have been so different than what he'd experienced at home."

"We all have our deep worries, our highs and our lows—that's life. We must do the best we can under the circumstances and keep moving on," Jerry said, leaning into her.

"The circumstances were as bad as they could get. If only we could have been in exile together," Otilia said.

"Please stop torturing yourself. He was stuck in a community where nobody took note of what he was going through. It would've been beneficial if he'd had access to counseling then, but that was not meant to be. He's unburdening himself and will get back on the right track."

"I worry about the consequences."

"I understand. My parents fled when they were persecuted, as they learned early on that they had no chance to survive if they stayed. For my mother, those experiences were more daunting than for my dad, and I feel I bore some of the consequences. But we all react differently, and we do what we can," Jerry said.

A young, skinny, long-legged woman passed by; Otilia nodded but the girl turned her gaze sideways.

"I wish Salva didn't have such a high-stress job," Otilia said.

"I take it he's content; it's a connection to his past. He has no apprehensions. Working is good; it gets him connected to others and keeps him from obsessing on his inner self."

"I know you want to put my mind at ease," Otilia said.

"Do you think they would consider moving to the US?"

"Now?"

"Or sometime in the future. They both have good skills."

"The language, jobs—it takes a while to adjust, and they've just had a baby. The paperwork, the expense . . . This country is moving forward. I think they have a better future here."

▲ ▲ ▲

During the following days, Salvador and Carmen spend lots of time with Otilia and Jerry. Salvador was sharing his stories and Jerry was seeing Salvador for who he was. Salvador told Otilia that he felt Jerry listened to him in a nonjudgmental way.

Salvador and Jerry watched fútbol games on television and played chess. One day Jerry commented to Otilia that Salvador had invited him to his office to show him around. "I'd like to see the lab, how they collect and preserve evidence, learn about the course of an investigation," Jerry said.

"That's good," Otilia replied. She was happy that her family, now made up of new members, were finding common ground.

▲ ▲ ▲

Late one evening, when Carmen had gone to bed, Salvador offered Jerry and Otilia a beer as they talked. Looking at Jerry, he said, "I want to thank you for caring for my mother."

"That is kind of you to say," Otilia said, and Jerry nodded.

"I have found a real companion in this special woman. We understand each other well," Jerry said.

"Life is about caring," Otilia said.

"I appreciate your visit. Do you visit your family often?" Salvador asked Jerry.

"Not so much. I was married for a short time a long time ago. We had no children—my wife died thirty years ago in a plane accident."

"I'm so sorry," Salvador said.

"It took me a long time to get over her death. I never married again, too many ghosts from the past to tackle. I am very sad I never fathered a child. But I am the great-uncle of a four-year-old," Jerry said.

Otilia interrupted Jerry to tell Salvador how Jerry had been surprised one day by the email from a Bolivian man who turned out to be his half-brother.

When a shrill cry came from Manuelito's room, Salvador stood up swiftly. He returned with the baby in his arms.

"Why don't we take him out for a stroll? It's a warm night and he is sweaty and uncomfortable. The fresh air will do him good," Otilia said as she touched the baby's forehead.

"I think it would be best if you could strap him in his baby carrier," Salvador said.

"I'll be happy to carry him," Jerry said, and he rose to put the carrier around his shoulders.

"That's great. I'll go shower while you are out," Salvador said with a smile.

▲ ▲ ▲

"I hope you are free on Monday, Mother. Sr. Malfi has asked if we can see him," Salvador said.

Otilia was glad. Sr. Malfi could bring them up to date.

At his office, Sr. Malfi first informed them that a legal complaint had been sent to the Evangelical Church Headquarters, describing the facts and reasons the previous property owners wanted to get in touch. "Of course, I included your signed affidavits where you swore that there had been an intentional misrepresentation of facts at the time of their purchase, since the property didn't belong to Tomás Campos, who purported to be the rightful owner, but to you. I made it clear that the church had relied on untrue statements of facts when deciding to enter into the real estate contract and that the transaction had led to damages to my clients. I also advised of a possible lawsuit to be brought against them if there was a refusal to communicate. I gave them weeks to respond, and I mentioned that if I didn't hear back, I would be sending an order to appear before a judge."

Sr. Malfi stopped to get a drink of water. He lit a cigarette and said, "Only a few weeks ago I heard from a lawyer, retained by the church, letting me know the sale was entered in good faith and the purchase was made according to contractual obligations. Therefore, charges were unjustified. The lawyer included copies of the binding contract proving they hold ownership. Furthermore, the church made significant improvements to upgrade the building, which was in disrepair, and since then property values have increased."

"In other words, neither the owners nor the law firm are willing to accept the claim," Salvador said.

"Organized land invasions have been a way of life for many Peruvians. They grew out of the massive migration from the countryside at the time of terrorism. Generations stayed put in these informal urban settlements and have benefitted from the Law for the Formalization of Informal Properties, which came into effect during Fujimori's time. They were entered into the national property registry. Now we are experiencing a similar situation in the Amazon, where homesteaders are illegally settling in, carving out plots in the dense jungle. If these people can show the Ministry of Agriculture that they are improving the land by clearing the trees and building their flimsy structures, they may get a claim to their parcel. That is today, when property rights have been tightened. I tell you this as there's been a precedent, offering freehold title to those who invade empty land and improve their living conditions," Sr. Malfi said.

"But this is a church, not a bunch of families in need," Salvador said.

"Remember that at the time, Fujimori's party was after votes," Sr. Malfi explained. "Abuses are still occurring and unscrupulous practices are going on. People who are moving to the Amazon realize they have a chance for cheap land and begin to stake out large plots with the expectation that they will be legalized. As land speculation gets underway, fraud raises its head. Sales take place, and if the next owners get the rights to the land, they win the lottery, but if they don't, they'll be kicked out and lose everything. Despite the uncertainties, settlers are putting down roots, as our laws allow those who are landless to gain rights when lawful owners aren't using their properties. Imagine, rather than fighting deforestation, the government is granting license to invade."

"So how does this relate to us?" Otilia asked.

"Well, there was an empty property in El Milagro, and then along comes Tomás with a child, whom he has to support. He has no intention of moving in, but thinks he ought to keep it until prices drive up. Then when Tomás hears about the possibility of invaders taking it over, he becomes concerned and thinks he better sell before he loses everything."

Now it would be up to the courts to identify who was at fault and the degree of complicity the municipality's employees had in facilitating the process. A lawsuit would be uncertain since they'd have to prove that Tomás was a savvy participant who had hoodwinked employees at the municipality. Tomás would be accused of forgery and obstruction of law, and the clerks would be considered accomplices.

"We could try our luck, but finding a judge and a court that would be favorable to our claim will be tough, as there are no clear guidelines on how to decide this type of case. The other day I spoke to a judge who was opposed to this kind of litigation. He mentioned how important it was to consider how things have changed since that time, and how Protestant churches have thrived. Nobody will want to see the courts rule against religious institutions. In this judge's opinion, everyone should take their losses and move on. It made me think that perhaps the government is still not willing to be implicated and will fail to address their responsibility. They are afraid that with everyone seeming to have a bone of contention, if they listen to all, they will need to go back to the time of the conquistadors. Would you be willing to wait? Because even if you win in court, it would take years before you would get the property back."

"Maybe," Otilia said.

"We could wait, since we have nothing to lose, but it would cost a lot of money, perhaps even more than what we could get for the land," Salvador said.

Then they were all silent.

# CHAPTER 25

## The East Bay, California; Tuscany, Italy; Berlin, Germany, 2014

One day Jerry began to talk to Otilia about taking a trip to Europe. By now they were living together at his place and had rented out her apartment in Lake Merritt.

"I'd like to see Italy," she said. "I've never been to Europe, so any country would be exciting to see."

"How come?" Jerry asked.

"Never had the income, never took the time."

"What intrigues you about Italy?"

"The art, the language—it's so musical, more pleasant to the ear than Spanish. I want to hear people speak, try homemade pasta, see the churches, the pope, the pomp and ceremony." She laughed.

"But I thought you weren't religious. Where would you like to go?"

Otilia had a few images of Italy: period architecture, Romeo and

Juliet, fashionably dressed people, succulent dishes. "Rome, the Vatican, Florence, the countryside," she said.

"We'll plan a trip to begin in Italy, then we can go to Germany. I want to explore my family heritage."

"But I thought they were Czech?"

"My mother's side of the family was from Germany, and so was my dad's family before borders changed."

▲ ▲ ▲

Otilia and Jerry were two of the thousands of tourists to head to Italy that fall. They began their journey in Rome where they spent a week visiting classic sites: ancient Roman ruins, the old town, and the Villa Borghese where they appreciated the art collection of Italian and European work. Jerry delighted in the exhibit, eager to tell her about the styles and the art medium used by the artists. They walked up and down cobblestone streets for miles passing stunning squares, then stopping to recover at a park bench. They went by enormous flowing water fountains where they stared in awe at the magnificent Baroque statues and other sculpted monuments. At lunch they ate pizzas and salads and in the later afternoon walked to get gelatos.

On the last day, they wanted to explore the different views the city offered, so in the morning, they took in the Spanish Steps, then climbed to the top of the church of Trinita dei Monti for a panoramic view. In the evening, before sunset, they caught the last magical glimpse of the city built on the seven hills from a rooftop bar.

"I wish we could stay here forever," Otilia said.

They looked at each other and smiled. "I love you," Jerry said, touching her hand. "One more picture," he said, reaching for his phone.

"I guess it's time to move to our next destination; we'll have our photos to remind us of the beauty and the good times." Otilia said.

They'd made arrangements to stay at a bed-and-breakfast in San

Gimignano, a quaint Tuscan town in the countryside. They had booked a room with a view to experience the "ultimate holiday," for pictures of a plain, restored two-story stone farmhouse, surrounded by vineyards, appealed to them. The advertisement promised tastefully decorated accommodation, a sunny breakfast room, and even access to a small swimming pool in a magical garden.

▲ ▲ ▲

Jerry drove the rented sedan down the slow lane of the autostrada, complaining about the cars roaring by. He preferred to be on country roads to peacefully navigate the low-lying valleys and hills. As they approached the town of Tori, Otilia spotted the road lined with cypress trees, the marker they were looking for. After driving up a dusty, unpaved road, Jerry pulled into the designated empty parking lot. They were surprised that there were no other cars. Further up on a driveway by the front door of the house, they noticed two old cars, badly in need of bodywork.

They walked up to the house, and Otilia caught a glimpse of a garden hose winding its way to an above-ground pool on an uneven patch of grass. A tricycle and a few toys were scattered about. Before Otilia could knock on the door, a man appeared behind a wrought-iron-barred window on the second floor. "They're coming," he yelled as a woman appeared moments later at the front door.

"I'm Barbara," she said. "I have some bad news." She talked very fast.

Otilia became worried. Was it news from home?

Barbara explained that they'd been unable to obtain a license to operate their inn. "You know how it is in Italy, such a bureaucracy. We have a saying here that we have more laws than people. But not to worry, I have found you a place nearby, a beautiful little hotel that has just been renovated with a full-size swimming pool, and its rates are cheaper than ours! You'll be very comfortable," she said, making gestures with her hands.

She invited them in for a drink, and they followed her through a long, cool, dark corridor and up a stone stairway to what appeared to be a living room littered with toys and clothes. Otilia asked if she could use the bathroom, and Barbara told her to wait until she got her son out of the bathtub.

"The *signora* wants to go pee-pee," she yelled as she disappeared from view.

"Come this way," she said, beckoning her over.

Otilia was shown to a large room where a toilet was located behind a washer and dryer and an ironing board stacked with dirty clothes. She stepped inside the small space without a door, and as she sat on the toilet, she saw the face of a young naked boy staring at her. Otilia laughed and the boy giggled, pointing his finger down at her private parts. Her dreams of a *bella villa* in a well-manicured Italian garden quickly evaporated.

▲ ▲ ▲

Otilia and Jerry walked hand in hand up the cobblestone alleyway to the hotel where, to their surprise, they found that little bit of the magic they had envisioned.

That night, they ate dinner at the hotel's dining room and Jerry ordered a half-liter of Prosecco to propose a toast to their first trip to Europe. "I hope this will be one of many," he said, leaning over to kiss her affectionately on the lips.

▲ ▲ ▲

Jerry said he was taking her to Germany to ensure she understood how their lives were entwined. In Berlin they lodged at a modern boutique hotel, with a tastefully decorated lobby with low leather sofas and glass coffee tables. Two television sets were on, one tuned to an English

CNN channel, the other to a local fútbol game. Their room on the fifth floor could be reached by a minuscule elevator with just enough space for the two of them and their suitcases.

The day after their arrival, the first thing Jerry planned was a bicycle tour of the city to see the sights. They would get a good feel for the many different sides of the city and its history as they pedaled through trendy neighborhoods and working-class areas, Jerry explained. "The city is flat with designated bike paths—you'll feel very safe."

A small group of people gathered in front of the bike shop to get fitted for their bikes. Otilia had started to ride once again after meeting Jerry. Jerry, an avid cyclist, had encouraged her to go out on short rides and, after she'd started to enjoy the activity, they took weekend getaways. She liked the freedom experienced through bicycling and the opportunity for exercise.

When the group was ready, the guide, a young man with cropped pale-blond hair and a polite bearing, explained the route and the breaks they would take. "After an hour we'll stop for a coffee and a 'Berliner' at one of our bakeries. In Berlin our 'Berliners' are called '*Pfannkuchen*.' Who has tried this pastry?" he asked.

A girl with a British accent said, "It's a donut."

"Correct, this is our famous sugar donut filled with jelly," the guide explained.

The guide led them single file down a nearby path to start their ride. He set a moderate speed with the group lining up behind him. It was a sunny day with only a few clouds in the sky and not too hot. Bikes and tandems began to pass. Otilia increased her speed, providing a wide margin between herself and the dog walkers and parents pushing strollers, to keep pace with the group. She looked in her mirror to see if Jerry was close behind, then wove by some joggers to remain on the far right-hand side of the path.

As they approached the Tiergarten park, the historic private hunting grounds for the royalty, they went by a number of foreign embassies.

When they entered the park, Otilia saw families barbecuing on a large open field of grass. The guide rode towards some benches and stopped. "Here we will stretch our legs."

"Let me give you a bit of the park's history. During the war most of the park's landscape, sculptures, and monuments were destroyed. After the war, the land was used for growing potatoes and vegetables for a starving population. Today, this beautiful place is where Berliners can rest and relax and where several memorials have been built. You may visit them another time at your leisure. You may want to see the Memorial to the Murdered Jews of Europe, also known as the Holocaust Memorial, which was finished in 2004 and holds the names of approximately three million Jewish Holocaust victims. The monument is composed of 2,711 rectangular concrete blocks laid out in a grid formation. Some say it was designed to produce a confusing atmosphere for the visitor, reflecting the despair and volatility of the situation for the Jewish people. It is located one block south of the Brandenburg Gate adjacent to the park.

We also have the Memorial to Homosexuals Persecuted Under Nazism, which opened in 2008, and the Memorial to the Sinti and Roma Victims of National Socialism, which was unveiled in 2012. A Memorial for the Victims of National Socialist Euthanasia Killings is scheduled to open in 2014."

The group walked to a circular pool of water with a triangular stone at its center. "The triangle refers to the badge that was worn by Roma and Sinti concentration camp prisoners. A flower is placed on the slab on a daily basis," the guide explained. "You should come back, take your time to explore and read the moving poem by a Roma poet, which you'll find inscribed in bronze letters."

They continued on through the historical city center and the Brandenburg Gate until they came upon an old patrol road with a watchtower along the remains of the Berlin Wall. Until 1989 the city of Berlin was divided by a wall topped with barbed wire entanglements cutting across streets and rows of houses. The wall had been erected in 1961 by the East German government to prevent the loss of their residents who were fleeing to the West. East German citizens were forbidden to cross over, and Westerners could only access the East at designated checkpoints.

They rode to the former section of East Berlin to visit the East Side Gallery where they walked their bikes to inspect a collection of murals painted by artists from all over the world. Jerry called Otilia to take a look at the back side of the murals facing the river Spree, crammed with gritty colorful configurations of varied forms. "This graffiti is excellent for encouraging public debate," Jerry said.

This was Jerry, Otilia thought, but she had trouble relating to how this hideous scribble grappled with the social issues of our times.

"The next stop is Checkpoint Charlie, a historical landmark," the tour guide announced. "And who knows how it got its name?"

"From the movies," a rider said.

Some in the group laughed. "Yes, it has been the setting of many films about the Cold War, but it got its name from NATO for Alpha, Bravo, Charlie. This was the third checkpoint opened by the Allied forces after the war, in and around Berlin."

The tour guide explained that there had been uncertainty after the fall of Communism, and today the young generation was confronted with the legacy of Nazism. "So, our situation is complex, having to come to terms with both 'isms' in our past."

They got on their bikes to pedal by socialistic-style housing projects. After a short time, the tour guide stopped again. "Please gather around. I want to show you one of the many Stumbling Blocks commemorating victims of crimes on these cobblestone-sized brass plates. As you can see, they are inscribed with names and locations where people were killed or deported to concentration camps."

Otilia froze, and her voice wavered as she called Jerry to come to her side. She pointed to the plaque in the pavement with the name of a person's last residence. She couldn't speak, for this bike trip was turning out to be too heart wrenching. She asked Jerry to hold her bike as she bent down to trace the name on the plaque with her forefinger. A man, approximately Manuel's age. She thought of his wife left behind, perhaps to be killed somewhere else soon after.

"Such a waste, all of these wars, true insanity," Jerry said when Otilia took hold of her bike. Placing his free hand on her back Jerry gently gave it a pat. "I'm sorry."

"There are so many memorials. So much effort has gone to recognize so many individuals," Otilia said as she started to cry inside. "Why hasn't Manuel been acknowledged by others? I'll never know when and how he was killed."

She closed her eyes and opened them again when she heard Jerry say, "We have to go, they've started pedaling."

"I'll settle down once I get moving."

She grasped the handlebars tightly and pedaled hard but, for the rest of the ride, she had trouble dislodging unpleasant thoughts from her mind. Telling the truth was a social good. When lies were spread through society—society crumbled.

That evening they decided to order room service.

"This was exhausting tourism, to learn about how things got so bad, how the Nazi's caused so much harm. I do admire how Germany remembers the Holocaust though," Otilia said.

"Today we got an education. Hitler certainly defined tragedies in people's lives and became despised. Now, the Germans have done a good job trying to honestly confront their history. But let's not forget that it has taken Germany a long time to come to terms with its past and to finally acknowledge their shared responsibility for the legacy of Nazism. Not until those Germans who came of age in the 1970s and 80s confronted their past, and the country was once again reunified, was the Nazi era publicly repudiated."

"No wonder your parents had bitter feelings about their countries of birth."

"I think my dad felt he was quite courageous to have left when he did, but wished he had joined the Allied army to fight the 'swine'— he despised the enemy. So much extended family was lost. He told me once he liked to see movies where the Germans got defeated and a lot of their soldiers died."

That night Otilia and Jerry looked for a comedy to watch on television. Otilia had trouble falling asleep. The sights she had seen remained in her head, and she thought about the horrific consequences of the Nazi regime.

▲ ▲ ▲

The next morning, Otilia woke up earlier than Jerry and reached for the Berlin travel guide on the night table. The morning light pushed through a gap in the blinds so she was able to read. Jerry continued to sleep for the next forty-five minutes, and when he awoke, he pulled her into his arms.

"What should we do today?" he asked, nuzzling.

"I'd like to visit the museum of the city of Berlin. I've been reading about it and it gets high reviews; it's all about everyday life in a communist country. It's interactive—you can touch, feel, react. Thinking how Peru might have turned out under a Maoist regime, this exhibit will be very enlightening."

"Good grief, Maoism was so much more extreme. In both types of regimes there was a climate of fear, I suppose. I don't think you'll get a true picture of day-to-day life but, sure, let's go and explore."

▲ ▲ ▲

They visited the German Democratic Republic Museum devoted to everyday life at the time the city was divided. They walked through an exhibit of a model apartment with a living room, a bedroom, and a kitchen and the comforts available. They peered into glass cases at products sold only to East German consumers. Jerry went over to pull out one of the drawers in the kitchen to look at the cutlery people used, while Otilia put on headphones to watch an East German television show. They went to sit on a Trabant, a car with no gas gauge that people had to wait up to ten-years for, then walked into a high-ranking Communist party member's office and a secret police interrogation room. They read how the state controlled the economy and its policies, how the media broadcasted news to remind citizens that everything was better in the Eastern European nations than in the West.

They learned how preschoolers were toilet trained in groups with the objective of reinforcing collectivist ideals, and that tourism was only allowed to other countries behind the iron curtain.

"It says here that East Germany didn't accept culpability for the Nazi past as they considered it to be the result of Western capitalism. Only since the 1990s, after reunification, did they start thinking about their responsibility to do their part in memorialization," Otilia said.

"It wasn't easy living in Communist countries. So many people lived in fear. Jewish people didn't talk about their backgrounds, afraid of being accused of spying for the West. My relatives in the Czech Republic went through a similar experience," Jerry said.

At dinner at a small restaurant close to their hotel, they sat at a table quietly contemplating the events of the day. Jerry reached out to Otilia and kissed her hand. Tentatively they started to talk about how it was indispensable to provide a platform to those whose lives had been shattered by deeply distressing events. "There are so many difficult issues involved in the aftermaths: justice, accountability, bringing about peace," Jerry said.

"Placing blame," Otilia said.

"Holocaust survivors place blame but don't seek revenge. I always wonder how come they don't. Is it strength or do they just want to move on and away, never to set foot in the country where they came from? Their only pledge seems to be to try to keep their memories alive and support Israel," he said.

"It's about forgiveness, isn't it? Revenge doesn't help. A tooth for a tooth . . . Right now, what people seem to be doing is erecting monuments. Do they help?" Otilia said.

"To remember."

"I don't think people forget. They quiet their demons but never forget. They carry their trauma forever in silence," Otilia said.

"But those who had the bad luck of living in times of terrible danger pass their trauma on to the next generation. I'm an example of this fact. I deal with my own helplessness, even though I'm part of the second generation, I can't let go. It's an upshot of persecution and war."

"In Peru the Truth and Reconciliation Commission provided a platform to make people's stories heard, but this turned controversial, and thereafter any attempt to discuss the conflict, every monument erected to the victims of violence, has become contentious." Otilia shook her head in frustration.

"It took West Germany years to mark that period of history, and look at East Germany: They controlled how the past should be presented to fit the regime's needs; they blamed Western ideology for causing the Nazi regime without taking responsibility and confronting the issue until recently," Jerry said.

"It's good that they are reaching out to make people sensitive to all injustices. Our generation has the responsibility to teach historical facts. The shame is that I don't see any of this taking place in Peru. There is some talk going on about how to understand and remember our war, since many young folks don't have a clue as to what went on. Then, we have people who pretend not to know. Our society is fractured and some still question who were the victims and who the perpetrators. What people mostly talk about is whether President Fujimori was a hero who destroyed terrorism or whether he was a criminal trampling on human rights."

"But the state had a duty to protect their citizens from terrorist violence," Jerry said.

"Yes, but when the Truth and Reconciliation Commission assigned responsibility for the conflict, they found that there was a great deal of lawlessness on the part of the government, so it was hard to place an exact blame."

"That is what the photographic exhibit *Yuyanapaq* documents, all of the human rights abuses by both sides."

"One exhibition is not enough," she said.

"Of course not."

"There are just too many dissenting voices. The lines between heroes and victims are blurred. How do you build monuments in that climate? And there is still a strong belief that talking about memory is somewhat subversive."

"People would rather leave memories behind," Jerry said.

"Reconciliation is still far away."

"Building memorials has become very popular here in Europe. They're part and parcel of the country's reparation programs and function as historical apologies to teach and pave the way for better understanding," Jerry said.

"I'm too exhausted to continue this conversation," Otilia said as they finished their meal. "It's too heavy for me to think about right now. Let's get the bill—it's time for a good night's rest."

# CHAPTER 26

## The East Bay, California, 2014

Today Gertrude Muller, Otilia's former neighbor, was coming for tea. She had an apartment on the fifth floor of the building where Otilia had lived before moving in with Jerry. She wanted to hear all about the couple's trip to Berlin. She'd been a friend of Michael's for years and dedicated time to care for him when he became ill. Otilia and Trudy had maintained a friendship ever since.

Trudy was born in Berlin and carried the shame of having spent her childhood under the tutelage of madmen subjecting her to the ideals of the Third Reich philosophy. She had shared selected stories from her past with Otilia, as she felt a certain bond with her, both having forged new lives for themselves. Trudy left Germany at twenty-three and hadn't returned since coming to America in 1952. Trudy was wary about German people, angry at her parents who'd participated and obeyed delusional Nazi leaders, leaving her feeling humiliated by their conduct. Shame had caused Trudy to become somewhat of a hermit, as she believed that as soon as she told people where she was from, they stopped seeing her for who she was, judging her for being one of "Hitler's children."

"My accent gives me away," she'd said.

Over the years and little by little, Otilia learned that Trudy's father, unable to find steady employment in the early 1930s, had joined a Nazi organization, and once Hitler was in power, a job quickly materialized for him. Trudy remembered her father as a gentle person, dedicating time to his children and enjoying family life. However, once war commenced, he was conscripted and sent to the front, only to return home sporadically. As soon as her father departed, her mother responded to a call for housewives to work outside the home, and the children were left as latchkey kids.

The early years of the war had little impact on their daily lives, other than missing their dad. Whenever their father was permitted to visit, Trudy's mother would throw big parties, inviting friends and relatives. Trudy remembered that food was plentiful then, and the partygoers drank beer while singing and dancing through the night. But as the war progressed, things began to change. When they learned that their father had died in battle, her mother and the two daughters had to separate. "Mother was sent to Essen, the capital of German industry, and we were sent to a special school in the countryside. As we prepared our clothes to be packed, our mother told us we would travel to a faraway place because the Führer wanted to keep all of his children out of harm's way."

Before Trudy and her sister departed, there was a great amount of excitement, as her mother, her teachers, and other acquaintances congratulated her for this accomplishment. "To be chosen to live in one of the children's homes Chancellor Adolf Hitler had set up for girls like us was a gift, people said. We were made to believe that we were in for a big surprise and would be granted many advantages. Only later did we find out that we were among the 'privileged children' groomed to enhance the Aryan race, and I felt greatly betrayed."

Otilia was shocked when she heard her story.

"Can you believe those bastards? While they were killing the Jewish children, they were secretly breeding and selecting blonde, blue-eyed girls to better the race."

On the day the sisters boarded the train to take them to their new destination, they were greeted with the Hitler salute by their chaperones. Their mother did not seem sad to say goodbye, as she said it was all for the glory of Germany. Mother gave each daughter a paper cone filled with sweets and fruits and settled them down at their assigned seats, offering last-minute hugs and goodbye kisses.

"We got good care and good food, but there were strict rules. Girls were given some basic language and social science instruction, but more important was to learn to become proper *Mädchen*. True German women honored and loved their country, were loyal to the Führer, and respected the spiritual and ethical values of the nation. Girls were expected to remain pure, pledge marriage only to Aryan boys, and become good and plentiful mothers for the Fatherland. We were informed that now we belonged to one big family of German girls and were part of the master race. We were educated to be the wives of leaders of the next generation and were to take our responsibilities seriously."

Otilia thought of the accounts that had come from those who'd been forced to participate with the Shining Path. They also weren't given a choice.

"To this day I am quite neurotic," Trudy said, the day Otilia found Trudy in pain, bent over trying to make her bed. "At the children's home we had to be precise; if not, we were punished and they would remove the sheets. I still look for creases," she said as she laughed and folded her pillow in half to neatly place inside the cover.

The girls were taught to be obedient and service-minded, and when the war escalated, they were taken to harvest potatoes to help the farmers in the community. Trudy did not see her mother much, as she was an essential worker in the war effort. Her mother would not succumb to what would be seen as an "unpatriotic act" if she were to put her daughters before the nation. When it became too dangerous for her mother to travel at all, Trudy had to be content with hearing her mother's voice on the telephone. The sisters rarely complained, but on the few times they became wistful, they were told by their favorite teacher that victory would soon come, and when the war was over, they'd be free to travel back to their family home.

When the Russians began to advance west, pushing the German army back towards their border, the teachers began to worry that they might be attacked and engaged the girls in daily drills the minute they heard the wail of the sirens. "We were so scared of the Russians, we heard bad things about them, how they pillaged and raped." By the end of the war there was little damage in the village, and the girls were sent back to where they came from. "We were in for a shock," Trudy said.

Otilia didn't know the details of how Trudy was reunited with her mother, but she knew they felt terribly scared living back in Berlin, three women alone. The period right after the war ended was one of terror—dangerous times for single women of all ages. Otilia was not privy to how Trudy had been able to immigrate to America, she only knew that when an opportunity presented itself, Trudy left Germany. Trudy felt revolted and shortchanged by having to exist in an autocratic and awful regime that prevented her from living freely and then having to survive among the ruins. "I wanted to live respectably in a new place where I could be a better human being," she said. In America, she desperately looked for ways to make up for missed opportunities.

▲ ▲ ▲

Trudy was wearing a gray-and-pink Chanel-style two-piece suit with a string of pearls. Her gray hair was cut blunt just below her ears. She was a strong woman who'd transformed her regrets into accepting her past and carried herself with a sense of dignity. She waited for Otilia to pick her up in front of her building, holding her head aligned with her spine and her shoulders back.

"So good to see you," Trudy said when she got into the car, placing her purse on her lap.

Otilia opened the door to the loft and helped Trudy go up the stairs to the airy living space. "Please come in and make yourself comfortable," Otilia said.

Otilia had placed slices of banana bread, small chunks of cut fruit, and scones with butter and jam on the coffee table. "What have you done?" Trudy exclaimed when she saw the display of food.

"We will have some tea."

Trudy settled herself into an armchair, and Otilia placed a pillow behind her back. Trudy reached out to squeeze Otilia's hand.

"Would you prefer coffee or tea?" Otilia asked.

"You are a very gracious host," Trudy said.

When Otilia returned from the kitchen carrying a pot of tea, she said, "Let's have something to eat, then I'll get my iPad and show you the photographs from our trip."

"This is delightful, Otilia, I've not been out for weeks—getting old is difficult."

"You're dressed so nicely," Otilia said and saw a smile on Trudy's face. "Is your arthritis acting up? I'll have to get you to our acupuncturist."

After Trudy had a few sips of tea, she asked, "Were you able to find the address I gave you?"

"I'm sorry, we didn't. We asked around but nobody knew where the street was; they told us so many street names had changed going way back."

"I understand, it was so long ago, and Berlin had to be rebuilt; it was in a state of complete destruction. As I grow older, I have recurring fantasies that one day someone will send me a picture of the building where I was born. But it hasn't happened yet. I can't remember it well, but I don't know why I keep thinking about that apartment building. Of course, it is unrealistic; the city was totally bombed and most of the people I knew then are dead," she said, her tone one of begrudging resignation.

"The city is beautiful now, with its canals, and transportation is excellent with easy access everywhere," Otilia said. Then, looking straight into Trudy's eyes, she added, "The Berlin you knew is different today . . . I understand how, when you lived there, life must have been very bleak."

"Times when the leaders were thugs," Trudy said.

"We went on a bike tour, saw a lot," Otilia said. "We visited a church that was left partly in ruins as a reminder of the war."

"The Kaiser Wilhelm Memorial Church. They retained the spire of the old church and Berliners nicknamed it the Hollow Tooth," Trudy said.

Her blue eyes seemed to gaze into the distance. "I remember the horse-drawn wagons on our street."

"You don't see any of them today, Trudy. Why don't you tell me about the building where you were born?" Otilia said.

"I remember the steel-gated arched entrance leading to the center square surrounded by several six-story buildings. There was a sandbox. We lived on the third floor, no elevator. I don't know how many bedrooms there were, but I recall the large bathroom and the toilet with a tank mounted high on the wall. I was afraid to sit on the hard seat as it was much too wide for a three-year-old's bum. I was fascinated by the long chain that my mother forbade me to touch. I would run away before she flushed, and the water began to flow into the bowl. What if I fell? I didn't know where I'd go if I was sucked in. And we had a large water heater to fill the bathtub. Every Saturday my father would use wood to fire it up so the family could take baths."

"I come from a culture where we had hot springs practically in our backyard, and if we could, we would jump in the hot water every day," Otilia said.

"Oh, Otilia, while you were away, I recalled this South American girl I met when I lived at the children's home. She was from Chile; her family lived in the southern part of the country and were from German background. When the war broke out, her father wanted to help Hitler—imagine that! The family came to Germany, where the father enlisted in the military, leaving the mother and children with relatives in the village where I was."

"How did you meet her?"

"She was around thirteen years old, and she played piano beautifully. She came to give concerts. She played along with our school orchestra."

"Did you play an instrument?"

"No, I had no talent. I was involved in sports. This girl, Johanna was her name, was shy. Didn't talk much, her German was poor. One day she stayed for lunch and sat at my table. We asked her to teach us some Spanish."

"I knew that Nazis went to South America after the war, but never heard that they went from South America to Germany to help in the war effort," Otilia said.

"I guess that isn't written up in the travel books, but Hitler had a program called 'back home to the Reich' and was happy to accept South Americans with German ancestry."

"I wonder what happened to them."

"I read that South American Germans came mostly from Chile and Argentina, and when the war was over, they returned to their countries with their tails between their legs."

"I'm intrigued by how people make peace with themselves after that type of life," Otilia said.

Trudy didn't answer and Otilia went to get her iPad. She picked up a chair from the dining room table and brought it over to sit closer to Trudy.

▲ ▲ ▲

Jerry had returned from the gym when Otilia arrived home, back from delivering Trudy. "How was your visit?" he asked.

"Trudy always baffles me with her stories. As always, she is very apologetic for her life, expressing regret for having been a child of the times and how happy she is that she will be buried in America."

"She actually says that?"

"She seems to tire easily and is a bit confused, trying to grapple with her memories and alleviate her personal sufferings. She was not interested in looking at so many photographs."

After Otilia cleaned the tea dishes, they moved to the living room to sit on the couch.

"We talked about the German people apologizing for the genocide, and she lamented that there should have been apologies to the innocent German people who were taken advantage of."

"The only ones to apologize to her would have been her parents. They were the ones who made bad choices," Jerry said.

"She feels that when her mother was alive, it was common for people not to talk about the war. That generation expected their children to get on with their lives. She regrets not having the opportunity to talk to her mother about how she survived. Although she says she has overcome her hurt, I think Trudy is still troubled."

"She lived through a period she could not control," Jerry said.

"She lost her family, was molded by frightful values, and carried her silence alone. She's only started to tell her story recently and hasn't moved forward. Now she seems to be haunted by memories she'd rather forget."

"It's too bad she didn't visit Germany. Maybe then she could have made some peace with her past."

# CHAPTER 27

## Lima, Peru;
## The East Bay, California, 2015

"An Empty Place of Memory," the headlines announced one Saturday morning in March, when Joachim Gauck, the German President, arrived in Lima for the inauguration of a memorial space. A controversial idea since its inception, but as the tide turned, after a period of much discussion, the site to be known as Lugar de la Memoria, la Tolerancia, y la Inclusión Social (The LUM)—Place of Memory, Tolerance, and Social Inclusion—was built. The word "museum" wouldn't appear in its name to ease tensions and address the issues brought forth by advocates of various political sentiments. An offer of a German monetary donation had come through early on, around 2008, but a feisty government had declined it. After a change in administration, the idea of creating a space to provoke thoughtful understanding of past events was welcomed. Construction took time, and still the building stood barren of contents, waiting for its purpose to be hammered out.

Mr. Joachim Gauck, a former Lutheran pastor, came to prominence as an anticommunist civil rights activist in the former East Germany. He did not enter politics until 1990, when he became involved in examining the German Democratic Republic dictatorship, hunting past communist secret service Stasi agents and exposing their crimes. Recently the German press called him "the president of hearts," as this son of a Soviet Gulag prison survivor was one of the founding members of the Prague Declaration on European Conscience and Communism, and a great defender of freedom and human rights. Today, he'd come to Peru to promote the importance of bolstering historical memory to close the wounds left by war and give voice to the victims of conflict. But his appearance reawakened the heated debate, impelling some people to come face-to-face with the past, while others were indifferent.

For years, senior government officials had resisted building a structure as a reminder of what had occurred, but after much public pressure from intellectuals and human rights advocates favoring the idea of a public place to memorialize the internal war, they pulled it off. How should the story be told? What to include in the space? Whose point of view should it present? Would the space be a place of remembrance to pay respect to lives lost or would it only recount the historical facts? There were so many questions. Yet the overarching one was how to arrive at a consensual truth.

▲ ▲ ▲

Carmen called Salvador to the living room to watch the televised broadcast of the inauguration. She was excited, as she'd worked for the Truth and Reconciliation Commission. One of their first recommendations to move the country ahead was to rectify past bitterness among citizens. A memorial would be the right step.

An imposing three-floor concrete structure placed at the edge of a

cliff facing the Pacific Ocean came into view when Salvador came to
sit next to his wife.

"Designed like a tomb emerging from the earth," a reporter
informed while he stood on the curb as a motorcycle raced past. "The
building is meant to evoke memory, in a broad sense. It is designed as
a reflection of a pre-Columbian system of terraces and fields in sloping terrain."

"Built among the ravines, stark but beautiful with such defined
lines—and look at the theater," Carmen said as the camera zoomed to
the auditorium.

The camera angle changed from a long shot to a close-up of a well-
known anchorman. "We have just learned that our President Ollanta
Humala will not be accompanying the distinguished foreign dignitary
to the inaugural ceremony," he said.

The focus went to hundreds of protestors who had taken to the
streets, contained behind concrete dividers, agitatedly moving their
arms holding signs denouncing the German president meddling in
the country's internal matters.

"Germany—your money is wasted on us," Carmen read. "Can you
believe this crap," she said.

"What an embarrassment," Salvador said.

"His attendance is seen as controversial, polarizing the debate to
the president's political detriment," the anchorman said.

"I knew it," Salvador said. "Humala is an ex-army colonel, too
closely tied to the armed forces to graciously accept Mr. Gauck's
presence."

"They're still reluctant to own up to it," Carmen said.

"Sure, they don't want to risk taking responsibility for the violence they inflicted on their own people for fear of losing support,"
Salvador said.

"It will be a museum, a cultural center, a place of reconciliation and
reflection on the Shining Path's reign of terror. We will open it up for

discussion, since for some of our citizens there is an intense discomfort in talking about what occurred," the museum's point man said.

"Will the museum show the struggle of reclaiming the land, rebuilding homes, mending relationships?" the news anchor asked.

"The specific content of our special exhibits is still under review," the spokesperson said.

The reporter who'd been at curbside was back on view, skipping up the staircase to the roof deck. "Here we are on the Balcony of Anguish, a place for visitors to reflect as they gaze out to the open sea."

When a second reporter approached him, he said, "I agree with my colleague, not discussing the role of the military in the conflict gives rise to suspicious behavior. This is not what a democracy is about, President Humala must show he is governing in the interest of all, not that he owes loyalty to the military. This museum is meant to not only to remember the past but to explore the notion of truth. It will take on the task of representing and instilling a sense of memory for its visitors. It's meant to give the viewer a feel of what people went through, a public condemnation of violent times. But, as of now, with no exhibits on the floors, the notion of truth remains a conundrum, and our society polarized."

Carmen and Salvador exchanged glances.

The camera moved to focus on Mr. Gauck, who was sitting next to several government ministers on a stage. He rose and walked up to the podium to take the microphone. "Ladies and gentlemen," he said. "I don't come here very often, and we Germans want to stand by your side. I would like to share with you our experiences and tell you how we were able to strengthen our nation by discussing our past."

The German president told the audience that Germany concealed its atrocities at first and not until the late 1960s did it begin to question issues of responsibility and guilt. "Where were the parents during the Hitler regime, the new generation asked, and we were forced to speak." He talked about the process of moving from fragmented remembrances to a collective culture of memory and how building memorials did not break his nation.

"Good speech," Carmen said after the speaker was shown going back to his seat. "Are we under the illusion that in Peru they will recognize that there is no future for the country without considering our past?"

A second speaker followed the German president, and these were his words: "It's not about placing blame, it's about having an understanding of what occurred and accepting responsibility. Turning a blind eye on past events is unhealthy, as what is buried will resurface in the next generation. History needs to be observed from all points of view"—he looked at the audience and continued—"also those of the victims."

"It remains in one's DNA. Those that experience turmoil will carry the consequences for their lifetime and maybe pass it on to generations to come," Carmen said, shaking her head.

"If the concept of a museum sounds daunting, it's because for sure it is. Officials here are still grappling with the complexities of memorializing armed conflict," said the reporter who came on the screen.

Reporters clustered around the German president as soon as the ceremony was finished, and Carmen went to turn the television broadcast off.

Salvador tiptoed to his son's room, took a peek, and saw his baby peacefully stretched out on his back in his crib. In his heart all he wished was that Manuelito would be able to thrive in an untroubled world.

▲ ▲ ▲

Otilia looked at her watch and went to prepare dinner while waiting for Jerry to arrive. When she heard the sound of his key turning in the lock, she hurried out to tell him the news.

"I got an email from Salvador saying the opening ceremony of the new museum of memory took place today, and he attached a video of the German president's speech. I'd like us to watch it together."

"Give me a few minutes."

Gripping her iPad, her chin jutting forward, Otilia opened her email and waited for Jerry on the couch.

"It will be exciting for you to see the finished building. Here is the chance to showcase your history," Jerry said as he sat beside her.

She felt her heart race as an unsettled feeling overwhelmed her when she heard the German president's voice.

"I feel anxious," she confessed after they'd watched the piece.

"Why? Aren't you pleased that old transgressions will be redeemed?"

Suddenly she burst into tears. She hadn't cried this hard for months.

Jerry placed one arm on her shoulders and pulled her closer into his chest. Looking him straight into his eyes while sniffing, she said, "Nobody's realities can be fictionalized."

"Listen, my love, people's memories fade away over time; this way they will be put in place."

"No two people experienced the same thing."

"Museums are a place where people can discuss and question, they can keep history alive. Those that were skeptical that events took place can be awakened to the facts."

"It will be *their* stories," she said, sitting upright.

"What do you mean? Whose stories?"

"The dominant class. It'll be political, just watch."

"Museums are a trustworthy source, it'll encourage interaction. You have to understand that there is a partnership of historians, curators, architects, and members of the community who have a vision and a perspective to make it as factual as possible. It'll attract people from all walks of life and all over the world, and they'll walk away with new knowledge and a better understanding."

"A place for tourists, is that what it's supposed to be? Another commercial venture? Terrorism tourism?"

"What's wrong with that?"

"What do you mean what's wrong? Making money out of our tragedy? Making a mockery of terrorism? That is wrong. Nobody will care or understand what I went through."

"I know what you're thinking, how when we were in Germany, we looked at some sites with a mixture of lurid fascination and disgust," Jerry said.

"I hope it will be a public condemnation of a violent past."

"Let me tell you about this one exhibit at the Museum of Memory in Santiago de Chile, where the visitors can deeply engage. Try to imagine walking down to an underground room. You take thirty-three steps, open the door, and you are in total darkness. The doors are locked shut. You can't leave the space. Hundreds of silhouettes of heads gradually light up on a screen. You find yourself standing among the victims, some who died, some who disappeared, others who are alive. You stand there for three minutes. When the doors open up, you can walk directly outside into the light. This installation is called *Geometry of the Conscience*, and it's a powerful memorial to the Chileans who are alive today, trying to understand the consequences of history," Jerry said.

Otilia was silent.

"Visitors will interpret the stories they see, especially those which give rise to an emotional response. Exhibitions must seep into people's consciousness to teach valuable lessons, even if the collective memory reduces events to a myth."

"We'll wait and see," Otilia said.

# CHAPTER 28

## Lima, Peru, 2015

The following weekend, on Saturday night, Salvador and Carmen would step out to attend Salvador's seventeenth class reunion. They'd cancelled their fifteenth due to poor attendance, and the social committee didn't want to wait until their twentieth anniversary for a gathering. Salvador had remained friends with a few of his classmates but hadn't seen others since their tenth reunion, and tonight would be a great time to reconnect. The social committee had rented an old colonial mansion turned into a restaurant in a bohemian neighborhood; the place would be theirs until the early hours of the morning.

Carmen was wearing a tight, low-cut black dress with a slit up the leg and doing her makeup when Salvador entered the room with an ironing board under his arm. "You look gorgeous. The dress fits you like a glove," he said after giving a whistle.

"I hope the night won't end with you guys playing cards and the women having to gossip while sitting at one side."

"Why don't you try Mahjong," Salvador said as he ironed his white shirt.

"Will you be bringing the tiles?" she asked.

"Too heavy. I promise we'll come home early," Salvador said.

▲ ▲ ▲

A glass chandelier hanging low illuminated the beautiful polished wooden floors at the entrance. A doorman escorted them up the open marble staircase to a room on the second floor, furnished with overstuffed armchairs and heavy antique pieces. Salvador picked up a sheet with the list of his graduating class from an ornate baroque table and stopped for a moment to study it. Two of his classmates were listed as deceased; one, he knew, had died in a car accident, the other of cancer recently. He looked past dark paintings of historical figures that hung on the wall and saw his friend Mario. He couldn't recall when he had talked to him last—precise dates were becoming difficult to recall. He had given him a call at his law practice to ask for advice on obtaining an attorney when the Reparation offices were first set up. Mario was one of his high school classmates who'd applied himself, had high aspirations, and done well. Family wealth had also helped.

Two waiters emerged through a swinging door from the back with trays of pisco sour and wine, while several waitresses walked around with trays of canapes. An instrumental piece hummed in the background as Salvador guided Carmen hand in hand across the room to mingle with classmates bestowing open smiles.

It was hot in the room, even though the ceiling fans ran at full speed, and one of the men yelled, "Let's open the windows." His wife went to pull the heavy curtains aside when a waiter quickly approached and said, "Miss, please let us take care of this."

Rafael gave Salvador a warm hug, slapping him on the back, "How have you been, *pata*? Up for tomorrow's game?" They still went out to play fútbol once a month.

Roberto came close and shook hands. With his gray sideburns and goatee, he appeared older than his thirty-five years of age. Perhaps it was due to the fact that he worked 24-7 in his family's demanding fruit wholesale business. Rumor was he never took breaks so as to afford to send his five children to private school.

Alberto was talking to Agustin when Salvador walked up to them, while Carmen moved over to chat with Sofia, Alberto's wife. Salvador and Alberto had been good friends in school, but after Alberto became a mining engineer working in the backcountry, they lost close contact.

During the cocktail hour, they and other classmates talked about their jobs and the great advances the country was forging.

"You've noticed the cranes. Have you seen how many there are?" Daniel said.

"Where are they?" Salvador asked.

"They are pretty hard to miss."

"The birds? Are they coming our way?" Salvador asked.

"No, my friend, we are talking about the machinery. Birds would make more pleasant sounds," another friend, Beto, replied.

"Do you know that there are no cranes in South America?" Salvador said.

"Thanks to the Chinese buying our minerals, our middle class is improving their quality of life," Alberto said.

"We are fortunate to live in a country that is on the rise."

"It's a boom, and I hope it'll last."

"Clearly the place to live with revenues going up, it's exciting to see our economy growing. And look how the food industry has put us on the map—a world-class cuisine we've got," Roberto said.

"Don't forget the world-class summer surfing competitions," Rafael chimed in.

"Just a minute, where did you guys get such damn foolish notions? Let's not paint such a rosy picture. There is economic growth reducing poverty overall, but still the rural poverty rate is close to fifty percent, and urban centers are riddled with crime due to impoverishment," Juan said.

"When did you become such a lefty?" Saul asked.

The head waiter announced that dinner would be served in the dining room, and Salvador went to fetch Carmen, who was engaged in an animated conversation with one of his classmate's wives. Carmen emptied her glass and stood to hook arms so that Salvador could escort her to their table.

They found their names on the folded place cards at a round table next to people they knew. Dinner unfolded in stages, with seafood appetizers and white wine coming first. Small plates of shrimp, mussels and clams were served with plenty of chopped onions, tomatoes, and cilantro. Later waiters brought out the reds to go with the goat stew on a bed of quinoa. By then the guests were relaxed, and conversation became more animated than ever—only to be interrupted by a photographer who came up to the table and asked the group to gather closer for a shot.

Mario wanted to know what people thought of the new museum to open in Miraflores and the inaugural speech given by the German president. The past was not the usual subject broached by this group, and Salvador was curious to know how they would react.

"Humala sure acted tough," Alberto said.

"Is that good or bad?" Sofia asked, needling him.

"The museum is about remembering. It's about interpreting the many stories," Mario said, raising his voice to get the attention of the group.

"The official, or the unofficial story?" Carmen said, exchanging glances with her husband.

"I have a problem with this—whose truth will they tell?" Agustin said. There was silence.

"So why wouldn't our President Humala attend the opening ceremony?" Alberto asked.

"Prosecutors filed charges against him for alleged human rights abuses to the Shining Path. Claims have arisen, the *milicos* are starting to panic," Roberto said.

"After all, Humala was stationed at an army base and committed violations against the civilian population. Wouldn't he be in a compromising position?" Salvador said.

"Or perhaps he's scared of offending the silent majority," Agustin said.

"I think you're right. He understands that he must play his cards carefully, and he'll see if this museum ever sees the light of day. I don't think it's a popular idea yet," Roberto said.

"Popular? Frankly, it's selective," Agustin said.

"What in the world does that mean?" Mario asked.

"You think people are going to be interested? They're not," Agustin said.

"It was a hopeless moment in our history, and we need to show we all did our best," Sofia said.

"We all were complicit," Carmen said.

"People knew what was going on," Sofia said.

"That's why it was good that we had a strong government that protected the people from terrorist activities," Agustin said.

"Fujimori was very aggressive; he countered terrorism in a brutal way," Mario said.

"Shining Path arose because they came from a place where people were exploited and dehumanized, denied a future, and that is what the museum will show," Carmen said.

"Getting back to Humala, he had a hand in the conflict; therefore, I don't believe he has any interest in disclosing what occurred at the time. He has a vested interest in keeping the events under wraps," Salvador said.

"Humala has disputed the claims. He became president in 2011, didn't he?" Agustin said.

"Yes he did, but that doesn't prove he wasn't guilty," Carmen said.

"The guerillas are despised. What they did was horrific," Agustin said.

"Gentlemen, let's not be judgmental—the only one here who can claim he had a real experience with violence is Salvador," Mario said.

"Some of us do as well," Sonia said shyly.

"Carmen has heard a lot of stories of terrible things that happened in people's lives. Haven't you, when you worked for the Truth and Reconciliation Commission?" Sofia said, turning to face Carmen with a glass of wine in her hand.

"That's one of the many stories that commie organizations pushed on us," Agustin said.

"Agustin Fierro, you should know better," Mario said.

"I'll be quiet then."

"I think it's important to have these conversations. Telling the truth is a social good. We must take into account that groups still discredit the work done by the Commission and denounce further attempts to document abuse. In the name of national security and economic growth, they're willing to grant perpetrators impunity. It seems to me that those people have developed amnesia, and it must be stopped," Carmen said.

"The truth is that some of us were oblivious to what went on—we were only kids," Sofia said.

"Do not say so. I heard a lot of stuff growing up," Clara said.

"I think people would now prefer to forget the facts," Carmen said.

"It's no wonder—with so much corruption around us, who can you trust? When I heard about Fujimori's government, that was an eye-opener, but it's still continuing," Roberto said.

"I, for one, studied history—and studied the official story at the time. What's recorded and given credence represents one point of view, the view of those who're victorious," Mario said.

"Now they want to discredit that version," Agustin said.

"You find that alarming?" Salvador said.

"Of course. They'll be responsible for tearing the country apart once again."

"No, they won't. There's a good reason we must talk about what went on because, let's be frank, there are always various versions. Let's look at Spain; silence prevailed in Franco's time and it lasted for years during his administration. Spaniards believed that it was best to create stability rather than pursue accountability. But it didn't last forever. Silence eventually became corrosive and now they've realized that a society can't bury its past forever. Consequences must be addressed at some point," Mario said.

"My father was in the army. He's a good honest man, was doing his job, thought he was doing the best for his country. Recently his boss was accused of criminal acts, and he is dragging my old man down with him," Sonia said, speaking very quietly.

"Tell us more," Agustin said.

All eyes were on Sonia, who realized she was revealing too much of herself. "I'm sorry, it's the alcohol talking," she said, bringing her hand to her thin lips, rising, excusing herself, and dashing out.

"Our stories, our collective memories, are important—what we know, what we believe, our fears, the dangers, the hate, the disgust, the anger we feel—are not to be dismissed," Carmen said, getting up from her chair to rush after Sonia.

"It's good for the new generation to have knowledge of that period in our history when life changed radically, when one day people were thrust into a different world and the word *terrorist* entered our vocabulary. But honestly, I think the term is being abused; we've distorted its image and it became cause for panicking. My parents have told me that when the Shining Path came onto the scene, neighbors stopped talking to one another, did not want to share information; in their distrust their only concern was if people shared their same ideologies, then they would open up," Sofia said.

"If they had become good *fujimoristas*, they would have trusted the rightful authority," Agustin said.

"Look who's talking—one who was safe in his gated home, up on the hills," Alicia said.

"I agree this is a topic that needs discussion. Unfortunately, for many it's a closed theme, *un tema cerrado*, a shame," Mario said.

"Elimination? Is that what it's all about?" Carmen asked.

"A page from Fujimori's playbook," Roberto said.

All but Agustin and Clara laughed. "Elimination" had been the term the authoritarian government of Alberto Fujimori misused to conduct operations to eradicate terrorism against suspected leftist rebel members, with the approval of senior officials. Elimination denoted getting away with illegally profiting from their positions of power for their own interest. Alberto Fujimori and his chief advisor and head of the National Intelligence Service, Vladimiro Montesinos, created a deep and wide network of thousands of people at every level of government, the military, and the business community who supported them and were kept on their special payroll.

"What happened to the refrain of 'Honesty, Technology, Work?' It turned out that they eliminated that ethos for the common good, and only Fuji and his buddies were able to stash away money in foreign accounts," Roberto continued.

"Good that all of their shenanigans have been exposed," Alicia, Mario's wife, said.

"Memorials are always politically charged," Mario said.

"Only Salvador remembers the details, the emotions he felt. Let's hear from him how he feels about a museum of memory at this time," Sofia said.

"Unfortunately, I am still not fully done with my past, but as for the new space, I am fully on board," Salvador said.

"Will our society become more just?"

"By building a museum, certainly not, but we need to have a

meaningful conversation about the events that took place—denial is an affront to our times," Mario said.

"The museum is a product of the left; too much attention will be placed on the terrorist," Agustin said.

"Bullshit. There is a need to create a reliable historical record of past abuses. But they have to be smart. They can't use the same enemy images that created distrust and suspicion, can't use the same rhetoric that created fear and anxiety in the general population. We need to portray leftist terror as well as the retaliatory terror of the army and police," Mario said.

"Are you making a good income defending those guys?" Agustin asked.

"We need to acknowledge the humanity of the adversary for us to coexist in a democratic society. We must debate and understand other points of view," Mario responded, ignoring Agustin's mockery.

"But why do you need a building—a great piece of architecture? Why not an online database with lots of material to help those who seek knowledge appreciate the tragedy virtually," Clara said.

"Not such a great idea." Mario shook his head.

"I think that's brilliant," Agustin said, turning to his wife with a smile on his face. "Video games to teach about wars, that's exciting."

"I read about a Czech company developing a game simulating the war in the Balkans, where players experience how things played out," Clara said.

"It's madness. That's the talk of a rich, educated fool. What about those who are illiterate? Do they have computers? Do they play games on their phones? Everyone should be confronting the past, whether you believe one side or the other," Mario said.

"Look here, by now we have plenty of evidence that both sides behaved badly. Both sides ignored the rules governing democracies and took wide liberties interpreting directives that benefited them without being held accountable," Salvador said, leaning to one side to allow the waiter to clear his plate.

"The museum will bring about divisions that will lead to confrontations and reopen deep wounds. For some, the museum is seen as favoring the terrorists," Alberto said.

"You are in favor of leaving past crimes and criminals alone to continue on?" Carmen asked.

"It's . . . it's not the guerillas they are celebrating, far from it—it's the brave people that were in the way," Mario said.

"But some cooperated," Agustin said.

Mario shrugged. "Bad decisions."

"Why rub salt into the wounds when the country's moved on?" Clara said.

"Secrecy is for fools," Roberto said.

"It's a stunt, attention drawing promoted by those who want to shed light on the conflict to optimize their claim, grab the opportunity for claiming their stake. We won't let the Shining Path get away with being heroes, showing how great a commitment to their cause they had. *Sendero*, after all, was insidiously oppressive."

"In my humble experience, the disappeared have gotten a bad rap—at times, the word *disappeared* has become synonymous with rebel sympathizer and considered an internal enemy, whereas many were not. I experienced this in my search for my dad. We need to clarify concepts, assign the disappeared the respect they deserve," Salvador said.

When dessert arrived, Carmen returned to the table with Sofia by her side. Carmen helped Sofia settle back in her chair next to her husband, Roberto, who reached out to hold her hand.

"I see you are talking about my favorite subject: the notion of inequality. I believe that in order to develop a shared history and be able to turn the page on this painful chapter, there must be a recognition of those who were greatly hurt. These were mostly people who'd had unequal opportunities, devalued for generations. People should be equally free, regardless of their differences. Hopefully, the museum will try to ensure it covers multiple points of view and experiences. The army might be considered heroes to some but not to the thousands of victims who suffered human rights abuses. There are multiple ways of looking at history, and each group wants to understand the events through their own lens. Exhibitions will tell about the experiences lived by all sides equally," Carmen said as she took her place next to Salvador.

"I agree, we have to support the idea. We live in a democracy that recognizes the past," Mario said.

"You bet your booty we do," Agustin said.

▲ ▲ ▲

Before the night was over, they all raised a glass to thank the organizers for the opportunity to reconnect with friends they'd lost touch with. Once Carmen and Salvador were in their car, they knew who they did not want to see again.

"A very opinionated group," Carmen said.

"I'd forgotten how some of them can talk your ear off," Salvador said.

"I didn't know Agustin Fierro was such a conservative," Carmen exclaimed.

"I think he became right-wing when he received an inheritance. Rumor has it that he was able to go to medical school, and do a specialty in France, after getting the funds."

"Did you notice how elegantly he dressed? A designer suit and golden cufflinks? He reeked of Paco Rabanne," Carmen said.

"He's an arrogant ass, thinks himself a step above the rest. I overheard him talk incessantly about buying an apartment right on the beach in Ancon. It was good of you to rush after Sofia by the way," Salvador said.

"I felt sorry for her; she does not seem the type who reveals much about herself. Talking about her family with a large group was difficult. She was very tense. When I reached her in the bathroom, she was about to pass out. She was flushed, her mascara was running, and she took her time freshening up after I gave her a few words of advice. She told me she carries a lot of shame about her dad. She has trouble coming to terms with who is considered the enemy. She feels her father was not to blame. A guerilla accosted his commander, held him at gunpoint, and her father had no alternative but to shoot, for otherwise both he and his commander would have died."

"Everybody has become traumatized," Salvador said, reaching out to hold Carmen's hand.

"I told her I wanted to see her again, see if I can be of help."

Salvador nodded in agreement.

# CHAPTER 29

## Lima, Peru, 2016

Otilia and Jerry were still on San Francisco time the day after they arrived in Lima and woke up later than planned. Otilia took a quick shower and dressed for the gray, cool October day. While applying makeup, she noticed her worry lines and tired-looking face. She brushed her hair, applied her lipstick, and rushed downstairs to get something to eat before leaving for the LUM. The museum, known as the Place of Memory, Tolerance, and Social Inclusion had opened its doors the year before, and today Carmen and Salvador were taking them to visit the site.

Salvador was leery about checking out a museum that was considered political, as much of the uproar that had arisen was over how Peruvian society should remember *that* time. But they had decided it was imperative that they should visit as a family.

"Breakfast is ready," Carmen said as soon as she saw Otilia coming down the hallway. The smell of simmering onions drifted in from the kitchen.

Carmen carried a platter of omelets to the dining room table and Luisa, who still helped the family out, followed with a basket of fresh buns and a pot of coffee.

Manuelito rushed in and went to sit next to Otilia with a bag of Lego bricks, which he dumped on the table. "Help me, *nana*," he said as he began to arrange the Legos according to color.

Otilia picked up a few bricks, put them together, and helped Manuelito stack them on top of his. She told herself to stay calm and not to look upon the visit with trepidation. It might be a slightly disquieting experience to watch and read information about what she'd lived through, but the exhibits were meant to bring to life evidence of the times. Hopefully there would be lessons to learn about restoring broken relations between victims and perpetrators to avoid repetitions down the road. She wanted to excuse herself from joining the others and stay home with the child, but she knew that wouldn't be right. Otilia then wondered whether the exhibits had been designed to shock or inform.

"I've been thinking that I have no childhood memories of those years. Nothing sticks in my mind," Salvador said when he took his seat at the table.

"You were too young to have understood the big picture. You just remember what you went through," Otilia said as she picked up her cup.

"Design is the key element of an exhibit," Jerry said. "Installations and presentations make a great difference to how the viewer will react. Maybe something will trigger a memory you might have kept hidden in your mind."

"Making the case that people were as much victims of Peruvian society as wicked perpetrators of crimes have infuriated some. You know that when areas of the country began to sink into chaos, when a community was terrorized, some folks were coerced to participate while others willingly joined the Shining Path. Curators are very concerned about making the visitor aware of the social context of the conflict, as the lines between who were the participants and who were victims became blurred when violence spiraled," Carmen said as she prompted Manuelito to drink milk from his glass.

People were wary that the manner in which the events were to be portrayed could be used for political aims, but press releases had made it clear that the exhibits convey the notion that there were no simple truths to explain the root cause of the problems that led to calamitous outcomes.

"It's about the need to give both sides a voice in an effort to make them see each other not as bad or good but as human beings caught in distressing and disadvantaged circumstances. People's memories over time are blurred, and the curators have made sure to show various perspectives about a single incident," Carmen said.

"I've read that activists have complained that versions of memory were carefully constructed to fit a particular bias. We shall see what we think," Jerry said.

▲ ▲ ▲

They parked in a lot close to the building and walked silently towards the museum. Before entering, they stopped to contemplate the modern tomblike structure with exposed rough concrete walls, sitting below the steep dirt cliffs facing the ocean. In the main lobby, they were guided to the registration counter, where a middle-aged man with a gold-capped front tooth explained that he needed to record their names. Entrance was free of charge. Otilia glanced down the hall to where a subdued display chronicled the events that had changed the course of her life.

*La Lucha Armada*—The Armed Struggle—depicted in the pavilion entitled "Origins of Violence," detailed the movement of the Maoist rebels who launched a plan of action to defeat the old order to bring revolution to the people. It explained how leaders were able to mobilize the masses and militarize followers to form a new state. Propaganda posters and accounts of rebel attacks were featured prominently. Next came information on how government forces stepped up their action to combat the enemy within.

"They could have averted this," Otilia whispered to Salvador as she went to stand by her son. She felt a lack of sympathy for both sides. "Why couldn't they have negotiated?" she asked.

While staring at the images, Otilia tried to shake off festering memories about how she set out on foot to search desperately for her husband and child the day after they hadn't shown up. How she walked through the streets of her village and the hills beyond to eventually get to police headquarters to file a missing person's report. "Another disappearance," the officer taking her report said with indifference when he looked up the records and discovered that there had indeed been a Shining Path attack reported in the village that night. Rumors had circulated that the authorities showed little interest.

Otilia followed Salvador down the corridor, feeling the rage the memories gave rise to. She looked at a photo of government soldiers showing no mercy towards a pregnant mother holding a child in her arms, while one of the soldiers pointed his rifle directly at her baby. It rattled her more than she had expected, and she began to walk through the halls with unexpected dread. She knew the history well, so why was she feeling so frightened? She was puzzled by the strong emotions she felt. She went to stand next to Jerry and took his hand and whispered, "Please stay by my side." Jerry released her grasp and slowly began to caress her back.

In the next room Otilia looked at a couple touching an interactive touch-screen map locating how many people were killed and disappeared throughout the country. She couldn't look at the horrifying figures. Disgusted, she asked Jerry to keep moving. "It gives me a chill; I can't comprehend death on that scale."

Photos, videos, artifacts, and news clippings provided a sense of how "One Village, Many Villages" were affected by the actions of the day. Neither Salvador nor Otilia nor Carmen wanted to hear all of the audio recordings of victims, and Jerry decided that his Spanish wasn't good enough to understand all the nuanced stories. "It's too bad there is no English translation," he said.

They followed the gradual sloping ramp upwards to the installations on the next floor, where tucked away in the back, in a twenty-foot-high cubicle with small showcases on all four sides, individual memorabilia was displayed. Clothes and blankets, photographs, watches, identification cards of victims who'd disappeared at the time gave evidence that they had lived. Visitors had left candles and flowers to remember their loved ones. "Unlucky victims of circumstances deserve respect," Carmen said,

In the section titled "Una Persona, Todas Las Personas"—"One Person, All of the People"—each of them placed headphones over their ears and stood in front of the individual hanging flat screen suspended from the ceiling to listen and see a human scale body of a person giving their testimony. Otilia apprehensively stood face-to-face to listen to a young man's story.

"This is very well done; each of us is worthy of being heard," Jerry said once he'd removed his headphones and had gone to stand next to Otilia. "It certainly gives the visitor a good idea of what people had to contend with."

"So many narratives. Different folks with their own stories," Carmen said as she reached for Otilia's hand.

Otilia felt impatient to leave and moved through the last display at a faster pace. "I don't need to see more," she told Jerry when he caught up to her. "I'll wait outside."

"I'll come out with you." Jerry said, stepping out onto the "Balcony of Anguish," the open-air roof patio overlooking the sea.

"It's good to breathe a little fresh air," Otilia said, taking a deep, long breath.

Salvador came out and muttered, "This is our sad history. It's hard to explain the magnitude of the events."

"I'm drained," Carmen said when she joined them. "It's so true how during that time every public service deteriorated, people's moral values changed, and everyone was out for themselves."

"Was all the trouble we went through for naught?" Salvador said.

"At least the exhibits will allow for conversations to take place. Brutal situations will be analyzed and hopefully continue to be addressed," Carmen said.

"This museum is important," Jerry said. "People have a responsibility to remember the events of the past and break the silence. I am the child of people who lived through the Holocaust and, when I was young, stories like these ones were not discussed. It's taken seventy years for Germany to pay homage to those who suffered injuries. History becomes distorted when an entire group's memories are not taken into account."

"This museum is meant for our children so they will not suffer like I did," Salvador said.

"I am pleased this place exists so we can bring Manuelito when he is older. He needs to know our history," Carmen agreed.

"It's a place that honors the survivors and the dead," Jerry said.

"The drama and the ambiguity of the conflict is still with us. I think they did a fair job displaying people's pain." Carmen nodded her approval.

"What is unusual is that one of the museum's focal points is to show how the past shaped what took place and to question how the country should move forward. The curators want to point out that reconstruction and redress are as important as the destruction itself," Jerry said.

When they left the museum, the clouds had moved, clearing the sky, and as Otilia felt the sun shining upon her gloominess, she felt happier. They walked back to the car, and Salvador suggested they stop for a bite on his way to his office.

▲ ▲ ▲

Once back in their home, Carmen and Otilia went to check on Manuelito, who was content playing with a young neighbor in his room. This bright, active child had come into the world and was linked to her family's past, Otilia thought as she remained by the door watching the boys. Sighing, she was thankful that children now lived in better times.

Before going into the living room, Otilia stopped to look at the photographs displayed on the wall in the hallway. As she studied a particular one of Carmen, Salvador, and herself, looking much younger at a nearby mountain resort, where they'd gone to get away from Lima's winter fog, it surprised her how fast the years had slipped by.

"The way that a country presents itself to the outside world is important to its international and national identity, and by opening this museum, Peru will be considered more of a democracy," Otilia heard Jerry saying when she joined them in the living room.

"For me, the museum confirmed what I knew, and I hope that for a visitor it will be a revelation—a testament of what took place. If the objective is to trigger remembering, I think it fulfills the purpose," Carmen said.

"What is gratifying is that it clearly portrays the abuse that took place during Fujimori's corrupt dictatorship. It gives me great satisfaction to know that Fujimori, the all-powerful president, sits in jail, powerless," Salvador said.

"Time and time again we see how social issues, financial hardship, moral confusion and leaders who behave in questionable ways can lead a country astray," Jerry said.

Carmen frowned in thought. "How the opposition will understand is anybody's guess. Each of us sees the world with our own prejudices," she said. "Some people believe that this wasn't their war; they were apolitical and didn't participate. And since they sat on the sidelines, they have trouble appreciating those who suffered and still struggle with its aftermath."

"I wonder if transmission of history is a curse or a legacy. Does it provoke anxiety or is it a source of inspiration to make the world a better place?" Jerry tilted his head at Carmen.

"Historical memory is a movement," she replied. "Countries need it to remember, it can't be ignored. Telling their story is an act of redemption."

"I want the next generation to know their past," Salvador said.

▲ ▲ ▲

The next day Otilia felt a great need to escape to a solemn place. While alone in her bedroom behind a closed door, she straightened out her belongings and made the decision to go to church. She felt drained of energy, both angry and saddened after yesterday's visit to the museum.

Rarely these days did she think of going to pray, but today she felt a great need to be on her own, to reflect on how her society had let her down. In prayer she could alleviate her hurt.

When Jerry entered the room, Otilia told him she wouldn't be long. He didn't argue, instead wrapping his arms around her waist to hold her close. She kissed him and remained in his embrace with her head nestled on his chest. "It's hard," she said, moving closer. He squeezed her body, offering his silent support.

Otilia released a long sigh. She longed to understand how it had all come to pass, how their lives had become so complex.

# CHAPTER 30

## The East Bay, California, 2016

I n Peru, where there was a culture of informality and a handshake was good enough to bind a contract, it was difficult to
believe that the courts would be able to solve the family's legal
argument. Accepting gifts and small courtesies was common practice
in a country where the penal code did not criminalize facilitation of
payments and, in some cases, bribes were imperative in exchange for
expediting paperwork. With a judicial system claiming they were
lacking resources, why would they want to hear their case?

The family trusted Sr. Malfi, a well-meaning advisor who proudly
stated he formulated strategies to put forward various angles in a dis-
pute. But he'd not been able to convince the current owners of Otilia's
property that they should be placing a joint case against the municipality for breach of contract, as they had in effect purchased stolen
property. The current owners claimed they were an Evangelical presence in the community, providing Christian service, and they were
there to stay. Their lawyer had stated that they had no intention of
getting involved in a court hearing, arguing that they justified their

ownership considering the substantial money they'd spent in mainte-
nance and improvements.

Sr. Malfi had written to the head of the public record office, stating
they had irresponsibly allowed for the transfer of property, only to be
told that the department always abided by high ethical principles and
procedures and would never have authorized such misconduct. Otilia's
allegation had been taken seriously and checked out properly, but after
a thorough investigation they were sorry to advise that there was no
proof of wrongdoing.

It had been four years since Sr. Malfi had alerted Otilia and Salvador
that new legislation was underway in regard to better protection of
property rights, but no such enactments were yet in sight. Otilia and
Salvador remained exasperated, and Sr. Malfi puzzled over this. Their
unflappable lawyer was now recommending that it would be best not
to continue throwing money away, and to consider dropping the case.

Salvador felt extremely discouraged and at the end of his rope,
pretty much convinced that if they sued the authorities, there would
be another long wait.

Otilia was in her office when she heard her cell phone ring. It was
Salvador calling her on FaceTime.

"I was with Sr. Malfi today, and it's not looking good. Judges are
having trouble managing caseloads and few courtrooms are being
made available. Time is a big roadblock, as the more time passes, the
less there is the will to proceed. In the final analysis, with our limited
evidence it makes it hard to know. Getting a guilty verdict against the
public record's department is not an absolute certainty. With our terms
so unclear, they will need to study the conditions that surrounded the
contract. Even if we win, it would take years to get the property back."
Otilia could see Salvador shrugging his shoulders.

"*No hay confianza.*" Otilia could hear Carmen's voice as she
appeared on the screen next to her son. "Sure, you can place the claim,
but rest assured, the government will not be implicated, as there's no

trust. Even though they may be well aware of their negligence, the Judicial will not make the municipality assume responsibility for what happened so long ago."

"Jerry's been reading about land reform in the *pueblos jóvenes* on the internet and found out that by 2007, more than three million properties in the shantytowns were titled for those who'd invaded public lands. They even provided the second generation with titles," Otilia said.

"I've read about it as well. Title to properties allowed people security from eviction, and squatters with titles could use homes as collateral to obtain loans to start businesses. Titles improved people's security and their economic outlook," Salvador said.

"And we've been left in the cold?" Otilia said.

"It might have been different if a neighbor had appropriated the land. But it was family, that's the issue. Even in the case of those who invaded lands, the government felt that it was good enough to have a family member offer their son or daughter an oral commitment and the land was theirs. Since they were family, nobody questioned them," Salvador said.

"Tomás—family? Ha! His actions were despicable. He never even apologized." Otilia didn't know why she should have expected him to do so.

"Let's talk tomorrow, we have to go now," Salvador said.

Otilia said goodbye to her children and felt irritated. *We've come to the end of the road*, she thought. She turned off her computer and, when the screen turned black, she reached for her coat.

▲ ▲ ▲

Otilia and Jerry had made arrangements to meet in the late afternoon at a Starbucks close to her office. When she walked in, music was coming over the sound system, and she saw Jerry sitting at a table by a window, looking at his phone. She felt the bustling energy of the room and wished they would be having their conversation in a quieter space. She waved and he smiled. She walked over to plant a kiss on his lips. Jerry had a paper cup with a latte, and she noticed a half of a scone on a plate. "I've left this for you," he said.

Otilia went to the counter to order and looked at the pastries on the display case but decided against them. She walked back to the table to sit across from Jerry, leaned closer, and placed both hands around the warm mug of mint tea. Jerry pushed the plate towards her. She felt tired and wasn't hungry; she just wanted to talk to Jerry before it got late and he had to rush out to his meeting nearby.

Tomás was a figure from the past, and she felt completely detached from him, but she was unable to imagine how he could have pulled such a thing. It was pure greed. The sale of her house to the church had been done speedily, and all of the legal back and forth over the years was overwhelming her. She was exhausted and recognized that prolonging the legal battle would be useless. She had known it all along, but hadn't been willing to admit it. Otilia felt a sense of anger and resentment brewing inside and didn't know where to begin. She paused to take a sip of her tea, lowered her voice as she scooted her chair even closer to Jerry and said, "I've just talked to Salvador and it's sad to say that the authorities failed to protect us. Nobody seems to hold any responsibility for what happened to us, and I am supposed to walk away."

"You should stop worrying; it does you no good, my darling. You are going to be all right."

"I can't stop," Otilia said, shaking her head.

"It's about the resources available."

"It was about the protection of our welfare. The government isn't handing out much, but in my case the property was downright stolen from me."

"Look, our family had to forget about obtaining compensation from the property owned back in Prague," Jerry said, trying to give perspective.

Otilia cast him a troubled look and exhaled. "You don't understand. That house was not an emotional place for you, you never lived there, you are from another generation."

"I see that there's a critical difference, but I carry loss at a cellular level. Sometimes the world is not a fair place."

"Don't talk to me about fairness. I see that both of our families were vulnerable, and our lives were altered due to the circumstances, but you are a generation removed. It was not your home that was lost, and you've learned about pain, guilt, and shame secondhand."

"I agree. Yours was a much more painful loss, but our similar stories bind us and believe me, I get it," Jerry said as he tilted his head to the side and looked at her earnestly.

After the collapse of the communist government, the Czech Republic enacted legislation to restore properties to their rightful owners. Miles's house had first been taken over by the Germans when they walked into Prague and, after the war, confiscated by the communist government. Property restitution was one of the conditions taken into account when the Eastern European countries applied to join the European Union after the fall of communism. In 1994 a law providing restitution of property taken by the Nazis from Holocaust victims required that claimants be Czech citizens and residents. Czech-Americans like Miles were not eligible for dual citizenship. In the year 2000 the Czech Parliament authorized the government to transfer unclaimed properties to the Jewish community. Miles did not receive any money but felt honored to obtain a certificate for his donation of the property to the community.

"I'll tell you a story I heard about friends of my father," Jerry said. "When the family submitted a claim for compensation in the 1990s, the ministry of finance imposed additional onerous conditions. They told the family they would have to prove that they were the rightful owners or heirs to the assets and that no claim had been filed before the communists came to power. That was more than fifty years ago—the descendants did not know the history of the property and there were no records available; everything had been lost during the Holocaust, and the current government had no clues. Then came disputes between competing claimants, since there were several tenants living there who couldn't be evicted. It took the family several years of lawsuits to be vindicated, but the government appealed the court's decision, afraid that a precedent would be set. After another number of years, with mounting costs to the family, they got nothing. The economy at the time was weak, the property was in horrible shape, and their nightmare had not been worth it."

"That's what I'm afraid of," Otilia said.

"There are frustrations and complexities in your case, but one never knows how a court would rule."

Otilia nodded.

"There is no equality in this world. You are owed fairness before the law but may never receive it," Jerry said. "When I was last in Prague, roaming around the neighborhood where my father's house stands, I looked at it and wondered how much it would be worth today. It's in a prime location. In a similar neighborhood in Paris or London, it would be worth millions. Today, of course, the Czech Republic is moving forward, and I'm sure it's worth a lot more than what it was worth then."

"That's not the case in the village where I came from," Otilia said.

"There are no simple answers for what route you should take. Restitution is a moral issue." Jerry sighed.

Otilia felt an overpowering need to burst into tears but made an attempt to contain them. She ran through a long list of occurrences she'd lived through. Quivering, crying, in between hiccups and above the chatter in the room, she apologized to Jerry.

Jerry went over to hug her, suggesting they gather their belongings to get ready to leave, and helped her rise. On the street they hugged. "I love you," he said when they parted.

As she walked back to her car, she started to cry again, but quickly decided she wouldn't let the combination of anguish and anger linger on. Otilia made a hasty sign of the cross to slow down her mind and clear it of all the ugliness. She vowed to start straight away with *un lavado de cabeza*—a personal brainwash, in order to carry on with living a healthier life.

# CHAPTER 31

## The East Bay, California; Washington, DC, 2016

The surprising chances that people living in different parts of the American continents would come together and become a family marveled them. Nothing would stop them, and now they were planning a get-together, possibly in the summer, in Washington, DC. They wished to connect and have conversations about the chain of events that led them to meet.

It was remarkable that when Jerry mentioned the plan to Otilia she became excited, and the more they discussed the time of year and place, the more meaningful the discussion became, as it was clear that social upheavals were the cause of their disconnects.

"A very special fellowship," she exclaimed.

"Do you think that Salvador and Carmen would be able to come?" Jerry asked.

"We should find out—the only consideration would be monetary," she said thoughtfully.

"It'll be our invitation," Jerry said.

"Are you sure?"

"I've given it thought and I think it's important we strengthen the family ties."

"Will you ask Franz to come from Prague?" Otilia asked.

"Yes, I thought I would write to ask if he'd like to come. I'm sure Dario would be thrilled. He likes information about the Czech side of the family."

After back-and-forth messages suggesting location and dates, it was decided that Dario and Mary Margaret would host the guests. They would meet in August in DC, as it would be the middle of winter and a slow month for Peruvians, as well as vacation time for those living in the United States. They would make memories together at the Alvarez's home on the Potomac River, where they would focus on togetherness and getting acquainted with one another.

Franz had responded that due to his poor health he would not be traveling, while Salvador and Carmen appreciated the financial help offered to them. They agreed to meet at National Airport where Jerry would rent a car and drive to a nearby hotel. They would spend time with their new family members and then take a few days to explore the nation's capital.

▲ ▲ ▲

Jerry and Otilia sat in the front of the car, Jerry driving, at ten in the morning on August 8. Manuelito sat in the back in a child's car seat between his mother and dad. Excited, the small boy chatted about the plane ride the previous day. "We played cards and I won all the games. I ate all of my chocolates."

"Oh no, that's not correct; I won some games too, don't you remember?" Salvador said.

Otilia had purchased a coloring book, and when the child got restless, she pulled it out of her bag. "These are some of the places we'll see," she said, turning her body towards Manuelito with her out-stretched arm.

"Thank you," Manuelito said as he took hold of a wrapped package with a ribbon.

"Look at these scented markers, take a smell," Carmen said as she removed the plastic from the box.

"How much longer?" Manuelito asked after he'd tired of coloring and doodling on a page.

"It will take a little bit longer," Jerry explained as he drove speedily along the highway.

"Let's count all the blue cars on the road," Carmen said when Manuelito put the book aside.

"There are more blue cars in Lima," he said after pointing at a few.

"Let's sing some songs for *nana* and *tata*," his mother said, and the three in the back started to sing.

Otilia turned to look at them as their voices rose in unison and Manuelito swayed from side to side. Otilia's heart felt full, seeing Salvador with his wife and her grandson enjoying themselves. She laughed. She was so pleased that Salvador had been greatly helped by the psychologist and he could once again engage with his family in positive ways.

▲ ▲ ▲

Dario and Mary Margaret, she in a palm-leaf print floor-length cream dress, and he in a matching shirt, waited on their wraparound porch by the front door to their home for their guests to arrive. The couple, married for more than forty years, had met at a party put on by the Spanish Department in their last year at the University of Maryland. They both had Spanish language in their backgrounds, since Mary Margaret had been brought to the States from Ecuador by her parents as a child.

Dario waved and indicated to Jerry where he should park. The family gathered their belongings and quickened their steps as they crossed the flowering garden to meet their hosts. Madelaine and Peter were just behind them. Introductions were made. They embraced and kissed each other's cheeks affectionately. Dario crouched down to offer Manuelito a high five, and the child was slow to react, unfamiliar with the gesture.

It was a hot, humid day, and Otilia felt her damp forehead. Mary Margaret, who had recently undergone cataract surgery to restore some of her vision, apologized for having to keep on her sunglasses to reduce the glare, while Carmen offered Mary Margaret the fancy wrapped package they'd brought. And after another round of embraces, Mary Margaret opened the front door and urged everybody to step inside.

It was cool in the house with the air conditioner blowing at full blast. From the room came sounds of soft jazz. Glancing around the spacious front room, Otilia noticed the beautiful wooden craftsmanship and modern paintings Jerry had told her about.

Dario escorted them to the family room where the guests milled around, while Mary Margaret went over to the kitchen to slice lemons from a pile, and Madelaine rushed to her mother's side to juice them. Peter placed ice into tall glasses, and Mary Margaret poured the fresh lemonade.

After a while, everyone was called to the dining room where there was a playful discussion by the younger members of the Alvarez's family about where they would sit. They would be ten adults and four children for a late lunch: Mary Margaret and Dario Alvarez, their daughter Madelaine with her husband Peter Murphy, and their daughter Paula, now seven years old; Dario and Mary Margaret's adopted son, William, and his wife, Grace, with their two children, Billy, eleven, and Sam, ten. William was Dario's nephew who'd come to live with the family when he was in his teens and now worked for the government. Dario and Mary Margaret's younger daughter, a physician working overseas, was not in attendance. Otilia, Jerry, Salvador, Carmen, and four-year-old Manuelito completed the gathering.

Once they took their seats at a long broad table laid out with a floral tablecloth and white dinner plates, Peter and Madelaine served mimosas.

"*Quiero jugo*," Manuelito yelled.

"You'll get your orange juice," Otilia said, bringing her index finger to her lip. "No need to yell."

Platters of antipasti with olives, cheeses, artichoke hearts, mushrooms, and cured meats were at either end of the table. Mary Margaret walked in with a basket of crackers and rolls in one hand and a bottle of champagne in the other.

Once they were seated, Dario lifted his glass to make the first toast. "To you who flew a long way to meet us. And to Milan, a.k.a. Miles, who is here with us in spirit—I want to thank him for our legacy. Miles, you were a smart man escaping from the horrors of the Second World War to build a good life for yourself in the American continent. I'm so sorry I never met you, a courageous and upright member of your community. I'm thankful you gave me a brother. To you, Jerry, you're a remarkable human being."

"Dario, I really don't deserve the praise," Jerry said, chuckling.

Salvador raised his glass. "*Salud*! I have to say that I feel I already know you. I've heard so much about you from Otilia and Jerry and seen you in photos and videos. I'm truly happy to be able to share this moment with you and have a chance to interact with my extended family."

When Otilia's turn came to speak, she told them that she would toast to the happiness she felt to have Salvador, Carmen, and Manuelito back in her life. "It could have been different if we hadn't met," she said, choking up. "My relationship with my family grows deeper each day, and Jerry's commitment to me is a dear gift. And now I find myself in the midst of meeting a new and beautiful family. Thank you so much for your lovely hospitality."

Jerry picked up his glass next. "Those who wanted to obliterate us couldn't achieve it. Now we have the proof: several generations here together. A family once again. We toast to our resilience."

"Jerry, I really want to thank you for cooperating with our request to undergo the blood test eight years ago. We were at a crossroad and you helped us when we needed you. I want to make a toast to you and to our beautiful daughter, Paula," Madelaine said.

Jerry stood and bowed, then proceeded to clap, and Madelaine asked Paula to clap to show her appreciation. One by one they stood and joined others clapping. Billy and Sam remained seated, clapping their hands on the table, and when the applause subsided and the adults turned to each other, raising their glasses and shouting "*salud*," the boys copied their elders, holding up their glasses of lemonade.

Once they were finished with their appetizers, Mary Margaret placed her napkin on her seat and headed to the kitchen to fetch a roast beef. Grace, a striking brunette, tall and slim with a warm manner, followed. She returned carrying a large platter of vegetables and roasted potatoes.

"You've gone to a lot of trouble," Jerry said, looking at Mary Margaret.

"My pleasure. You know I love to cook and was fortunate to have lots of help," Mary Margaret said, smiling at Grace.

After the roast and the vegetables were served, Dario began pouring glasses of red Malbec. Manuelito gobbled his meal before anyone else was finished.

Dario turned to Jerry and asked, "Now tell us, Jerry, where have your travels taken you lately?"

"I'm traveling less, staying closer to home, but was in the Czech Republic a year ago where I visited Franz, Miles's last living relative," Jerry said, looking at Grace and Madelaine. "His mother, Anna, passed away recently and, as I've mentioned, he's a recluse and was not up for the long trip to join us. But what I wanted to share is that when I'm in Prague, I have this curious experience—everything appears so strangely familiar. Mind you, I don't speak the language, but the way people speak, their mannerisms, their tone of voice, it's as if it all seems to be part of my culture," Jerry said, with a bitter laugh.

"I know exactly what you mean. When I went to Spain the first time, I felt I was familiar with their culture, for it held the best of the South American ways with a European flavor. Funny how for us children of immigrants, we carry the old country in our blood," Dario said.

"I have the same sense in Germany, where my mother came from, but it still does not mean that I would be comfortable living there," Jerry said.

Miles came up in their conversation over and over again, his astuteness, his strength to persevere through hard times, the way he threw himself deeply into his work, his cutting humor. His need to live in the present, casting aside memories of the past to fend off his suffering.

"He wanted to protect our family against misfortune, but he was not one who provided emotional comfort; for him it was all about finances. As I grow older, I can better understand where he was coming from," Jerry said.

"Do you still carry the burden of the Holocaust?" Peter asked.

"Interesting you should ask; only a Jewish person understands that particular context. You are a member of the third generation and still appreciate what it means. My answer to you is yes, I do. I do feel the burden of our people's history. When a tragedy hits, my first thought is, how would I have survived in the worst of situations as, for example, in a concentration camp? I know it's crazy, but it seems to be imprinted in my psyche. I guess I was told too many awful stories growing up. I'm haunted by those types of questions. Would I have run away? Killed myself? I find myself wrestling with those thoughts."

When conversation eventually veered toward Otilia's history, the children had left the table and gone to play on the lawn in the backyard with Peter's golden retriever. Otilia disclosed that, in the years after her husband and child disappeared from her life, she had many sleepless nights. Such uncertainty. Not knowing where they were tormented her. She'd spent months alone with no family or friends, with dreams shattered. She told them about her escape to the States and about her years trying to find her loved ones from abroad.

"And then I came back into her life," Salvador said.

"He was all grown up, had a wife," Otilia added, with a smile directed at Carmen.

"And that's me," Carmen said.

"Wasn't that a relief, to find him," Mary Margret said.

"Heaven sent, so exciting, but more than anything, a great consolation to know he had overcome an enormous burden. So much loss."

"Of course," Mary Margret said, looking straight across the table into Otilia's eyes.

"Weren't you in a panic?" Madelaine asked as she opened her blue eyes wide, smoothed down her hair, and tucked a few loose strands behind her earlobes. "I don't know if I could handle being separated from my child."

"It was extremely difficult for both of them. Otilia was very isolated and felt guilty, Salvador of course was troubled, not knowing about his parents' circumstances, moving through life the best he could. They are both strong people; they held it together remarkably well," Jerry said, wanting to veer the conversation to a different topic.

"We muddled along," Otilia said.

"An intolerable situation." Dario's forehead furrowed.

"Not knowing where your parents are is the worst that can happen to any child," Salvador said.

"When the mafia rules the world, you can't trust anyone. I searched and searched and found that every lid I would lift was in vain. Nobody bothered to help, the authorities claimed there wasn't any evidence that their disappearances had indeed taken place," Otilia said.

"They told you their disappearances weren't plausible?" Dario was aghast.

"You know how it is during warfare, when there's bloodshed—it was a chaotic time," Salvador said.

"They both had hard lives, but the crucial thing is that they've found each other, and our Manuelito has a grandmother and a step-grandad," Carmen said.

"But the government has apologized!" Jerry said, looking at Dario.

"They've only offered an apology?" Dario asked, flabbergasted.

"What about a recompense?" Peter said in his forceful voice.

"That's another long story without a happy ending," Salvador said.

Mary Margaret stood and stepped away from the table, and Madelaine and Grace followed.

The sun had moved towards the west, and they all went out on the deck. They stood to watch the spectacular views of the river as a blend of yellow, orange, red, and purple hues colored the sky. They'd forgotten about the children and found them engrossed watching a movie in the family room. Otilia looked at Manuelito picking up a handful of M&Ms from a bowl.

▲ ▲ ▲

Peter, a lawyer, approached Otilia when they gathered back in the living room. He was interested in talking to her about how Peru had dealt with compensating those who'd been displaced by the violence.

"I can't believe you've had so much trouble obtaining compensation. Didn't your country assign monetary figures to the various categories of suffering?" Peter asked.

She briefly explained how her lawyer had dealt with her claim, meeting fierce resistance from government authorities to their inquiries. How it had taken years before an evaluation had finally wrapped up. "I think they went through the motions and did what they'd planned to do from the start," Otilia said. "You see, the government preferred to give recompense to communities at large and didn't want to bother with individual situations."

"It must have been an emotionally draining process," Peter said.

"The big hurdle was our family falling out. I thought I'd be heard but found the Reparation office to be dismissive. They refused to take responsibility for our family's issue."

"Did you have another recourse?" Peter asked.

Otilia revealed the difficult situation they found themselves in and the approach they tried to take. "The amount of hours it took to delve into how my brother was able to steal our property from under us was tremendous. Dizzying paperwork. At the end nothing worked out, so finally, although we were reluctant to accept it, there came a time when Salvador and I decided not to endure further investigations or cross-examinations."

"I understand," Peter said.

"Our situation was complicated, as there was a history of trouble in the family business even before the conflict began. Then, when our main witness, the pastor of the Evangelical church that had acquired the property, became uncooperative, we had no recourse. With little evidence to back up the case and the bureaucratic culture in Peru unchanged, what could we do? Institutions are still corrupt, procedures are undermined, and we couldn't continue fighting them. There came a time when we didn't want to incur further expense."

"You must have been incensed that the system wasn't working for you and the mistakes weren't corrected."

"Sometimes you have to swallow the hurt. They say that reconciliation is about compromise," Otilia said, pursing her lips. "Life has its twists, and people play the cards they are dealt the best they can. We lost a lot and will not get it back, but Salvador and I found each other. We are moving on and what's important now is that we also have you in our lives."

"Did you ever consider returning to Peru?" Peter asked.

"Maybe one day when we retire, but Jerry and I haven't broached the subject. Peru isn't the same as the country I left. I was uprooted and learned to adapt. Sure, sometimes I feel nostalgic—I miss some of the festivals that dotted the calendar, the music, the food, but I think it's pure fantasy. I rebuilt my life, and it would be difficult to go back and have to adjust. Here I have my work, my friends; I'd lose my links once again if I left."

"But your family and your grandchild, you'd be with them."

"I never lived in Lima; there I've always felt like a tourist, and frankly I don't feel quite at home. Besides, Salvador and Carmen lead a busy life. We have good times when I visit," Otilia replied with a smile.

"I'm happy for you that you have found your place in California."

"I built a supportive community for myself with those who welcomed me when I arrived and formed close ties with people who substituted for my blood relatives."

▲ ▲ ▲

Once the children's movie was over, they all met in the kitchen for ice cream and pie. As they ate, while the children went off to play, Grace and Carmen began a conversation about Peruvian desserts. When Madelaine overheard, she said she was eager to learn how to cook Peruvian dishes.

"Peruvian food has become well-known as they've created a unique cuisine, blending ingredients from various cultures," Jerry said.

"It's said that the new cuisine has given Peru a new sense of identity," Carmen pitched in.

"Food has helped start restaurants and improve tourism. Peruvians are proud of their multicultural creations, mixing the traditional Spanish cuisine with African, Chinese, and Japanese dishes," Otilia said.

"How so?" William asked.

"We've had immigration from different countries for hundreds of years, and during the last civil war a lot of people from the highlands and the Amazon moved to the cities, bringing along the cuisine from their regions. They would remember the land left behind through the food they prepared. For the most part these people remained in the metropolitan areas and opened up restaurants. The cities already had Chifas, restaurants opened by Chinese immigrants, and Nikkei eateries, so young chefs developed the idea of taking bits of each to create new dishes," Carmen explained.

"A restaurant culture developed and now has become internationally well-known. San Francisco, New York—there are even a couple of restaurants in DC," Jerry said.

"In Peru, cooking schools started to expand as the Andean cuisine took off. The first cooking schools were set up by chefs as a way to get trained personnel and offer young people in the outlying areas a path for more opportunities to move their families forward," Carmen said.

"We're still a land of contradictions: nouveau cuisine for those who benefit from a good economy, and hunger and poverty for others," Salvador said.

"I had a meal planned for tomorrow night, but instead, how would our Peruvian guests like to introduce us to their specialty?" Mary Margaret said.

"That would be fabulous! I'd like to learn how to prepare some of your dishes," Madelaine said.

"I would too," Grace said.

"I'm in to cook with you," Dario said.

"Why don't we give Mother a break and let those who are interested in a cooking class do the preparation," William said.

"I'll do the shopping tomorrow morning. Make up a list and I'll be sure to get what you need," Peter said.

"Give us a moment and we'll try to figure out the menu. Does anyone have an iPad so I can check out a few recipes? Any allergies?" Carmen asked.

▲ ▲ ▲

On Sunday, when Otilia, Jerry, Carmen, Salvador, and Manuelito arrived at the Alvarez's home, bringing with them two bottles of pisco, Madelaine and Peter were unpacking groceries.

"Here are the lemons for the drinks," Peter said, laying them next to the bottles of liquor.

Their meal would consist of *anticuchos de pollo*, chicken skewers; roasted beets with Granny Smith apples and almonds in a *ponzu* sauce; fried yucca; and *locro con camarones*, shrimp with butternut squash, corn, yellow potatoes, and *queso fresco* in a chili pepper sauce.

Carmen suggested that they work in pairs, assigning each one a task.

"I want to learn how to make *locro*," Grace said.

"Here is the list of ingredients we'll need. Could you please start by peeling the vegetables?"

"Let me know when I should start the grill," Dario said.

"We first need to prepare the marinade for the chicken," Otilia said. "We'll need to cut up the meat in small cubes and then add the soy sauce, spices, and some chili paste."

"Do we have the wooden skewers? Who wants to learn how to make a fresh chili pepper sauce? We need a food processor, please," Carmen said, raising her voice above the chatter.

"William and I will need a blender to make the Pisco sours. We can sip as we cook," Jerry said, directing his request to Mary Margaret, who was walking into the kitchen with a large pot.

"In case you need another pan," Mary Margaret said, placing it on the counter.

"I'll do the chili paste with my partner," Salvador said, smiling at Madelaine.

"Please wait a minute," Mary Margaret said as she opened a drawer to remove a few aprons to hand out.

"I need one too," Peter said.

"I'm so sorry these are all I have, you'll have to tuck a towel into your waistband."

Carmen went over to the Alexa and asked to play a medley of Peruvian songs. "There's no cooking without music," she said as she began to sway her hips and swing her arms.

Salvador joined her, taking her into his arms, and they started to move to the rhythm of the beat. Manuelito, who'd run into the kitchen with Paula when the music began, started to shake his body vigorously.

"Look at the children," Grace exclaimed in surprise.

Peter asked his wife to dance, and William approached Grace as she set her eyes on Carmen to try a few awkward steps.

"That's cool," William said as Grace faced different directions and moved her arms.

"Back to work," Carmen commanded when the song came to an end, and they got back to their tasks.

▲ ▲ ▲

After a few hours of preparation: chopping, blending, and diligent stirring while sipping their drinks, dinner was served. By this time, they were hungry and couldn't wait to taste the colorful and delicious dishes that were spread on the counter before them.

Night fell gradually as they spent time together, appreciating their home-cooked meal and their camaraderie. Mary Margaret had surprised them with coconut cookies, her specialty, for dessert. Over animated conversation they'd learned more about how each one of them had been shaped by time and place and the beliefs that had surrounded them. They talked about the economic desperation people lived through in Latin America, struggling to survive day by day, and the number of illegal immigrants coming into the States for better opportunities. Then they discussed the Latino voters and how they would cast their ballots in the upcoming elections.

"There are twenty-seven million eligible Latino voters," Peter said.

"But we have a history of low voter turnout," Dario explained.

"I don't know about you, but Trump's anti-immigration rhetoric disturbs me," Madelaine said.

"I am thinking of voting Republican. I like what he stands for, Christian family values. Trump would bring in change," William said.

"Are you my relative?!" Dario exclaimed.

"Values, man? Look at his values. He calls Mexicans *bad hombres* and is going to build a wall on the southern border; he's unscrupulous, full of rhetoric," Jerry said.

"What Latinos care mostly about is the economy. We lost big in the recession back in the late 2000s during the housing crash. People need better-paying jobs," Dario said.

▲ ▲ ▲

The children were becoming rambunctious, and it was time to leave when Dario walked over to Carmen as she opened the front hall closet door to pick up her purse. "You opened my mind to facts I had little knowledge about," he said, wanting to let her know she'd enlightened him about the history of Peru.

"As you can see, I truly believe nobody should be trapped by their past. Concealment of trauma is wrong and individuals who were denied a good life need to be treated with dignity. It's not right to carry out heinous acts, shatter people's lives and sense of security without offering something in return. Victims who faced dire challenges have a right to reparation, don't you think?" Carmen said.

"I fully agree, we can't push the memory of tragic events out of people's consciousness. I'm so pleased Peru has stood strong against national forgetting," Dario said.

"Recent studies have shown major tragedies that create a traumatic impact on a society will be felt by later generations as well. This research is beginning to show that our genes can turn on and off and be passed on. People can inherit the fears of a previous generation, which will determine the choices they'll make in life. One study found that concealment of trauma in past generations resulted in lower ability to engage in work and relationships among grandchildren," Carmen explained.

"It goes back that far?" Dario said, shaking his head.

"In the case of the Holocaust, they found that second- and third-generation survivors were more prone to stress disorders than those who had not had traumatic experiences in their families' backgrounds. And another interesting point was that when people talked about their past family history, they were better able to sustain good relationships."

"Are you saying that passage of time may not be sufficient to wipe out the impact of people's negative experiences?"

"Exactly, and neither is the deliberate policy of forgetting by a nation. Acts of remembrance are important for our mental health."

Salvador came over to Carmen's side to tell her they were ready to go and held out his hand to bid Dario goodbye. Dario patted Salvador on his back and said, "I've had a delightful time with your family. You have a beautiful, competent, and compassionate wife."

When Otilia approached, she noticed Salvador's genuinely happy smile. "One last hug," she said as she opened her arms to embrace Dario.

Walking towards the car, Jerry took hold of Otilia's hand before glancing back at their hosts to wave goodbye to them.

The reunion had been an affirmation that each one had come into each other's lives in different ways and they cherished the opportunity given to them. They felt lucky they could make plans to meet again next summer in The East Bay to continue building shared memories.

"We'll recreate ties and reclaim our need for closeness with people who care. They will provide the pleasures we've missed," Jerry said before getting into the car.

"In this family, our stories count," Otilia said as she buckled her seat belt. She was silent a moment, reflecting. "This is how we bring them back—the people, the memories we once thought were lost." She gave a sigh and felt a sense of relief as Jerry turned out of the driveway.

"We'll continue our conversations when we return," Carmen said.

# ACKNOWLEDGMENTS

I am grateful to so many people for believing in this story and helping it come into the world.

To Patricia Anderson, thank you for guiding me through the process.

To my editorial team: Jessica Reyes, lead editor, thank you for your positive disposition, insight, and care.

Leis Pederson, I appreciate your brilliant suggestions and feedback.

Amanda Hughes, thank you for refining and polishing the final product. It was great to discover we shared experiences that helped us connect.

Neil Gonzalez, thank you for your eye-catching cover image that captures the novel's essence.

I am grateful to my early readers for your friendship, encouragement, and enthusiasm. Thank you Susan Swanson, Myriam Waissbluth, Claudia Marshall, and Judith Plessis for your meaningful suggestions. Thank you to Blanca Sorribas and Stany Ayala for grounding me in Peruvian history and culture.

To Emilia Mantilla, thank you for your research and your organizational and computer skills.

I want to give a special thanks to my dear husband, Nate, for creating a supportive environment and encouraging me to turn lived experiences into a novel. This story, with some amounts of fiction and truth, is meant for you.

# ABOUT THE AUTHOR

**ELIANA TOBIAS** was born in Santiago, Chile, to immigrant parents who had escaped the Holocaust. She graduated from the University of Chile and later completed graduate degrees in the US and Canada. After working in the field of education in various capacities, including teaching at the National University in Trujillo, Peru, she discovered her love of writing.

Eliana's rich experience of political turmoil—listening to stories of the Holocaust when Jewish communities in Europe had been shattered, losing family in Chile under military dictatorship, and living in Peru during a time of intense civil conflict—fueled her passion to write about the ways people caught in devastation find to rebuild their lives. Eliana's first novel, *In the Belly of the Horse*, received an award from the International Latino Book Awards in 2018 and was also nominated for the Latino Book Into Movies Awards. Eliana splits her time between California and British Columbia.